CW01661457

Praise for Jen.

"With the pages filled with betrayal, lies of omission, and secrets, *All Our Next Times* makes for some very compulsive reading. And that ending? OMG!"

LL MEYER, AUTHOR OF THE WORLDS COLLIDE SERIES

"You *will* get hooked."

GLADYS CROSS, AUTHOR OF THE DEVIL'S DEVIANTS MC SERIES

"I'm rendered speechless. Wow."

BOOKEND GAL

"Wow! I was not prepared for that ending. This is a beautiful love story that will make you cry and gasp out loud."

L. AQUILA, AUTHOR OF *FLEETING TIME*

"The beginning of an action-packed [series] filled with unexpected and delicious drama..."

THE DRAGON DEN BOOK BLOG

All Our Next Times

LN
P

Also by Jennilynn Wyer

Fallen Brook Series

All Our Next Times

Paper Stars Rewritten

Broken Butterfly

Reflections of You

FALLEN BROOK SERIES
BOOK ONE

All Our Next Times

JENNILYNN WYER

All Our Next Times
Paperback Edition
Copyright © 2024 by Jennilynn Wyer

Love N. Books Press
An Imprint of Wolfpack Publishing
1707 E. Diana Street
Tampa, FL 33610

www.lovenbookspress.com

All rights reserved. No part of this book may be reproduced in any form or by any electronic or mechanical means, including information storage and retrieval systems, without express written permission from the publisher, except for the use of brief quotations in reviews. Any use of this publication to train generative artificial intelligence (AI) technologies is expressly prohibited.

This book is a work of fiction. References to historical events, real people, or real places are used fictitiously. Any similarity to real persons, living or dead, is purely coincidental and not intended by the author.

All brand names and product names used in this book are trademarks, registered trademarks, or trade names of their respective holders. Wolfpack Publishing is not associated with any product or vendor in this book.

Cover design by Jennilynn Wyer Designs
Edited by My Brother's Editor

All Our Next Times was originally self-published in 2020 by Jennilynn Wyer.

Paperback ISBN 979-8-89567-946-3
Ebook ISBN 979-8-89567-945-6
LCCN 2024951267

Dedication

To every woman who struggled to find her voice.
Never let go of your dreams.

Playlist

"Helium" performed by Sia
"Wonderlust" performed by Will Post
"Blurry" performed by Puddle of Mudd
"She Cries" performed by Will Post
"Alive" performed by P.O.D.
"The Distance" performed by Cake
"Before You Go" performed by Lewis Capaldi
"Beautiful Thing" performed by Benson Boone
"My Hero" performed by Foo Fighters
"Sugar, We're Goin Down" performed by Fall Out Boy
"The First Time Ever I Saw Your Face"
performed by Roberta Flack
"Stitches" performed by Shawn Mendes
"Circles" performed by Post Malone
"Gone, Gone, Gone" performed by Phillip Phillips

Reader's Note

Every great love story has a beginning, a middle, and an end. *All Our Next Times* is the beginning of Elizabeth's.

Book one takes place during childhood through high school, is told in multiple POVs, and ends in a shocking cliffhanger.

Please refer to the author's website at www.jennilynnwyer.com/content-and-trigger-warnings for a list of potential trigger warnings. Recommended for mature readers.

All Our Next Times

LNP

Prologue

HAILEY

Present Day

YOU. Such a simple word. An everyday word. A word that sounds like a letter but isn't. A letter that begins words like unloved, useless, ugly, unwanted. That is what I hear every day. In my head. In my heart. You are unloved. You are useless. You are ugly. You are unwanted.

The fifteen-minute warning bell sounds, blaring obtrusively through the school halls, alerting everyone that it's time to get to their next class. Lockers bang shut, voices get louder, footsteps become hurried. I scurry and scamper around people, my head lowered, my eyes averted to the scuffed beige linoleum floor. I want to be invisible. I want to be unseen. Please don't notice me. Please leave me alone.

I know what will happen if I look up. I know what I will see, what I will hear, what I will feel. Ugly. Unwanted. Useless. Unloved.

Unfolding the crumpled piece of lined notebook paper, I read over the poem I wrote to my sister, Elizabeth.

Broken Butterfly

She wanted to fly but her wings were broken.
She dreamed big dreams, but they weren't allowed to be spoken.
Her feelings pushed down her throat left her choking.
He beat her down, but she was still hoping.
Body, soul, spirit, all burned,
Wishing that her family would see and be concerned.
Fighting him isn't a battle, it's a war,
Every breath is now a chore.
She can't get air, can't fly, can't soar,
Can't leave this dark room, Can't even find the door.
Loneliness consumes her,
She sees all the darkness, never the light.
She doesn't see a tunnel with an end in sight.
She sees the pitch black that the world is at night.
No one is there to tell her everything will be alright.
She's dead inside but no one knows.
How the blood boils, how the heart slows,
Because this was not the life she chose.
When she sleeps, she dreams, she can still hear her screams.
Her sister replaced her.
The pain he inflicted chased her.
His love is like a disease.

No one hears her cries, no one hears her pleas.
In her dark world, fallen on her knees,
Thinking death is better than life,
Help me please!
One final blow is all she can take,
Before she dies for good with a final shake.
Now all those people who called her a mistake,
Can finally rest at ease when they go to her wake.

I wipe away the lone tear that streaks down my cheek.

I'm sorry. I love you. Forgive me.

Neatly folding the paper into fourths, I slip it inside my sister's locker.

"Hailey!"

Elizabeth's voice rings loudly from across the hallway.

My steps quicken. One look at my face and she'll sense something is wrong. She'll stop me. She'll want to know. I can't tell her. I don't know what to do. I'm broken, and nothing can fix me.

I ignore my sister and keep walking. I pass the cafeteria doors, walk past the gymnasium, push open the back doors, and once outside, sprint across the baseball field. The smell of fresh-cut grass stings my nose. The bright sunlight causes my eyes to water. A movement to my right catches my eye.

I stumble to a standstill when I see him.

How did he know I was planning to ditch school? How did he know I would come out this way?

Parked in the senior lot next to the baseball field, he leans against his car door, hands tucked casually in the side pockets of his frayed blue jeans. But there is nothing casual about him.

His cold eyes follow me. Watch me. Taunt me. Smile at me.

Fear sends my heart thrashing inside my chest like a trapped bird. My legs won't move, even though my mind screams *run, run, run*.

The corner of his mouth tips up, and he crooks his finger for me to come to him.

I have no choice. My body reacts to his simple command as if I was one of Pavlov's dogs. My legs involuntarily move toward him, even though my mind warns me to stop. To run away. I can't.

When I get close enough, he says, "Good girl."

I used to love his voice. Now that voice is one from my nightmares. A voice that is soft and deep but full of darkness and cruelty.

He opens the car door, and I get inside. I know what's coming. I know what to expect. And I know the words he'll use when he brings the pain. *You are ugly. You are useless. You are unwanted. You are unloved.*

YOUNG LOVE.

COMPLICATED.
BEAUTIFUL.
AND HEARTBREAKING.
THIS IS THE BEGINNING
OF MY LOVE STORY.

Chapter One

ELIZABETH

Summer Before First Grade
The Day I Met My Moonlight

DADDY'S CHEST is warm against my back as he helps me position my fingers over the guitar struts.

"Like this." His large hands engulf mine, and our fingers work in tandem to push down the chords. "Good. Now you try by yourself."

I wiggle in his lap to get more comfortable, the acoustic guitar cumbersome to hold and heavy on my slim thighs. My tongue sticks out in concentration when I try to form a barred C chord—and fail spectacularly when a loud bang from outside causes me to jump.

"Let's take a snack break," Daddy offers, but I shake my head and reposition my fingers.

Daddy started giving me guitar lessons when I was two, after he found me in his music room making disharmonious chaos with every instrument he owned. I have a clear memory of him sitting me in his lap and showing me how to pluck guitar strings. Even as a baby, I was instantly captivated by the different sounds each instrument made. Guitar, piano, drums. I can play them all. Not as good as Daddy, but hopefully one day.

Another bang, followed by loud voices.

"Sounds like a new family is moving in," Daddy comments.

Excited curiosity has me pushing the guitar off our laps and scurrying to the window. I squish my nose against the glass, little plumes of condensed vapor clouding the windowpane with every breath. Sure enough, there's a large moving truck in the driveway next door. The family that used to live there moved out a month ago. I hope the new family has kids my age. It would be nice to have new friends to play with.

Bouncing on my tiptoes, I shout an exuberant "Yes!" when I see two boys come out of the house and run across the front lawn, a tall, bearded man jogging after them.

With gleeful anticipation, I dash out of the room.

"Where are you off to, puddin'?"

Bounding up the stairs to find Hailey, I shout, "I'm going to meet the new neighbors!"

I hear Daddy's fading chuckle as I leap up two steps at a time in my haste to get to my bedroom. Running as fast as my little legs can carry me, I throw open Hailey's bedroom door, startling her awake from her nap.

"Hailey! Hailey! Come on! We have new neighbors! Get up! Get up!"

I run through our jack-and-jill bathroom to my room and fling open my closet to grab my blue Easter dress. Mommy says I look like a princess whenever I wear it.

Bleary-eyed and grumpy, Hailey shuffles into my room and yawns sleepily.

"I don't wanna go."

I wriggle out of my shorts and shirt and slip the blue dress over my head. "Fine. But I'm going."

Mommy taught me how to braid my hair, so I quickly comb it and then braid it into two pigtails. Seeing the gold plastic princess crown I wore last Halloween sitting on my dresser, I grab it and carefully place it on top of my head. I rush past Hailey into the bathroom, do a quick check in the mirror, decide I look awesome, and run downstairs.

Grabbing a bag of fruit candies, I shove them in my dress pocket, and sprint out the front door, only to skid to a sudden stop once I see my mom talking to another lady on the front porch of the house next door.

My darting gaze searches everywhere for the two boys I saw from the window, but I don't see them.

"Lizzie-bear, come meet our new neighbor, Freda."

Climbing the porch steps of the neighbor's house, I gracefully curtsy in front of the beautiful woman.

"I am Princess Elizabeth, ruler of the magical forests beyond," I announce regally, gesturing to the copse of trees that jut up against our backyards.

Freda's face lights up in amusement, but it's her eyes that transfix me. They are light-colored and metallic looking, like the shiny quarters I get for my birthday.

"It's so nice to meet you, Princess Elizabeth. You are a very pretty princess in a very pretty dress."

I beam at her and give another curtsy. "Thank you."

"Your mom was just telling me all about you and your sister. I have twin boys, Jayson and Julien." Talking to Mommy, Freda says, "My husband just took them to grab something to eat. I haven't had time yet to go to the grocery store. They should be back soon. I would love to introduce them to your daughters. Get them out of my hair for a little while, if you know what I mean."

"I understand completely," Mommy replies, and I scowl when she pats the top of my head and makes my tiara slip forward.

Taking off, I leap down the steps and head toward my forest fort in the backyard. "Tell my princes to come rescue me when they get home!" I yell.

"Do not go far, young lady. Dinner is in an hour!"

I reach the fort hidden among the trees that Hailey and I started building at the beginning of the summer. Our fort is made from anything we find lying on the ground, along with some plyboard Daddy gave us, with an added hodge-podge of dead tree limbs, pine cones, and rocks to complete the makeshift structure. Mommy bought us a plastic tarp to cover the top of our fort. Daddy chopped some firewood, and we use the bigger pieces for benches to sit on. Hailey and I try to work on the fort every day. We made paths along the ground by taking sticks and scraping aside fallen pine needles. And we constructed ladders up the trees by nailing broken tree limbs into the bark.

Since we love collecting things we find in the forest, Hailey and I have an assemblage of glass jars along the back wall of our fort. The jars sit atop their own stumps, and I made labels for what is inside each one. One jar is for rocks we find along the creek bank. Another jar is for freshwater shells. We keep a few empty ones to catch fireflies.

Wanting to impress the boys when they arrive, I make sure everything is in place. Deciding to tidy a bit, I sweep the floor with a pine branch to get rid of the dead leaves that have fallen to the ground. Taking out the bag of fruit candies from my pocket, I place it on an empty stump, half-tempted to open it and sneak a few.

When I hear the distinctive noise of twigs snapping on the ground, I straighten my crooked tiara, push the tarp aside—and give a startled shriek when I come face-to-face with two upside-down heads.

Dangling from their knees on a low-hanging branch from the tree in front of the fort's entrance are two brown-headed twin boys with silver-gray eyes and wearing the same clothes. I know what identical twins are from my kindergarten class. We had a deck of picture cards with words on them of different people, and twins was one of the words. The image for twins was of two identical blonde girls with matching red bows in their hair.

My huge smile shows my two missing front teeth. They smile back, also gap-toothed just like me.

"Hi," I say, suddenly shy, brushing my right foot back and forth along the dirt on the ground.

One of the boys reaches up and grabs the tree branch, flipping over and landing on his feet in front of me.

"I'm Julien."

The other boy waves. "I'm Jayson. Our mom said we had to come rescue Princess Elizabeth. You her?"

"Yep," I say, popping that 'p' good.

"Okay. You're rescued." Julien grabs my hand and takes off toward the creek.

Jayson swings down from the branch and runs after us, grabbing my other hand. Feeling like I'm a human rubber band tethered between them, I laugh as we stumble across the forest floor, weaving between the trees until we reach the water's edge.

Jayson lets out a loud *whoop* and charges for the water, fully clothed with his tennis shoes on, taking Julien and me with him.

The creek isn't deep, the water only coming up to our ankles, but the bottom of my dress gets soaked.

"Your dress is all wet."

I look down at myself and shrug. Hailey and I have come home looking much worse.

"Here. Help me lift this rock," I say.

I bend over and grip the sides of a partially submerged chunk of what Daddy told me is granite. I have a jar full of rounded pieces, some pinkish in color, some with big clear crystals.

Julien and Jayson immediately squat down to help. Together, we're able to tilt the rock at an angle, and I see what I'm looking for.

"Don't squash me," I tell them, sinking a hand under the water to snatch the tiny crawfish trying to hide.

"Is that a lobster?" Jayson asks, his eyes big when I victoriously hold up the wiggly creature.

The rock makes a big splash when they let go and gather in close.

"Crawfish. My daddy calls 'em crawdads. I guess they do look like tiny lobsters."

I place the little crustacean in his open palm. He uses his thumb and middle finger to gently pick it up and smiles at me when its claws and legs squirm wildly. Once Julien gets a chance to hold it, I put it back into the creek.

"They like to hide under the rocks. You can find all sorts of things in the creek. Turtles, water striders, dragonflies, minnows. See?"

I point to three small minnows darting around a swirling eddy where a large tree limb has fallen into the water.

"Hey, want to build a dam?" Julien asks, finding a large stick on the ground.

Jayson and I begin hunting around the bank and within minutes, we have built a substantial pile of wood. As we work, I ask the twins about where they're from and why they moved here, what their favorite game is, favorite color, favorite food. I learn they moved here from Knoxville, Tennessee because their dad got a new job, and that we're the same age. Jayson says his favorite food is pizza, and Julien's is tacos.

"I'll be right back," I say, remembering the bag of candy that I left in the fort.

When I return, I divvy out equal portions between the three of us. Picking through the remains in the bag, I remove the purple ones and shove them in my dress pocket because, yuck, grape is gross.

Watching me do this, Julien takes my grape candies and gives me his orange ones. Jayson swaps his yellow ones for my red ones. Satisfied, we sit cross-legged on the spongy, leaf-littered ground and gaze out over the water.

"Do people mix you up and call you the wrong name?"

"All the time," they answer in unison, voices so in sync that I can't help but giggle.

Julien leans in and whispers something in Jayson's ear, a grin playing on his lips.

"I bet you can't tell us apart," Jayson smugly says.

Licking the sticky sugar from my fingertips, I meet his challenge with a smug smirk of my own.

"Bet I can."

"Close your eyes."

I roll them instead. "Why?"

"Just close them," Jayson insists, a playful edge to his voice.

Reluctantly, I oblige and squeeze my eyes shut.

Running footfalls thunder around me in dizzying circles, and laughter bubbles up in my throat as I try to follow their movements.

"Okay, open your eyes."

When I blink them wide, they're grinning like they've pulled off the greatest of tricks.

"What's my name?"

"Julien," I say confidently.

His grin falters and is replaced by a frown. "Lucky guess. Close your eyes."

With an exaggerated huff, I do as he says. More footfalls, the swish of leaves under their feet, the sensation of a breeze tugging at the loose wisps of my hair.

"What about now?"

I quickly study their faces. "You're Jayson," I declare, locking eyes with the twin on the right. "And you're Julien."

Their mouths drop at the same time, clearly shocked at my superpowers of deduction. It's kind of funny to watch.

Jayson narrows his eyes, clearly suspicious. "How can you tell?"

They may look the same, but there are a lot of things different about them. Jayson's eyelashes are slightly longer, and Julien has a small scar above his right eyebrow. Jayson has seven freckles across his nose, but Julien only has four. I counted.

Standing up, I dust off the dirt and crumpled leaves clinging to my dress. "I just can. Want to play castles and dragons?"

We abandon the half-built dam by the creek and dive into an afternoon of grand, imaginary adventures. Julien becomes the brave knight, Jayson the cunning wizard, and I—naturally—am the princess, leading them into battle against a fearsome dragon.

By the time we defeat the beast, the sun has dipped low, casting long shadows through the forest canopy.

"Lizzie! Boys! Time to come in," Mommy calls from the backyard.

Hailey's shouts, "Daddy's grillin' burgers!"

We scramble to the creek, frantically washing the mud from our hands, though it's no use against the sticky residue of candy. Our clothes are a lost cause, smudged with dirt and grass stains. But none of that matters as we link hands and head toward the house together, our laughter floating up into the warm summer air.

Walking hand in hand, my heart swells with the kind of happiness that fills every corner of my chest. I glance at the twins, and something inside me instinctively knows that meeting Jayson and Julien has changed my life forever.

That night, after Mommy and Daddy tuck us in and kiss us good night, Hailey tiptoes into my room. The soft creak of the door makes me smile even before I see her. She climbs onto my bed, the pink covers cool against our bare legs, and wiggles in beside me. The familiar scent of her shampoo, like sweet cherries, fills the air as I snuggle deeper into my pillow.

"What do you think about Jayson and Julien?"

Her nose scrunches. "They're okay for boys."

She says *boys* like the word is infected with cooties.

I flop over onto my back and stare at the twinkling stars cast on my ceiling by the nightlight on my dresser.

"I like them a lot."

I go on to tell her about the adventure we had in the forest. The silence from Hailey doesn't bother me—she's always the quiet one, letting me spill my stories without interruption. After I finish, she slips out of bed and pads back to her room. I hear her rummaging around before she returns with her sparkly pencil and orange-scented paper, the smell wafting over as she settles back beside me.

"What are you doing?" I ask, watching the pencil move swiftly across the page.

"Shh," Hailey whispers, pressing a finger to her lips.

I lean over to peek, but she turns her shoulder away, guarding her secret.

Giving up, I climb out of bed and go to the window. The moonlight bathes the yard in a soft glow, and across the way, past the oak tree that grows between our two houses, Jayson and Julien's faces peek out from their second-story window. The moment they see me, they lift the glass. I do the same and immediately feel the fragrant breeze sweep in, carrying the sweet scent of honeysuckle.

"Good night, Princess!" Jayson calls out.

"Sleep tight," Julien shouts.

I blow them each a kiss. "Good night!"

"I'm done," Hailey softly announces from the bed.

I wave bye to the twins and crawl back under the covers.

"This is a story about Elizabeth and her two princes..." Hailey begins.

Her voice becomes softer and softer, the words like a lullaby. My eyelids grow heavier as her story lulls me into sweet dreams, and the last thing I remember is the echo of Jayson and Julien's laughter as we run barefoot through the forest.

Chapter Two

ELIZABETH

Third Grade
The Day I Met My Sunshine

THE NEXT MORNING when I take my place on the reading rug in our classroom, I daydream about last night.

When I went to my window to say good night to the twins, I discovered cut-out construction paper stars, and a moon taped on the outside of the window glass. Each star had a letter written on it that spelled out P-R-I-N-C-E-S-S.

As I inspected the paper starry night, wondering how it got there, the branches on the oak tree started to move. That was when I noticed two brown-headed boys smiling at me through the window. Jayson and Julien had been stuck at home with the flu all week, and Mom wouldn't let me go over to see them.

Opening the window, I held out my hands to help Jayson as he climbed through first.

"What are you doing?" I whispered.

"We're tired of being stuck inside...and we missed you," Jayson replied, turning to help Julien.

My little heart melted. "I missed you, too."

"I'm stuck," Julien said, trying to clamber over the sill.

We pulled him inside, and his long legs accidentally kicked my ladybug nightlight lamp from my bedside table.

"Be quiet. You're going to get us in trouble." Jayson picked up the lamp and placed it back where it belonged.

"Sorry."

Hailey must had heard the noise because she came through the bathroom, her eyes widening when she saw Jayson and Julien.

"Mom is going to be so mad if she finds them in here."

"Love you Hales, but scram." I shooed her away.

"Your funeral," she replied and retreated to her room.

Once she was gone, the boys and I snuggled down together on my bed. Jayson doubled a pillow over and rolled onto his stomach beside me, propping his head on top of his folded arms. I reclined back against my headboard, and Julien laid his head on my lap. He sighed when I slid my fingers through his soft brown hair.

"Would you rather eat a bowl full of maggots or three spiders?" Jayson asked.

We loved playing this game.

"So gross!" I threw my stuffed dog at him.

Considering the question, Julien said, "I'd eat the spiders because they're small and there's only three of them. I don't think I could eat an entire bowl of maggots."

"Still gross." I pretended to fake vomit. "But I see your point. I agree. Okay. My turn. Hmm." I spent a second thinking and then it hit me. "Would you rather...kiss a girl or kiss a toad?"

Jayson slid his eyes to Julien, then looked at me and said, "We'd kiss the girl, but only if it was you."

I was nine years old, but after first grade when Jayson, Julien, and I became friends, I discovered that boys were not as icky as I once thought. I also saw Samantha kissing boys all the time behind the jungle gym on the playground at recess. It had me thinking about whether I wanted to kiss a boy or have a boy kiss me. My mom and dad kissed all the time. Mom said that people kissed when they really liked each other. Samantha must have really liked a whole bunch of boys.

Would I want a boy to kiss me? I didn't think I would. But then I would see Julien running across the playground after Jayson, or I would think about the color of their eyes that had always fascinated me, and I would change my mind. Yes. Yes, I did want to kiss a boy. Well, two specific boys with gray eyes. And yes, I'd want them to kiss me back.

I had talked to Hailey about it one night. She thought I should keep my feelings a secret. That if they knew I liked them in that way, they would stop being my friends.

Hailey reappeared in the bathroom doorway. "Mom's coming up the stairs."

Little sisters could be so annoying.

"How do you know that?"

"I went downstairs for a glass of water."

Julien pecked my cheek with a quick kiss and crawled off my bed. "Come on, Jay. I don't want to be grounded again."

Jayson kissed my other cheek.

As they disappeared out my window, Jayson poked his head back in.

"Samantha tried to kiss us on the playground, but we told her no." Then he smiled at me and disappeared.

Seconds later, I heard their voices from the darkness say, "Good night, Princess."

I touched both cheeks where they kissed me, and it was Hailey's turn to make fake vomit sounds.

Coming out of my daydream, I absentmindedly pluck at a stray piece of fluff on the reading rug as I wait for class to begin.

Jayson and Julien are still out sick, and the room feels emptier without them.

Beside me, Samantha and Jacinda giggle-gossip about a boy they saw in the hallway. I catch fragments of their conversation—something about his dirty clothes and his weird eyes. I really hate it when people talk about others behind their backs. It's rude.

"Sorry," Maria mumbles beside me, her knee grazing mine as she shifts.

"No prob," I reply, my attention already elsewhere.

The sudden clap of Ms. Pauling's hands snaps us all into focus. She stands at the front of the classroom next to a boy I've never seen before. His dark hair falls into his eyes, his head tilted down as he stares at the floor. He's wearing a light blue, long-sleeved button-up, the fabric wrinkled and stained with faint brownish smudges. Samantha and Jacinda's snickers grow louder, and the boy's head snaps up, a scowl firmly set on his face. The sight of him tugs at my chest.

"One, two, three, eyes on me." Our teacher chants the familiar words she uses to get us to focus.

"One and two, eyes on you," we recite in unison.

"Good morning, class," Ms. Pauling says brightly, her tone light as she gestures to the boy. "I'd like to introduce our newest classmate, Ryder Cutton. Ryder is from Virginia and will be joining us for the rest of the school year."

Choruses of "Hi, Ryder" and "Welcome, Ryder" sing out from the reading rug.

"Since it's November, and Ryder hasn't been here for the past three months, who would like to be his class buddy—"

Before she's even finished her question, my hand shoots up. "I can be his class buddy, Ms. Pauling," I say, my voice clear.

"Excellent, Elizabeth. Thank you."

She instructs Ryder to sit next to me on the reading rug. I try to scoot over to make room for him, but Jacinda and Samantha refuse to move. Ms. Pauling doesn't notice because she turns around to retrieve the bin that contains our assigned reading books.

"Make room for Ryder," I tell Jacinda.

She barely acknowledges me. Instead, her eyes flick toward Ryder, and she cups her hand over her mouth to whisper something to Samantha. Their muffled giggles drift through the air, making Ryder's shoulders slump a little. He frowns, the corners of his lips turning down, but stays silent.

Annoyance prickles my skin, and I can feel my patience thinning. I glance at Ms. Pauling, who's still busy sorting through books, and decide to take matters into my own hands. I swivel around, bend my legs at the knees, then plow Samantha and Jacinda out of the way. Once a space is cleared, I grab Ryder's hand and pull him down next to me.

"Ignore them."

He smiles at me.

Ryder has really pretty eyes. Catching the sunlight streaming through the window, they're a light shade of brown. Their color reminds me of fall sunsets, the kind that make the leaves in the backyard glow in shades of gold and amber.

Ms. Pauling finally turns around, her sharp gaze landing on Jacinda. The subtle narrowing of her eyes is enough to send the message. Jacinda straightens up at the silent reproach.

Samantha leans back and sticks her tongue out at me. I roll my eyes and pretend I didn't see it.

Ms. Pauling passes out our assigned reading books but doesn't give me mine. "Ryder, until you take the reading test so I can assess your reading Lexile level, why don't you and Elizabeth go to the school library and pick out a book to bring back to class. I will let Mrs. Heard know you are coming." She points to the clock hanging on the wall. "Please be back in thirty minutes, no later."

As soon as we step into the hallway, the muffled chatter of classrooms fades, replaced by the distant hum of the school's air vents.

"I'm sorry that Samantha and Jacinda were so mean to you."

Ryder shrugs but doesn't say anything.

Trying to lighten the mood, I show him where the important things are located. "That's the boys' restroom." I point to the blue door on our left. "And the water fountain. I never use it because... *ick*, germs. I bring my own water. The cafeteria and gym are down at the end of the hall. We usually go outside to play, but when it rains, we use the gym."

At the end of the corridor, I pull on the heavy glass door and gesture for Ryder to enter.

"This is the library. It's my favorite place."

The smell of books fills the large, airy room. Tall wooden shelves stretch toward the ceiling, and the soft glow of the fluorescent strip lights gives the space a warm, welcoming feel. Mrs. Heard, the librarian, sits behind her curved desk in the center of the room, her glasses perched low on her nose as she types away at her computer.

"Hi, Mrs. Heard!"

"Hey, sweetheart. Ms. Pauling said you were coming. It's nice to meet you, Ryder. Let me know if you need any help finding a book. We'll get a chance to talk more during library time on Friday."

With a nod, she returns to her computer, leaving us to browse. Ryder wanders quietly down an aisle, his fingertips brushing the spines of books. I watch him for a moment.

"What do you like to read?" I ask.

He shoves his hands inside the pockets of his jeans and shrugs his shoulders again. I decide to try a new tactic. I grab a *My Little Pony* picture book from the shelf and hand it to him.

"You like magical talking rainbow unicorns?"

The horrified look that overtakes his face when I place the book in his hand is just too funny. It gives me the encouragement I need to continue teasing him.

"What about this one?" I say, handing him *When the Crayons Quit*.

He surprises me when he replies, "Do they have *The Hungry Caterpillar* or any books about the American Girl dolls? I like the ones with Josephina and Felicity."

Ryder has a nice voice. It's deeper than Jayson's or Julien's.

"You know the names of American Girl dolls?"

"Who doesn't?"

Well, okay then. Who am I to judge? I walk over to the American Girl book section and take a couple of books off the shelf. Ryder clutches his stomach and bends over laughing.

"I'm just messin' with you, Elizabeth."

I put my hands on my hips and give him a piercing look. He gazes up at me and starts laughing all over again. Wiping tears from the corners of his eyes, he straightens up and grins.

"I have two sisters. My little sister, Brea, collects them. Our living room is covered in American Girl dolls. It's creepy the way they all stare at you," he says with a shudder.

"Sounds like your sister and my sister will love each other. She has these dolls with huge eyes that freak me out."

Mrs. Heard finds us in the stacks and hands me a paperback. "This finally checked back in, and you were next on the wait list."

It's *Where the Red Fern Grows*. I do an imaginary fist pump. It's been checked out of our public library for forever, so I asked Mrs. Heard to put me on the wait list for it here at school.

"Thanks so much!"

Ryder shuffles closer. "I've been wanting to read that one. My older sister said it was really good."

I thrust the book at him. "Here. You can read it."

My offer seems to baffle him for some reason. "Thanks, but you should keep it. I'll go find something else to read."

"Seriously. Take it. I can read it after you're finished."

"How 'bout we share. Deal?"

"Deal."

Ryder smiles, and it's such a nice smile that I can't help but smile back.

Ms. Pauling pokes her head around the corner of the stacks. "Hey, you two. It's time to head back to your class."

The rest of the school day goes by quickly. Ryder and I talk. A lot. I tell him about Jayson and Julien. He tells me about his old friends and school in Virginia. His dad opened an auto shop in town, and that's why they moved here. Once school is dismissed, we part ways, and I go find Hailey, so we can catch the bus home.

While standing in line, waiting to get on, someone bumps my shoulder.

"Hey," Ryder says.

"Hey! Is this your bus?"

He nods.

"You must live in our neighborhood. What street?"

"Our new house is on Fallen Brook Drive."

"That's where we live," Hailey pipes up.

"Ryder, this is Hailey, my sister I told you about. Hales, this is Ryder. He's in my class, and I'm his class buddy. He has a little sister named Brea, and she *loves* American Girl dolls."

That fact gets her excited. "Really? How many does she have?"

Ryder looks up into the sky to do a mental calculation. "About fifteen."

"What? No way! I only have three!"

Hailey must be super impressed because as we load onto the bus, she begs Ryder to come over to his house and meet his sister.

"Why don't you guys get off at my stop and walk home with me? Brea should already be there. She's in kindergarten, and Mom picks her up at one. Aisle or window?" he asks when we get to the first available bench seat.

This boy is just so nice. "Aisle, please. Thanks."

"Yes!" Hailey exclaims, always happy to sit next to the window.

I drop my backpack onto the floor and hug it between my feet. Ryder nudges my shoulder again and shows me *Where the Red Fern Grows.*

"Want to read with me?"

"Sure."

Halfway home, I remember that I promised the twins that I'd meet them in my room after school.

"Do you mind if we drop by my house first before we head to yours?"

"*Lizzie,*" Hailey whines. "*American Girl dolls,*" she emphasizes gravely like it's a life-and-death situation if she doesn't get to see them as soon as possible.

I'm sure Jayson and Julien won't mind if I'm a little late.

"Where have you been?" Jayson says as soon as I open my window for them to climb inside.

"Who's that?" Julien asks, his tone wary, eyes narrowing the moment he spots Ryder standing just behind me.

Ryder gives a chin jerk in greeting. "S'up."

"You guys sound so much better." I reach behind me and grab

Ryder's hand, pulling him forward. "This is Ryder. He joined our class today. Oh! And he lives right down the street. His dad owns a garage, and they have this awesome car in their garage. It's black with a yellow stripe down the middle. Ryder's dad let me sit in it. The car is amazing! It has this really big thingy sticking up from the hood."

I wave my hands around in an exaggerated motion, trying to show just how big it was.

"It's called a supercharger," Ryder helpfully interjects.

"Yeah, that," I reply, growing more animated as I talk. "His dad let me sit in the front seat and rev the engine. It was so freakin' loud! The whole car vibrated, like it was alive, and the windows rattled. It was awesome! You guys *have* to come see it."

I really want the twins to like Ryder and welcome him into our group.

Jayson sizes him up. Julien does the same, then holds out a fist. "Any friend of Liz's is a friend of ours."

Chapter Three

ELIZABETH

Seventh Grade
The Beginning of Change

THE HUMID, chlorine-scented air is electric with excitement as Jayson slices through the water with ease. His legs and arms pump rhythmically, and his head tilts for a breath after every third stroke.

Standing on the bleachers, I cheer him on, barely able to contain myself.

“Faster, Jayson! Go! Go! You can do it!”

Beside me, Ryder purses his fingers between his lips and lets out an ear-piercing whistle.

Jayson is neck-and-neck with one of the swimmers from the opposing team in the next lane, and it has come down to the final seconds.

“You’re almost there!” I shout.

Jayson surges forward with a sudden burst of energy, his muscles rippling beneath the water’s surface. He stretches out, fingertips grazing the touchpad at the end of his lane an arm’s length before his closest competitor, and the air around us explodes with noise.

He rips off his goggles, looks up at the board to see his time, then scans the stands before his eyes find our group. The smile that lights up his face is blinding. I am so freaking proud of that boy. Jayson just demolished the district's freestyle record for his age group.

I grab hold of Julien's shoulders and shake him silly. "He did it!" I shout, my voice barely audible over the uproar of celebration.

As soon as Jayson hauls himself out of the water, his coach and teammates swarm him in an ecstatic group hug.

"He's not going to have any bones left," Ryder says, taking pity on Julien and prying me off him.

As soon as Jayson heads in our direction, I leap off the bleachers and tackle him in a fierce hug, not caring one bit that he's dripping water all over me.

I grab his face. "I am so super, duper, awesomely proud of you!"

His hands press over mine. "Thanks, Liz," he says softly.

Jayson's opponent, the second-place finisher, comes over.

Swiping a hand through his damp, blond curls, he says, "That was pretty epic. I thought I had you, and then you shot away from me. I didn't stand a chance. I'm Elijah. I go to Highland Middle."

"Thanks, man," Jayson replies, tapping Elijah's proffered fist. "I had to push myself hard just to stay even with you. You're really good."

Elijah's hazel gaze shifts to me. "Is this your sister?"

My stomach does a little flip, my cheeks instantly warming. I tuck a loose strand of my pale hair behind my ear, suddenly self-conscious.

"I'm Elizabeth, the best friend, not the sister."

Elijah shuffles his bare feet on the wet concrete. "Um, so, my team's heading out. Our coach is taking us for pizza." He pauses. "I was wondering...maybe I could get your number, so we could, you know, text sometime?"

Before I can respond, Ryder says, "Yeah, that's not happening."

Wait, what?

Elijah's face falls, and he gives me a small, awkward smile. "Oh, okay. Well, it was nice meeting you," he mumbles, then turns to rejoin his teammates, looking dejected.

I turn wide, incredulous eyes toward Ryder. "What the heck was that for?"

Ryder just grins and casually slings his arm around my shoulders, steering me toward the exit before I know what's happening.

"Who's ready for some burgers?" he asks no one in particular.

"That wasn't very nice. Did you see the look on his face?"

Jayson scoops me up, laughing as he practically shoves me into Ryder's mom's minivan.

"You were rude to him," I continue, but my admonishments fall on deaf ears.

"Not happening, Liz," Jayson says, grabbing a hoodie off the passenger seat and pulling it over his head.

Ryder's mom, Faith, finds me in the rearview mirror. "Who was rude?"

"Them," I accuse.

Climbing into the back row, Julien drops into the seat and buckles up. "I didn't do anything."

Ryder goes to the back with Julien, and Jayson slides in next to me.

"Dude asked for her number," Jayson says.

Ryder's dad, Randy, chuckles from the driver's seat as he pulls out of the parking lot. Faith smacks his shoulder.

"Not helping, dear."

Not done with our conversation, I vocally huff and cross my arms over my chest to show my displeasure.

"Elijah was really nice. He even came over to congratulate you. So what if he wanted my number?"

Apparently, I'm now invisible because the boys start talking about the swim meet and the new dirt bike Ryder got.

I take out my phone to text my friend Maria. She'll listen to me.

Me: Ugh! Boys!

It doesn't take long for her to reply.

Maria: Who?

Me: Who do you think? The three idiots I'm being forced to share a car ride with right now.

Maria: What did they do?

Me: What is it Jamie's boyfriend says all the time when Brea hangs around and won't leave them alone?

Maria: Have no clue what you're talking about.

Me: This cute boy from Highland asked for my number. Ryder shut him down before I could say anything.

Maria: OMG!!! Tell me!! Did you get his number?

Me: NO!

Maria: Was he cute?

Me: Yeah. Curly blond hair. Tall. Pretty hazel eyes.

Maria: Doesn't sound like someone you'd go for. Not your usual type.

Me: I have a type?

Maria: Jayson. He's more your type. Dark hair. Broody.

Me: You're crazy.

I surreptitiously peek at Jayson, then snap back to face forward when he glances over.

Maria may have a point. But it's not only Jayson. I've been crushing hard on him *and* Ryder for a while. It sucks being best friends with guys you also want to kiss. But that's *never* going to happen. I know that.

For the rest of the car ride, I sit quietly and do a little brooding myself as I stare out the window. When we arrive at Ryder's house, Jayson is the first to hop out.

Grabbing his duffel from the back, he says, "Going to take a quick shower to rinse off the chlorine."

Ryder tosses him the keys to the house. "Don't use all my shampoo like last time."

Jayson catches them midair, and without missing a beat, shoots Ryder the middle finger.

The rest of our group pulls in behind us, my parents and sister in our SUV, and Freda, Mitch, and Brea in their truck.

Hailey and Brea skip off hand in hand, their laughter fading as they disappear inside the house. Ryder, Julien, and I follow the paver-stone pathway that leads to the backyard.

The sun sinks lower on the horizon, casting a blend of pink and soft orange light across the sky. Puffy clouds, tinted in the same pastel hues, float lazily overhead, their edges catching the final glimmers of daylight. The sun won't set for another hour, but Ryder gets to work on lighting a fire to help keep the mosquitoes away.

Settling into our Adirondack chairs circling the firepit, a gentle breeze rustles the leaves of nearby trees as late afternoon quickly deepens to the bluish-purple of dusk. While Ryder and Julien talk about cars, I look up at the sky and count each star as they appear.

The tranquil quietude is broken when the back screen door bangs open. Jayson strolls outside, wearing one of Ryder's Randy's Custom Auto T-shirts and a pair of gray sweatpants, hair slicked back and arms loaded with canned drinks.

Handing everyone a soda, he collapses into the chair beside his brother with a relieved sigh and hooks a leg over the armrest.

"Coach told me after my heat that they would do an assembly on Friday to celebrate my record-beating time."

Ryder raises his can of soda. "You are a badass."

I'm so proud of each of their accomplishments. Jayson smashes it at swimming. Julien plays soccer. Last year, his team made it to the state finals, but they lost by one point. Mr. Cutton has been teaching Ryder how to drift at the Fields, a dirt track built on one of Mr. Jacoby's abandoned agricultural fields that sits between Fallen Brook and Highland. Even though Ryder has three more years before he gets his license, he already drives like a pro. He's that good.

The twins and I frequently go out to watch him. Sometimes, his dad lets us sit in the back seat while Ryder spins the car around the dirt track. It feels like being stuck on the Tilt-a-Whirl at the amusement park. Maybe Ryder will teach me how to drive like that someday—crazy and wild, and a little dangerous.

"Are we going to talk about what happened earlier?" I blurt.

"Nope," is the simultaneous answer I get back from my three best friends.

"Seriously?"

Julien pops open his soda and takes a sip. "Some guy comes over when he sees you with three other guys, and without checking with us first, decides it's okay to ask you out. That's not cool." He points his can in my direction and takes another sip.

"Says who? The no-fun police?" I grouse.

"You're too young to date," Ryder says.

I aspirate my drink. "You don't get to decide when I start dating. You can't control my life like that. It's not fair. I don't tell you which girl to like," I choke out.

Jayson pats my back until my cough settles down, then squats on his haunches in front of my chair, those silver-moon eyes boring into me.

"Do you really want to go out with Elijah?"

I look down at his hand touching mine. For some reason I feel like I want to cry.

"No," I whisper.

I don't want to date Elijah. I just wish everyone would stop acting like they have a say in my life. It feels like I'm never given the chance to make my own decisions before the guys jump in and take over. I know they mean well, but it's frustrating.

Julien nudges my foot with his shoe. "You good?"

He's always been the more empathetic one and can easily pick up on my feelings.

"Yep."

I go back to watching the stars.

Once Jamie, Ryder's older sister, and her boyfriend Jack arrive, the parentals congregate on the back deck, enjoying their beer and light conversation as Mr. Cutton mans the grill. No one cooks a hamburger like him, and my stomach is already growling in anticipation.

Soon enough, dinner is in full swing, and I join in the banter and happy laughter that circulates the firepit. I smile at Daddy when his eyes find me. He's on break for a month from touring with his band. I miss him so much when he's gone, so little moments like this, even tiny ones like a shared smile or quick glance, mean the world to me. Video calls and text messages help when he's away but having him physically here with us is so much better.

Just as I'm thinking about heading inside to grab stuff to make s'mores, Dad's voice cuts through the comfortable hum.

"Want to put on a show, puddin'?"

I look up and notice the two guitars he's holding by the neck in each hand. He had disappeared a few minutes earlier and must have gotten them from the house.

Happiness explodes like a glitter bomb inside my chest. I love performing with my dad.

"Absolutely."

He hands me my acoustic first, then loops his guitar strap around his neck. Taking out two picks from his pocket, he offers me one.

I lightly strum my guitar and adjust the tuning pegs.

"This is something I've been practicing."

I play the intro to "Stitches" by Shawn Mendes. Dad waits a beat, then joins in as the percussion parts of the song, slapping and thumping his hands on the body of his guitar. His deeper voice melds with mine, and we sound like John Cozart's *a cappella* cover of the song. Freda and Mom take out their phones to record our impromptu concert. Jamie, Brea, and Hailey provide background vocals, and I'm completely shocked when Ryder joins in as well. He hates singing in front of people. Jayson and Julien whoop it up, stomping their feet and hitting the arms of their chairs to the beat. When we get to the end of the song, everyone sings the last lyrics.

Jayson reaches across the gap between our chairs and brushes a hand down the length of my hair. It's his quiet way of apologizing. And just like that, our disagreement and my hurt feelings from earlier evaporate into mist.

As ten o'clock approaches, Faith brings out blankets for us to lie on, so we can watch the meteor shower forecasted to happen. The best viewing times are supposed to occur after midnight, but hopefully we'll get to see one or two before then.

Once Ryder and Julien stretch our blanket out flat, I lie down. Jayson rolls in next to me, and I use his shoulder for a pillow. Julien reposes back and rests his head on my stomach, his face gazing up at the sky. Ryder extends his long legs and gets situated on the other side of me, our hands gravitating toward one another, pinkies linking.

We lie there, tangled in the quiet, the stillness between us perfect, like we've always known how to fit together this way. In these moments, nothing else matters. Just being here, together, is enough.

Yawning widely, I catch the tail end of a faint flicker of light streaking across the inky darkness.

"Make a wish," Jayson says.

I close my eyes and wish upon a shooting star.

"What did you wish for?" he asks when my eyelids blink open.

I just smile.

Chapter Four

ELIZABETH

Summer Before Eleventh Grade
Choices and Regrets

WE'LL BE HEADING to the Outer Banks next week for July Fourth. Our families—mine, the twins', and Ryder's—rented a huge ten-room, three-story beach house on Topsail.

North Carolina has the best beaches, but Topsail Island is my favorite. It's sandwiched between the green ocean of the Atlantic to the east and the placid waters of the sound to the west. Serenity Point at the southern end of the island is nothing but flat, fine-grained sand that goes on as far as the eye can see. When at the beach, I wake up every morning before sunrise and walk down to the point just for the chance to see a pod of dolphins play in the waves or swim up the channel.

Between Topsail and the mainland is Banks Channel and a network of channels and sandbars. Julien and I love to walk along the sandbars to find hermit crabs, sand dollars, and conch shells. My jar collection now takes up all the shelves on my bookcase in my room.

"I'm not feeling this one," I tell Maria and take off the swimsuit I just tried on.

"Decent?"

"Yep."

My dressing room door cracks open, and I pass her the red two-piece to put on the discard rack.

"Try the yellow one."

Knowing I'm not going to like it because yellow clashes with my pale skin and blonde hair, I humor her anyway. Just as I expected, I hate it.

"I think I'm done."

I get no answer.

"Mar?"

Taking off the hideous yellow monstrosity, I go through my pile of favorites—a bright blue bikini with matching halter top, a long-sleeved swim shirt that zips up the back and comes with matching bikini bottoms, and a muted green one-piece paired with black board shorts—and cringe when I add up the total. There goes all the money I saved babysitting for a year.

When my phone chimes, I check my messages. Hailey sent a heart GIF and Julien sent a thumbs up, but nothing from Ryder or Jayson yet. I took mirror selfies of the winning pieces and sent the photos to the boys and Hailey for their opinion.

Maria stampedes into the dressing room just as I'm zipping up my denim shorts.

"Sexy boy alert!"

"What?"

"Sexy. Boy. Alert!" she whisper-shouts.

She scares the crap out of me when she pounds on the stall door.

"Hurry up!"

"Chill. I'm coming."

I give my reflection a thorough once-over in the mirror. My hair has really grown out over the past few months. It's halfway down my back and keeps a permanent wave—which I love by the way—but the temperatures are too hot right now for me to do anything other than tie it up into a high ponytail. I'm considering cutting it. I wonder if I'd look good in a short bob.

Sliding my feet into my sandals, I grab my stuff and unlock the door.

"Jayson and Ryder just walked in." Maria bounces on her toes as she peeks around the corner.

Ryder seems to make her nervous. She said it was because he was totally and utterly hot, and she couldn't deal with all his hotness. Those were her exact words verbatim.

I don't disagree. He *is* hot. Jayson, too. Unfortunately, as they've grown older, their level of hotness has exploded exponentially—as have my crushes on them. Once all three of them hit their growth spurt, Jayson and Julien shot up to over six feet. They're so active in sports, their muscle mass compensated for the sudden height gain. Ryder filled out as well, mostly due to all the heavy lifting he does on the regular in his dad's garage. The cute boys I grew up with are turning into devastatingly handsome men, and I'm stuck as the ugly duckling best friend.

My sandal catches on a bump in the carpet and flies off.

"Hurry up. They're coming this way."

Hopping on my left foot, I redo the strap and buckle. "Calm down."

She glowers at me over her shoulder. "You calm down."

I roll my eyes. Sometimes, she can be a major drama queen.

Grabbing her arm, I pull her from the dressing room.

Chapter Five

JAYSON

"I NEED SUSTENANCE. Want to grab something from Ruby's?"

Ryder's head emerges from under the hood of the sleek muscle car he's been working on, a thin smudge of grease streaking his cheek.

"Almost done."

Wiping his forehead with the back of his hand, he goes back to figuring out why the engine won't crank. We spent most of the day fine-tuning his bike, getting it ready for tonight's race at the Fields.

I truly believe Ryder has it in him to go pro—whether it's bikes or cars, the guy has a natural-born gift. Like all true adrenaline junkies, he says he races for the thrill of it and has no plans for his hobby to become something more. He knows what he wants in life, and that future includes taking over his dad's auto shop. Simple. Defined. Unlike me.

I wish I had my life mapped out that clearly. Instead, it's just a maze full of twists and turns that all seem to lead back to the same place: Liz.

My phone buzzes at the same time as Ryder's. A quick glance at the screen, and my breath catches in my throat.

"*Fuck me,*" I mutter under my breath, staring at the pictures Liz just sent.

I hold my phone out to Ryder. He takes one look and lets out a groan.

Wiping his hands off on a rag before reaching for his own phone, I watch him swipe through the images, his fingers pausing on each one a little longer than the last.

"What are you doing?" I ask, but I already know.

"None of your business," he replies, saving each picture of Liz to a file on his phone he thinks Julien and I don't know about. We all have one.

"I like the green one. It's the same color as her eyes."

I bite back the territorial growl that rises instinctively. I don't comment because...yeah. Not going there. Not now. Not ever. The truth? Liz should feel like a sister to me after all the years we've spent together. We've been best friends—me, her, Ryder, and Jules—for almost a decade. We've had sleepovers, shared inside jokes, cuddled on couches during movie nights, and I've snuck through her window countless times just to be near her. Normal things friends do.

But Elizabeth Penelope Fairchild has never felt like a sister to me. Not once. She's been the center of my universe since I was six years old. From the moment I first laid eyes on her.

But here's the catch—the part that keeps me up at night.

I glance at Ryder.

He's in love with her, too.

And that knowledge digs into me like a sharp thorn I can't pull free. I've tried to bury my feelings. Ry's been my closest friend for longer than I can remember.

But damn it, Liz makes it hard to stick to those friendship

boundaries. Especially when she sends pictures of herself dressed in only a bikini. She's clueless to the effect she has, and the temptation to cross that invisible line is always there, waiting for me to slip. But fuck if it wouldn't be a fantastic fall.

"You coming?" Ryder asks, already walking out of the garage bay.

I know what he's thinking because it's exactly what *I'm* thinking.

However, I'll be the guy buying her the swimsuits because I'll get to see her wear them at the beach next week.

Maybe that'll be enough to keep my heart in check.

Yeah, not likely.

Chapter Six

RYDER

RIGHT BEFORE JAY plows into a parking meter, I jerk him out of harm's way.

He looks up, says "thanks," and goes back to staring at pictures of Liz on his phone.

The boutique clothing store is located only four short blocks from my dad's garage, and he'll be lucky to make it there alive.

"You know distracted walking is against the law."

"You're shitting me. Really?"

Jay is too easy to mess with and will believe almost anything I tell him. I don't take that for granted. The level of trust between us wasn't just built—it was forged over years of loyalty and friendship. It's the kind of bond where you instinctively know the other person has your back, no questions asked. That same trust is why it makes it even more imperative for me to talk to him and Julien tonight about my feelings for Elizabeth.

She's on my mind constantly. The thought of asking her out isn't new; it's something that's been lingering for longer than I care to admit. The idea of us, of more than just friendship, has been like an itch I can't quite reach. Every time I work up the courage to tell her how I feel, something stops me. Or rather, someone.

I see the longing glances Jay throws her way. The intense way he watches her when he thinks no one else is paying attention. It's impossible to miss because it's the same way I look at her.

And it's not just that. They've known her longer. Before I came barging into the picture, they were an inseparable trio—Julien, Jayson, and Elizabeth. I remember that day so clearly, stepping into their world for the first time, feeling like I was intruding on something sacred. But I couldn't stop myself from gravitating toward the girl who had instantly won me over with her kindness and sweet smile.

That first day in class, Elizabeth stood up for me, loaned me that book she'd been waiting weeks to read—like I mattered more than the story she'd been dying to dive into. She brought me into her circle without hesitation. I've always been grateful for that. Jayson and Julien became my brothers in every sense of the word, and Elizabeth...became my everything.

I give Jayson's shoulder a nudge, trying to shake the weight from my thoughts. "Yes, I'm shitting you. Were you asleep during driver's ed?"

He barely glances up from his phone. "Pretty much."

"Heard Elijah is racing tonight."

We first crossed paths with Elijah three years ago when he was going to Highland Middle and swam against Jayson. He started racing at the Fields last year. Dad has been giving him some pointers, and Elijah and I have met up a few times to mess around on our bikes. The guys think that he's still hung up on Elizabeth. I'm not so sure.

Jayson shrugs, but his voice is flat when he replies, "As long as he stays away from Liz, I don't have a problem with the guy."

When we reach our destination, I catch movement behind the

glass storefront of the boutique. Maria freezes when she spots me through the display, then quickly ducks out of sight.

"Jay, there's something...I want to talk...to you about."

His eyebrows raise at my faltering tone.

"Okay."

I open my mouth, but nothing comes out. When it comes to Elizabeth, I can't seem to find my voice. I've tried—God, I've tried so many times to tell them how I feel about her, to bring it up in some casual, offhanded way. And every time, the words get stuck, like now.

My eyes catch Elizabeth through the window, and my heart beats a fast staccato triple beat.

"After the race, can you and Jules drop by my house?"

He glances through the window, then back at me, his brow furrowing as if he's already figured out my big secret.

I just pray that he doesn't hate me for it.

Chapter Seven

ELIZABETH

SEVERAL YEARS AGO, Mr. Jacoby installed towering pole lights around the dirt track he built, and something that was done for fun on the weekends turned into regular Friday night races where anyone with a dirt bike or a fast car and the attitude that comes with either could meet up for friendly competition. It's a weekly ritual we've clung to ever since, as if the dust and adrenaline have seeped into our bones. The North may have hockey, the Midwest their football, but our tiny slice of nowhere North Carolina is all about fast cars.

I don't know how they arrange the line-up of racers, but Ryder always gets a text days before, giving him just enough time to prepare.

Watching him race is both exhilarating and terrifying, like riding a rollercoaster without a seat belt. My stomach twists into knots when I see him tear through the turns, clods of dirt flying in his wake. But no matter how badly I may want to throw up when I watch him race, I'm still the loud, crazy girl cheering her guts out with pride on the sidelines.

As we approach the Fields, I twist in my seat and glance out the back window. Mr. Jameson is trailing behind us in his truck, Jayson and Julien crammed in the back seat. I wave, but they don't notice—Ryder's old KTM dirt bike is in the way.

"We're here," Mr. Cutton says.

The sight of the track's glowing lights sends a jolt of anxious energy through me.

Ryder cuts me an amused side-glance. "Why are you nervous?"

"Not nervous," I lie. "Just excited."

To prove his point, he places a hand atop my knee to still the pogo-bouncing of my leg. At his touch, I become hyperaware of the cascade of goose bumps that ripple in waves over my skin.

"Hold on," Mr. Cutton warns.

He somehow pulls off a perfect three-point turn on the narrow dirt road, kicking up a swirl of dust before parking along the side. It's an ideal spot, making it easy to unload Ryder's bike.

Ryder jumps out first, then reaches up to help me down, his hand steady as he guides me to the ground before heading to the back of the truck to pop the tailgate.

With a honk of the horn, Mr. Jameson drives by, slowly hunting for a parking spot large enough for his long-bed.

"Anything I can do?" I ask.

"We got it, sweetheart," Mr. Cutton says with a grin, already unhooking the straps holding the bike in place.

I stay out of their way, leaving them to their work, and let my eyes wander. The place is packed, and the atmosphere hums with anticipation, the air thick with the smell of damp earth and car exhaust.

I spot familiar faces milling about—kids from our school, others from Highland, and even two county deputies, one of them Elijah's dad.

Speaking of Elijah, I spot him walking his bike toward the track.

"Elijah!"

He looks over and waves.

"Be back in a sec," I say and jog off.

I've gotten to know him better over the past year after he started coming to the Fields. He's a really nice guy. Funny, too. I think the guys are wrong about him wanting to date me. He hasn't shown me any obvious interest, other than friendly conversation.

"Hey! Haven't seen you in a while. How's your summer going?"

Elijah has been absent from the Friday night races for a month, so I haven't seen him since school let out for summer break.

"Shit," I groan in disgust, and I mean that in the literal sense.

The long field grass tickles my calves, and I'm glad I'm wearing tennis shoes because I think I just stepped in a pile of cow manure.

Several months ago, the herd from an adjoining field got loose during a race and sauntered across the track. It made for a memorable night. Tonight, not so much.

"You okay?" Elijah asks. He props his bike on its kickstand.

"Yeah. Yuck. I think I just stepped in cow dung."

Balancing precariously on one leg like a human flamingo, I lift my foot, trying to peer at the smeared mess on the sole of my shoe.

"Gross," I say with a grimace.

Elijah rushes forward just as I wobble, his arms catching me before I topple over. For a moment, we end up in a ridiculous, off-balance pose, like awkward dance partners frozen mid-step.

"Thanks for the save." I giggle up at him.

"No problem."

The frivolity of the moment quickly evaporates when a strong arm snakes around my waist and pulls me upright in one swift motion.

"Don't touch her," Jayson says in a tone I don't recognize, and Elijah's hands shoot up in confused supplication.

Jayson's grip tightens, his chest pressed against my back. I feel the warmth of his breath fan across my neck when he drops his head and huskily murmurs in my ear, "You good?"

And dear god, my body combusts in a wildfire of shivers that I have no control over.

My mind scrambles for a coherent thought. I'm going to die. Just drop dead right in the middle of a field and die. *Get a grip, Elizabeth!*

"I, um...stepped in something and lost my balance," I stammer, trying to focus. "Elijah caught me."

Julien and Ryder stroll over, and my embarrassment deepens. The tension between Jayson and Elijah is palpable, but Julien defuses it with a casual fist bump and a quick, "Hey man."

Jayson still hasn't let go, his arm a firm band around my middle. Every muscle clenches tight at the featherlight, almost imperceptible circles his thumb traces over my stomach. I bite my lip to steady my breathing but it's almost impossible when his touch sets my nerves on fire.

"Jayson," I whisper, turning my head slightly.

Our lips are scant inches apart, and the sudden spark that leaps between us snaps Jayson out of his stare off with Elijah. His hand suddenly drops as if burned, and for some reason, that confuses me even more, especially after what happened with Ryder in the truck.

"Catch you on the track," Elijah says to Ryder, making a hasty escape.

"Hold up," Julien calls and catches up to him.

Ryder bumps Jayson's shoulder. "Come on. Help me and Dad with the bike."

The guys leave me standing there, alone, in a daze of confusion, struggling with a maelstrom of emotions I don't have the first clue how to process or even comprehend. Something changed between me, Ryder, and Jayson tonight.

"Boo!"

I jump like a startled cat getting doused by a water hose. "Jesus, Mar. Don't do that."

She hooks her arm through mine. "There are so many hot guys here. No wonder you come every week."

Her eyes widen when she realizes her double entendre, and she snickers.

"You're so juvenile, Mar."

This girl is a jumble of crazy. Mostly good, sometimes annoying, but I love her just the same.

We talk as we walk, following the crowd of people making their way over to the track.

"Oh, he's fine as fuck. Who's that?"

I glance in the direction of where she's pointing. Tall, blond, blue-eyed, and someone you never want to mess with.

"Fallon."

He's a friend of Ryder's from Highland, but there's something about him that always makes me turn and run in the other direction.

His family is loaded. Montgomery Pharma is one of the largest pharmaceutical companies in the nation, and their headquarters are in Research Triangle Park; not to mention, about half our state is employed in one way or another by his family's company.

She lets out a lusty hum. "*That's* Fallon Montgomery? Holy hell. Yes, please."

"Liz!" Julien shouts, waving us over to where he and Jayson are standing.

It doesn't escape my notice that Jayson keeps his distance,

which only confuses me even more. But those thoughts disappear as soon as Ryder straps on his racing helmet.

"Babe, you're crushing my hand."

I look down at our joined hands and immediately let go.

"Sorry."

Needing something to anchor me, I wrap my fingers around the rough wood of a nearby fence post. The texture digs into my palm, grounding me as my heart hammers an erratic rhythm inside my chest.

Ryder, Elijah, and several others line their bikes up at the starting mark. The track is slick with remnants of the week's summer storms, the mud clinging to their tires.

Fallon takes a megaphone from one of the deputies and walks out onto the track.

"Who's ready to see some racing tonight?"

The gathered crowd responds with a wave of excited shouts and cheers that vibrate through the ground beneath my feet.

"I can't hear you! Who's ready for some heart-pounding, loud as hell, strap-yourself-to-your-seats racing tonight?"

The screams and whistles erupt into a roar, the sound swelling to a deafening crescendo that pulses in my ears.

Fallon hands the megaphone back to the deputy and signals for the racers to mount their bikes.

With a twist of their handlebars, engines roar to life, their revs crashing into the night like thunder breaking loose, each rumble sending a thrill through the crowd.

Through the noise, I strain to hear what Fallon says.

"You know the rules. If you don't, tough shit." He steps out of the way of the bikes and raises his arms in front of him. "On your mark."

My eyes are cemented to Ryder's profile, my palms sweaty. I

can't see his face because of his helmet, but I know he's completely focused.

I grab hold of Maria.

"Seriously?" she says and dislodges her arm from my death grip.

Lifting his arms above his head, Fallon shouts, "Get set!"

Ryder tenses. I tense. Everything goes pin-drop silent. Not even a cricket dares to make a chirp.

Fallon drops his arms.

"Go!"

The bikes scream away from the starting line, and a loud whoosh of breath I didn't know I was holding comes rushing out of my lungs. The action on the track is a cacophony of chaos. Two riders slide out of bounds around the first corner. One rider gets taken out when his front wheel hits a rut, and he clips the bike next to him.

Somehow, Ryder and Elijah make it through unscathed. By the second lap, the racers seem to have gotten used to the conditions on the course. Two laps down, two to go.

On the last lap, Ryder takes first position. He leans into the last curve, his leg stretching to the ground to help turn the bike as it skids around the bend, and then he's off like a bullet. He takes a quick look behind him, then slows down when he passes by our group and pops a wheelie as he crosses the finish line. Elijah follows thirty seconds later, with the remaining riders close behind.

"Oh my god! That was epic!" Maria screams.

Me? I'm speechless. That boy. That wonderful, crazy, magnificent boy.

Fallon saunters onto the track and throws Ryder's arm up in victory.

"Jay, come on," Julien says and jumps the fence.

My cheeks hurt from smiling so hard as I watch them celebrate.

After things settle down and the track is cleared for the next race, the guys help Mr. Cutton load Ryder's bike into the bed of the truck.

"Be right there." Ryder stops in front of Maria and me, his copper eyes locked on me as if I'm the only person who exists in the melee surrounding us.

"Hi."

"Hey." He runs his hand through his dark hair and grins.

Maria's gaze pings back and forth between us.

"You were incredible," I tell him, a huge smile exploding across my face.

"Yeah?"

"Yeah," I breathe.

He links our pinkies together. "There's something I'd like to talk to you about tomorrow. Can I come over around one?"

Maria leans against the fence and pretends that she's not blatantly eavesdropping.

"Oh, sure, yeah...did you want to talk now?"

Ryder considers it. "Tomorrow. Jay, Jules, and I have got something to do tonight."

Secret guy stuff. Figures.

"One is fine, or come over whenever. I don't have any plans."

His pinkie squeezes mine before letting go.

As soon as he leaves, Maria turns around. "What was that about?"

That foreboding sense of change comes back with a vengeance, and I don't know if I'm prepared for it. I should talk to Hailey about it later. She'll help me figure things out.

"I don't know, Mar. I guess I'll find out tomorrow."

Chapter Eight

RYDER

RECLINING back in the weathered Adirondack chair, I let the humid evening air settle around me. Scrolling through photos on my phone to pass the time, I mindlessly flick past memories that span almost a decade.

I pause on a group photo of the four of us, staring at it for a moment. My thumb hovers over the screen before I finally press the power button, the glow of the phone fading into black.

I keep second-guessing whether openly confessing my feelings about Elizabeth is a good idea. The conversation I'm about to have could go one of two ways: they could understand and give me their blessing—or I could lose my two best friends.

The memory of seeing Jay grab Elizabeth earlier flares up again, the same bitterness bubbling to the surface. That pang of jealousy, sharp and unsettling, had been hard to swallow. But it quickly quieted the second the race started, and her eyes were fixed solely on me. I love having her attention. I love it when she cheers me on. And the smile she graced me with at the end when I walked over to her...I thought my heart was going to explode right out of my chest.

The back patio door creaks open, then slams shut.

I wipe suddenly damp palms on the front of my shorts and wait.

"Guess what?" Julien leans against the stone façade of the firepit, looking smug. "I posted a video of your race, and it's gotten over ten thousand views."

Jay drops down in the chair next to me, legs outstretched, arms crossed over his chest. "You were reckless popping that wheelie at the end."

"I knew the conditions of the track. I made sure to compensate," I reply, not understanding why he's so upset.

And yeah, I may have been showing off a little for Elizabeth.

He sits forward and laces his fingers together, his disapproving eyes landing on me.

"That stupid stunt almost cost you the race."

"It's just a race, Jay. It doesn't mean anything."

"Liz was watching. She was worried."

Julien kicks his brother's shoe. "No, she wasn't. Stop being a dick."

"Speaking of Elizabeth," I say, gathering my courage.

Jay's head snaps back. "What about her?"

I silently give myself a pep talk to man the fuck up and get the words out. I don't think I've ever been as apprehensive about anything as I am right now.

Taking a deep breath, I decide it's now or never.

"That's why I wanted to talk to you tonight." My chest gets tight, but I plow ahead. Needing to stand and pace, I start over. "Okay. Look." God, this is hard. "Okay."

"Will you just say whatever the fuck it is you want to say?" Jay snaps.

From the look he's giving me, the firm set to his mouth, the clench of his jaw, suddenly his surly mood makes sense.

He knows.

Time to rip the Band-Aid off—and it all comes out as a complete tumble of word vomit.

"We've been friends for a long time. A very long time. It's always been us and Elizabeth. You guys are my family. I consider you both my brothers. I would never, *not ever*, betray you or do anything that would hurt either of you."

I stop and make eye contact to emphasize that point, to show them I'm serious about what I just said.

"This is difficult. Has been difficult for a while. The best friend thing with Elizabeth isn't working for me anymore. I want more."

I stop in front of Jayson, but he keeps his head bowed low between hunched shoulders, his hands gripped tightly together in his lap until his knuckles are white. He won't look at me, so I ramble on, needing to get it all out.

"I love her. I am in love with her. I've kept my feelings to myself...because I know you're in love with her, too." Emotion chokes me until I can't breathe. "I'm tired of fighting my feelings. I'm tired of feeling guilty about wanting to ask her out. So here I am, laying it all out, hoping that you both will forgive me. Hoping that you don't hate me for loving her."

Julien is the first to break the strangling silence.

"If it was any other guy, I'd kick his ass because *it's Liz*. But you're not any guy. I trust you implicitly, and I have no problem with you wanting to date her, Ry. I *will* have a problem if you hurt her or break her heart."

Relief floods me. "I promise. I won't. I swear. I told Elizabeth that I wanted to talk to her about something important tomorrow, but I had to talk to you guys tonight. I needed to make sure we're all good first." I silently beg Jay to look at me. Give me a reaction. Something. "Jay? Are we good?"

He remains quiet, his posture rigid, angry.

"Jay, you're being uncharacteristically non-verbal," Julien says when his brother remains stolid.

One minute goes by. Two.

Suddenly, Jay springs out of his seat and bolts across the yard.

"Jay!" I shout as he sprints out of view around the side of the house.

Julien cuffs my shoulder. "Give him some time. He'll come around."

I don't cry, but damn if the tears don't come.

That possibility I had feared just came true.

And things will never be the same between us ever again.

Chapter Nine

JAYSON

MY MIND HAS GONE BLANK. Anger grips me, and I can't fucking breathe. I don't remember anything after leaving Ryder's backyard. I don't remember how I got here.

I sat and listened to him pour his heart out to me. Every goddamn word he spoke mirrored my own thoughts because my heart was saying the same thing. His words were my words. But knowing those words were coming from his mouth, his heart, I couldn't sit there any longer.

I knew it was coming. I knew it the moment Ryder told me he wanted to talk to Julien and me about something important. But when he finished talking, when my twin brother gave him his blessing, I just ran. Fucking jumped out of my seat and ran. I had to get out of there. I had to escape before my world fractured apart into a thousand jagged pieces.

I grip the sides of my head, hands fisting my hair. My mind races, thoughts blurring together. Images of him and her. I'm in agony.

Shit! Fuck! Dammit! I'm going to lose her. I'm about to lose my reason for getting up in the morning. I exist because she is in my life. Without her, I don't know what the hell to do. Ryder is going to take her away from me. He'll be the one she kisses, the one she gives her heart to. The one she gives her love to.

The thought of her being with someone else—no, not just someone else. Him. My best friend. I should be happy. I should have patted him on the back and stepped aside. Allow Liz to choose for herself. I have no rights to her. She doesn't officially belong to me. I have no say in what she does or who she dates.

But goddamn it! She's mine. I have loved that girl for half my life. I can't let her go, not even to be with my best friend. A guy who is like my brother and part of my family. Ryder has always been the better man. He had the courage to step up and tell Julien and me how he felt. I wish I was that selfless. I wish I could be more like him, but I'm not. I'm just a scared boy, who at the age of six found his soulmate. And I can't step aside. Not even for him.

Looking up at the old oak tree that stands between our houses, I peer up at Liz's window. It's open like usual, and I can hear her voice floating down to me like a song whispering through the leaves of the tree as it glides upon the night's breeze. She's talking to Hailey. I stand there at the foot of the tree and listen.

I don't know how long I'm there lost in my world of misery and questions. I hear a click and then her bedroom goes dark. I watch as Liz appears in the frame of her window, her long pale hair loose around her shoulders, looking like a goddess come to life. While my mind is still running on a loop, my body takes over and decides to move on its own. Without thinking, I leap up and grab hold of the bottom branch of the oak and start to climb.

Liz notices the tree shudder from my efforts, her face full of confusion, wondering what's climbing the tree in the middle of the night. She leans over the sill to get a better view, then startles when she sees me.

"Jayson?"

Chapter Ten

ELIZABETH

WHEN I GOT HOME from the Fields, full of confusion and doubts, Hailey was waiting for me in my bedroom. I had texted her on the way home asking if we could talk. She has a way of making me feel better about things that bother me.

"What do I do, Hales? Things seem to be changing between us, and I don't know if it's a good change or not."

Fragrant summer air filled with the scent of honeysuckle vines wafts through my open bedroom window, fluttering the curtains.

Hailey takes a brush from my bedside table and glides it through my hair. She opens her mouth to say something but doesn't. I know she's trying to find the right words, like she does when writing her poems. Hailey wants every word to have meaning.

"You, the twins, and Ryder have always had a special bond. And I know you love them in different ways. But is that love the type of love that goes deeper? You need to ask yourself that question first."

I think about Julien, his quick smile and kind spirit. But my feelings for him don't go further than profound friendship.

Then there's Jayson. He makes my heart pound. I look into his light-gray eyes and every part of me tingles. Ryder is my amber-eyed daredevil, the keeper of my heart.

What would happen to us if I chose one and not the other? Would Jayson hate me if I dated Ryder? Would Ryder never talk to me again if I chose Jayson?

Nose scrunching in thought, I exhale a sharp sigh. "I don't want to hurt anybody."

Hailey puts down the brush and embraces me in a warm hug. "What do *you* want, Lizzie? What would make *you* happy?"

I lean back into my sister's arms, accepting the comfort she's giving.

"I wish the choice was taken out of my hands, so I don't have to constantly worry about it, but I also just want things to stay the same."

I'm a coward.

She stifles a yawn and climbs over me to get off the bed.

"Sorry, sis. I'm exhausted and at a loss on what you should do. Get some sleep and hopefully the answer will come to you in your dreams."

"Good night, Hales. Thanks for listening."

"Always. Love you."

Hailey walks through our jack-and-jill, closing both bathroom doors.

My mind is too busy running ragged circles, and I know sleep won't come anytime soon. I click off my bedroom light and walk over to the open window. Even though it's the middle of the summer and the air is sticky with humidity, I keep my window open at night. I started doing that when the twins moved in next door.

The branches and leaves of the oak tree shake. Sometimes raccoons or opossums climb the tree at night. I peer out to get a closer look and jump a foot off the floor when a tall figure appears, scaring the crap out of me.

"Jayson?"

He climbs through the window and into my bedroom. His metallic eyes bore into mine, their glow in the darkness rivaling that of a full moon. I'm forced to look up at him since he's several inches taller. He's breathing hard, fists clenched at his sides. He looks angry, wild, but his eyes hold something else. Something that causes my heart to skip a beat.

"Jayson?" I ask again, unsure, and raise my hand to touch him.

As soon as my fingers graze the side of his face, his eyes change, his pupils dilating, making his irises look almost black. He takes a step toward me. I take a step back. It's almost like we're dancing. My pulse quickens even more.

Jayson's heated gaze tracks across my face like an intimate caress. He takes another step forward until his body is mere inches from mine. An unfamiliar spark ignites between us. It's electricity charged by lightning. Heat fired with an internal flame. Air from our lungs comes out in short, sharp puffs.

Even though Jayson isn't physically touching me, I can feel him *everywhere*.

He takes another slow half-step toward me. Those mesmerizing eyes hold mine, and I couldn't look away from him now if my life depended on it.

Slowly, very slowly, as if he's about to touch something precious and fragile, Jayson cups the side of my face, fingers wrapping around the nape of my neck, thumb curling under my chin. With gentle urging, he tips my face up, his thumb tracing the contour of my bottom lip.

I go motionless, absolutely still, knowing what's coming but disbelieving it's about to happen.

"I love you, Liz."

He closes those final millimeters and presses his mouth to mine.

I get just a moment to feel the softness of his lips before he claims every thought in my head with a kiss that shakes the foundation of reality and tilts my world upside down.

It's like an out-of-body experience.

My first kiss.

My first kiss with Jayson.

I've never kissed a boy before. I have absolutely no experience to fall back on to help me figure out what I need to do. So I relinquish control to Jayson, knowing that he will guide the way.

He guides me where he wants me, kissing me deeper. I never could have possibly imagined being kissed as thoroughly as Jayson is kissing me right now. It's as if we can't breathe unless we are taking in the air of the other. It's heady and intoxicating.

His phone chimes with a notification, ending the surreal moment. I'm the first to pull away.

Seconds tick by, but it's enough time for my brain to clear from the sensual fog of Jayson's kisses—and panic sets in.

What have we done?

"Liz."

My panic rises. "What have we done?"

"Something we should have done a long time ago," he replies softly, pulling me back for another kiss to prove his point.

A kiss that weakens my knees and fuzzes my brain.

No. We can't do this. I push against his chest.

My voice rises when I start to cry. "You don't understand. You don't get it. This changes everything."

Without fully letting me go, he pushes me backward to my bed and sits down with me.

"Liz, look at me."

I refuse.

"Liz," he says more sternly. "Look at me."

Once he has my attention, he pulls my face to his and kisses me slowly—once, twice, three times.

"Nothing is going to change. I promise."

"But—"

"I love you. I have loved you for a long time. Tell me that you feel the same. Please tell me that we can be together, that you'll be mine. I'll do anything. *Anything*. Just tell me."

One of the boys I have loved since I was six years old is in front of me, declaring his heart to mine, trusting that I won't break it. And I won't. I can't.

It seems that fate is stepping in, making the decision for me.

So, I let it.

Jayson waits patiently for my answer, but a part of me hesitates —the part that's in love with Ryder.

You can't be that selfish.

I don't know what to do.

"Liz, *please*."

Jayson's anguished words pleading with me to love him back tear down my walls of resistance.

"Yes."

His stunned face breaks out in a brilliant smile. "Yes?"

I kiss his cheek. "Yes."

I kiss his forehead. "Yes."

I kiss his nose. "Yes."

I stare into the eyes of the boy who has been my best friend since I was six years old.

"I love you, too."

Chapter Eleven

JULIEN

SITTING IN THE BEDROOM, my back against my headboard, I stare up at the ceiling while I wait for my brother to come home.

I just spent two hours with a distraught Ryder. He was upset, thinking he had destroyed our friendships with his declaration about his intentions for Liz. I reassured him that everything would be fine, that Jayson just needed some time to process.

I pick up my phone and check the time. *Jay, where the hell are you?*

On automatic pilot, my thumb scrolls through my photos until I come to the one that I took of Ryder and Elijah on their dirt bikes. I hit the circle on my screen to pull up my contacts.

Don't do it. Don't press the—dammit, Julien.

Me: Hey. You up?

I send it before I lose my nerve. It takes mere seconds before a reply comes back.

Elijah: Yeah, I'm up. Just watching some TV in bed. You?

I relax into my pillows, the swarm of butterflies in my stomach calming.

Me: Things turned to shit tonight and... I don't know. I just needed somebody to talk to.

My phone vibrates in my hand, and I almost drop it when Elijah's name pops up.

"Hey," I answer, then I hold my breath as I wait for his reply.

"Thought you might need to hear a friendly voice instead of a text."

"I'm sorry for bothering you so late. I don't know what I was thinking. You were probably about to go to sleep," I prattle.

"Julien, it really is no problem at all. I was up."

I hear rustling in the background, and I assume he's getting more comfortable in bed. Oh, the images that conjure up. I whack the phone against my forehead, hoping to reboot my brain.

"Julien? You still there?"

"I'm here."

"What's going on?"

"Tonight has been messed up."

"Talk to me. Maybe I can help," he gently prods.

I need a friend to talk to. I can't talk to Ryder about it, and Jay is definitely not a contender for a "shoulder to cry on." I can't go to Liz because she's the topic of conversation I want to talk about.

"Ryder told me and Jay something tonight, and my brother flipped the fuck out."

"Why?"

This is the hard part. "Ryder told us that he wanted to ask Liz out. That he's in love with her."

I hear him suck in a small breath before replying, "Ouch. How are *you* feeling about that?"

"It was weird at first, but I can think of no better man for her than him."

"How is Jayson handling it?"

"Not good. We all thought you liked her, so Ryder's big announcement took me by surprise."

"I never liked Liz like that. I like someone else."

The softness creeping into Elijah's voice has me on edge. Has me thinking things. Impossible things.

"What if that someone else likes you, too?"

I say it out loud without meaning to because there is no chance in hell that Elijah would ever be interested in me. He may send beautiful smiles my way, but that doesn't mean anything. Elijah is a nice person all around. He smiles at everyone.

Total silence ensues over the line.

"Julien?" Elijah whispers, and I hear him say my name as if he were sitting right here next to me.

"Yeah?" I swallow hard.

"I consider myself a pretty good judge of character when it comes to reading people. Someone like me has to be."

What does he mean, *someone like me*?

"If I read you wrong, then please say so. But I don't think I did."

Tiny beads of sweat pop up along my forehead.

"I'm not sure I understand what you mean," I tell him, even though my conscience was screaming inside my head, calling me a bald-faced liar.

"You caught my attention the first time I laid eyes on you at the swim meet. Do you remember that day?"

I remember every fucking second.

"That was almost three years ago," I reply.

"I know. That's how long I've been waiting for you to say something. To call me. To ask me out. Anything."

I pull the phone away from my ear and stare at it. Does he mean...? *No fucking way.*

"Elijah—"

"Go out with me this weekend."

My heart hammers like a bass drum. Want and desire consume me like wildfire, but disbelief and fear hold me back from saying yes.

Deciding to play dumb, I say, "I thought we already decided to hang out this weekend."

Stupid, stupid, stupid.

Elijah's gentle laughter rolls over me like silk. "You know that's not what I meant."

"Then I'm going to need you to spell it out for me."

"All right. Hi, Julien. I'm Elijah. I like you. *A lot.* And I think you like me, too. In fact, I'm pretty sure that you do. So, I'd like to ask you out on a date."

I want to say yes so badly. I've had a crush on Elijah for years, only now to find out the feeling was mutual.

"Julien?"

Pain seizes my heart as indecision claims me. What will people think if they see me and Elijah together? What will Jay think? Or Liz or Ryder? My parents? Fallen Brook is a small town and small towns can have small mindsets.

Feeling like I want to cry and cursing the universe for being so unfair, I choke out, "Elijah, I can't. I'm sorry. I'm not ready. I don't even know if this is what I want."

"Do you like me?" he asks.

Yes! I dream about Elijah almost every night. I dream about how it would feel to kiss him and touch him. Every single time I see him, I swear, I swoon like a fucking Southern belle. He's gorgeous and kind, and my body has a visceral response to him whenever he's within a hundred feet of me.

"I *can't*," I reply, wanting to say the exact opposite, but too chickenshit to do it.

He sighs, and I want to crawl through the phone and wrap my arms around him. I'm not rejecting him. I'm scared. I've never told anyone, not even Jay or Liz, about my feelings because *I* don't even understand them. How can I be attracted to girls *and* to guys?

"I understand," he eventually says, but I can hear his disappointment.

I try to meet him in the middle and be as truthful as I can.

"I *do* like you, Elijah. I want to say yes. But I just can't right now. Is it okay if I asked for more time? Can we see how we are as friends first?"

Without hesitation, he replies, "Yeah, Julien. I'd like that. I would love for us to be friends."

All the tension that had been coiling inside me, ready to explode, expels in a deep exhale. "Thank you."

"Can I tell you three really important things?" he asks.

"Go for it."

"Thing number one. You have the most beautiful gray eyes I have ever seen. I dream about your eyes. The way they look like liquid silver, and how they shine when you smile."

My breath hitches, and it feels like all the blood drains southward to my dick.

"What's the second thing?" I literally groan.

"Everything will be okay. Things with your brother. Things with Liz and Ryder. I'm a believer that stuff happens in life for a reason. If it didn't, I wouldn't have met you."

I melt a little at his statement. "What's the third thing?"

"One day, when you're ready, I'm going to kiss you."

It was after three in the morning when Jayson sneaks into our room through our bedroom window. I figured out where he was after I got out of the shower and saw the outline of his silhouette inside Liz's bedroom. I lied to Mom when she saw me downstairs in the kitchen getting a midnight snack. She asked me where Jay was, and I told her he was already asleep upstairs.

When I finally settled into bed for the night, I texted Ryder to make sure he was okay. He was still a mess. He thought Jayson hated him. He thought he'd lost his best friend. I reassured him over and over that everything was going to be okay. Our bonds of friendship were strong. But like the stupid asshole my twin brother just made me when I saw he was with Liz—I was a liar. What I promised Ryder was now all a big, fat lie, and that infuriated me.

"Where the hell have you been?"

I glare at my brother as he strips off his shirt and shorts and climbs into bed. His nonchalance only adds fuel to my anger. I lob a pillow at his head.

"I asked you a question."

"Fuck off!" He turns his back to me and takes the pillow I just chucked at him, punching it a few times before resting his head on it.

Needing to see his face—knowing I will catch him in a lie if he tries—I sit up and sling my legs over the side of my bed, ready to confront him.

"Are you seriously going to pretend that I did not just see your fucking idiot self in Liz's bedroom?"

I get nothing.

"After everything Ryder said to us tonight. He laid his heart out, and you shit all over it."

That gets his attention. Jay leaps out of bed and lunges at me. My brother may be muscular, years of swimming giving him broad shoulders and strong arms, but I'm faster, my soccer skills and quick feet coming in handy. I easily dodge his attack. He immediately recovers and grabs my shoulders, shoving me backward. I know it's not me who he's fighting. He's fighting himself. He's at war with what he's done and needs to channel that aggression into something physical. Unfortunately, I'm his punching bag.

Jay catches me off guard with a punch to the jaw, but I give back as good as I get and clip him on the nose. We both freeze when we see blood. Some drips from the cut he opened on my lip, and some is from his nose. We both look over at our bedroom door at the same time, expecting Mom to barge in and catch us fighting.

"Does hitting me make you feel better? Want me to see if Liz wants to come over so you can pound out your guilt on her, too?"

Jay's face blanches. He quickly backs down and takes a seat on the side of his bed, his anger deflating right before my eyes. Like earlier tonight at Ryder's, his head hangs low as he refuses to look at me.

"I panicked. I fucking panicked. I heard what Ryder was saying and all I could think about was that I was going to lose my girl. *My girl,*" he declares, thumping his chest above his heart. "I know I should've told her how I felt ages ago. I know I should've talked to Ryder. The three of us have been dancing around the subject for years. I wasn't expecting him to finally grow a pair and pursue her. So yeah, I panicked. *Fucking hell,*" he finishes on a tortured groan.

"You need to fix this."

"I know. I promised Liz that I would take care of everything. I'll make sure she doesn't lose any of us. I made her a promise, and I will never break my promises to that girl."

"You didn't see what you running off did to Ry. He's devastated. He thinks you hate him. I promised him otherwise. Told him you just needed a moment. Now I'm a lying asshole, thanks to you."

If I thought Jay's head couldn't hang any lower in shame, I was wrong.

"Talk to me. No matter what, I am here for you. But I won't betray Ryder. I'm not going to lie to him."

"I love her, Julien. I can't live without her. I'm sorry."

I love my twin brother, too. I hate seeing him tying himself into knots about this. We all knew things would come to a head sooner or later when it came to Liz. Lines would have to be drawn, boundaries established, choices made. I only wish he had gone about it better. Talked to me and Ryder, instead of running off behind Ryder's back to stake his claim on her and steal her away from our best friend.

"He still plans on telling her how he feels tomorrow. You're going to have to suck it up and talk to him first before he sees her. Otherwise, it's going to cause a shitload of problems."

I touch his shoulder, and he reaches up, grabbing my hand like a lifeline. Sitting down beside him on his bed, I wrap my arm around his shoulders and pull him to me.

"Want to talk about it?"

Jayson wipes wetness from the corner of his eye and smiles. "It was beautiful."

"Okay, not wanting too many details because the girl is my

best friend, and I may decide to punch you again if you made any moves on her. But go ahead."

Jay tells me that Liz said she loved him back. Regardless of how screwed up the circumstances, she made a choice. I hope Ryder is strong enough to live with it.

Chapter Twelve

ELIZABETH

THE MATTRESS BOUNCES, waking me from the dream I was having. A dream of me, Jayson, Ryder, and Julien when we were younger. We'd been playing in our forest fort after coming back from the creek. I remembered Jayson had found this rose-colored quartz rock in the shape of a heart that he gave to me to add to my jar collection. He placed it in my palm and wrapped my fingers tightly around it. I could feel its smoothness and its warmth. When I opened my hand, the heart-shaped rock was broken, split and cracked down the middle. I looked up to ask Jayson what happened to it, but it was not Jayson in front of me. It was Ryder.

"So, which one was it?" a voice asks from beside me, pulling me fully from my dream.

I stretch my arms up and roll over. Images from last night instantly flood my brain, and I lift my fingers to my still tingling lips.

"Which one was what?" I ask, not fully awake yet.

I sleepily swat her offending finger away when she pokes me in the ribs.

"Which one was it? Jayson or Ryder? Or was it Julien?"

I crack one eye open.

"You know I can hear everything in my room even with the bathroom doors closed."

That instantly wakes me right the hell up. "What exactly do you think you heard?"

Her grin is more mischievous than the Cheshire Cat's. "Okay, well not everything, but I did distinctly hear the sound of a boy's voice and..." She puckers her lips and makes kissing noises.

Oh, dear god. I cover my mortified face with a pillow that immediately gets ripped away.

"Spill it, sister. Which one was it?"

I don't know if I'm ready to have this conversation yet. I haven't had a chance to wrap my head around everything that happened last night, the words that were spoken.

I love you, Liz.

I love you, too.

My fingers press against my lips again, and Hailey's eyes grow big, her mouth forming an *O*.

"I knew it!" she shrieks, bouncing up and down on my bed. "If you don't tell me right now what happened last night, I will never speak to you again, Elizabeth Penelope!"

"Yeah, right," I scoff, not believing that for one second.

"*Lizzie*," she whines.

What do I tell her? How much should I share? Once I say the words, once I acknowledge what happened, there's no going back. Am I ready for that? Am I ready for what's to come?

"He kissed me."

Hailey nods her head, waiting for me to continue. But that's all I get out. My brain simply shuts down for a second and focuses on that one thing: *Jayson kissed me*. The feel of his mouth on mine. The heady sensation that followed when my body fired to life, both hot and cold consuming me at the same time. I relive it all in that one second.

Hailey jumps on top of me. "You are such a bitch." She laughs. "That's all you're going to say?"

"It was Jayson," I whisper.

Using me as her own personal jumping pillow, she bounces in excitement. "And?"

I push her off.

"And I don't know what to feel. I wish I had your way with words. To be able to articulate everything the way you do in your poems. That's what it feels like. A poem filled with romance, beauty, angst, life, and heartbreak."

She lies down beside me and tucks my hair behind an ear. "You and your big, fancy words."

"Huh?"

"*Articulate*. You always talk like a grown-up. Sometimes I forget that we're only a year apart. And why would kissing Jayson be heartbreaking?"

"Because our kiss changes everything." And it will. One kiss will change four friendships forever. "Jayson said he loves me. He said he's loved me forever."

"Do you love him back?"

"Yeah, I do. You know that. I'm ecstatic. Over the moon. But then I picture Ryder and feel like shit."

Her eyes glisten with understanding. "Because you love him, too."

I nod, a single tear sliding down my cheek.

"But that's what you said you wanted, Lizzie. You said you wanted them to choose for you. It sounds like Jayson chose. He chose you. The next step is to talk to Ryder. Talk to Julien. Clear things up before next week because your teenage drama is not going to ruin our beach vacation."

"Ryder said he's coming over at one to talk to me."

"About what?"

I shrug a shoulder. "I have no clue."

"Well, then, there's your chance." She hops off my bed and smacks my thigh. "Breakfast is ready. Mom made pancakes."

"Hey, Hales?"

She stops in the doorway. "Yeah?"

"Thanks."

"Anytime."

A warm breeze floats through my open window, fluttering the curtains. I get out of bed, and my heart thumps wildly as I approach the window. I peek over and notice that, for the first time in nine years, their window is closed and the curtains drawn. Does that mean something? Is Jayson regretting what happened last night? Uncertainty settles over me, but I can't keep standing there worrying. After a quick shower, I head downstairs for breakfast.

"Morning, sweet pea."

"Morning."

I give Mom a hug and a kiss before taking the barstool next to Hailey.

"I'm going to the store to pick up the stuff we need to take with us next week. I figure we can wait to do the grocery shopping once we get to the beach house. Did you want me to grab any snacks to take with us in the minivan?"

She hands me my plate, and I grab the bottle of syrup, pouring a generous amount over my pancakes. Dipping a piece of bacon into the sweet gooey goodness, I bite into it.

"My usual."

"Candy and diet soda. Got it."

"I'll come with you," Hailey says, getting up from her seat. "The charger for my phone broke, and I need a new one."

"Do you want to come too, Lizzie-bear?"

"No, thanks." I lick syrup off the side of my thumb. "I'm supposed to meet up with Ryder later."

Hailey gives me a knowing look, but Mom is thankfully oblivious. I finish with the bacon and dive into my pancakes.

"I'll clean up. You guys can head on out. When is Daddy coming home?"

He's on the final leg of a four-month tour.

"Day after tomorrow. Their last show is in Austin."

Mom and Hailey gather the things they need to take with them, and I decide to head to the music room before I clean up the kitchen and put away the dishes. There's a piano piece I've been working on that I want to finish before Dad comes home.

Dad converted one of the back rooms into a music room. It's where he keeps his instruments and gives me lessons. I walk over to the piano—an old upright that belonged to my grandmother that my dad refuses to get rid of—and pull the bench seat out. Getting comfortable, I hover my feet over the piano pedals. Dad bought me a laptop and installed some music software on it. I use it to compose my musical pieces. Placing the laptop on top of the piano, I open the file that contains my latest composition.

I don't know how long I sit in front of the piano, composing, changing notes, playing, adding parts. Once I'm happy that the piece is finished, I play it from the beginning to hear it in its entirety.

Flexing and wiggling my fingers over the keys, I begin. Instantly, I'm lost to the melody, being pulled into the music. The pattern and flow of the notes, the way my hands float over the white keys, combine together to create something magical. As the song finishes and my fingers still, I shut my eyes to exist in the brief moment of silence that follows.

A noise behind me draws me out of the music. Jayson leans a

shoulder on the doorjamb, hands in his pockets, ankles crossed, looking as handsome as ever.

"That was beautiful, Liz."

He's wearing a Carolina University T-shirt over dark shorts, his hair damp and swept back off his forehead. We have an open-door policy, and the boys know they are welcome to come into the house anytime they want, using the key Mom gave Freda.

My heart soars as my eyes take Jayson in from top to bottom. That lean, muscled body was pressed against me last night. A blush spreads across my chest and up my neck before uncertainty weighs me down.

Jayson must feel my apprehension. He kneels in front of me and takes my hand, kissing each finger.

"Hi."

"Hi back."

Hands grab my hips and coax me off the piano bench. Once I'm straddling him on the floor, he tugs me forward until I'm pressed intimately against him, and a million goose bumps explode like confetti.

"I thought last night was a dream."

"No dream." He kisses the tip of my nose. "I talked to Julien last night."

He watches to see my reaction.

"Oh?"

"Yeah. We stayed up all night talking."

"And?"

"He's good with us being together. Everything's okay, just like I promised."

"What about Ryder?"

Jayson doesn't answer and brings my lips to his. It's a claiming. He's making sure I know that I am his, and he is mine.

The kiss starts simple, sweet, but turns into more as we lose ourselves in each other. I thought my first kiss with Jayson last night was the kiss to end all kisses. I was wrong.

Jayson pulls me in for a hug and softly nuzzles my cheek. Minute prickles of warmth scatter across my skin at the contact.

"I've been dying to kiss you again, but that's not why I came over. I know you said Ry was dropping by at one to talk to you. I wanted to see you first."

"Do you know what that's all about? Did he say anything to you last night?"

Again, he avoids my questions. Instead, Jayson takes my face between his hands.

"Last night, I promised you that I would make everything right. You will not lose any of us. I swear it. I'm going to head over to his house right now and talk to him."

Something is off. I can feel it.

He lifts me off him and helps me to my feet. After checking his watch, he twines our fingers together and leads me out of the room.

We walk to the front door, hand in hand, and down the steps to the front walkway.

"Everything is going to be okay," he reassures me once again.

It has to be. I can't lose Ryder.

Jayson bends down and kisses me.

"I promise," he says.

I take a deep, cleansing breath, one filled with hope.

But that hope shatters when I hear a deep voice shout, "You piece of shit!"

Before I can register what's happening, I watch in horror as Ryder tackles Jayson to the ground. They roll over in the grass a few times before Ryder gains the upper hand and pins Jayson down, his right fist smashing into Jayson's face.

"You son of a bitch! You knew! You fucking knew, and you stabbed me in the back!"

Another punch.

Why isn't Jayson fighting back? What the hell is going on? After standing like a statue, completely frozen, not knowing what to do, I finally find my voice.

"Ryder, stop! You're hurting him!"

I try to pull him off Jayson, but it's no use. He either isn't hearing me, or if he is, he doesn't care.

A car pulls up the driveway, but I don't look to see who it is.

Jayson's cheek is already swollen, and his mouth is bleeding. If I don't do something, I honestly think that Ryder might put him in the hospital.

Not knowing what else to do, I hug him from behind and hold tight. My instincts tell me that even in his uncontrollable rage, he would never hurt me.

"Please, Ryder. Stop."

Like a switch being flicked, his fists still and he stiffens.

Mom hurries up the walkway, a look of utter shock on her face.

"Ryder! Jayson! Elizabeth! What the hell is going on here?"

Freda runs over from their house next door. "Jayson?" she gasps.

Her son is on the ground, blood on his face, bruises starting to appear. Ryder stands over him, me clinging to his back. If this wasn't the worst moment of my life, it would look a bit funny.

"I'm so sorry, Elizabeth. I'm so goddamn sorry," Ryder chokes out.

He gently removes my grip, looks around in a daze, and then takes off.

"Ryder!" I yell after him, but he's already gone.

Chapter Thirteen

RYDER

I DON'T THINK I have ever felt such rage. I want to hurt something as badly as I am hurting right now. How could he do this to me? I poured my fucking soul out to him last night. I told him my intentions. He knew I was going to tell Elizabeth today how I felt about her. I understood that finally telling him and Julien about my feelings for her would cause problems—would hurt them, would hurt *him*—but I never imagined that Jay would do what I saw him do. They were holding hands. He fucking *kissed* her right in front of me.

Not wanting to go home, I take refuge in Dad's garage. I find him bent over the engine of a station wagon.

"Since you're here, mind handing me that work light?"

When I pull it off its hook, it slips from my fingers and crashes to the floor.

"Son?"

My legs give out like dead weights, and I drop to the concrete floor.

"Ry, are you okay?"

I shake my head.

"What happened?"

I shake my head again.

"Hey. Talk to me."

Dad joins me on the floor, rubbing his large, grease-stained hand up and down my back, helpless on what to do or how to comfort me. He doesn't know my life just exploded apart. My best friend betrayed me in the most awful way. The girl I love to the depths of my being has been taken from me. Other than last night, I haven't cried since I was four years old when I fell off my bike for the first time. But the anger, deception, and hurt eviscerating every pore of my body breaks me.

"Dad."

I turn to grip his shirt. And I cry.

"It's going to be okay. Whatever it is, you're going to be okay."

But it's not. *I'm* not.

Sensing someone is watching, I hastily wipe my face dry.

"Thought I might find you here," Julien says, his tone sober.

Dad gets up and murmurs something to Julien, then leaves us in privacy.

I rub my hands over my face a few times. "Did you know?"

My anger is like tinder, ready to combust with the tiniest of flames.

"I had no clue until several hours ago after he got home."

"What do you mean *after* he got home?"

Julien shrinks back, looking guilty. Then it hits me, and that ember of anger flares to life again.

"You're fucking kidding me. That's where he ran off to last night? He ran straight to Elizabeth's? He went to her right after I poured my goddamn heart out to him!" I punch the metal cabinet next to me. "*Motherfucker!*"

"Ry, it's a difficult situation for everyone."

Julien, always the peacekeeper.

"Like hell it is. I'm the one who manned up. I'm the one who put it all on the line. I didn't go behind his back. *Your* back." I jab my finger at him. "I put my friendships with you first. What he did...he's a fucking coward."

"Hey, I'm not going to justify his actions. I agree with you. What Jay did was wrong. I told him that. But what's done is done. They're officially dating, and we have to accept that. If you want to keep her in your life, if you want to keep me in your life, if you want to someday rebuild any type of relationship with Jay, you're going to have to learn to deal with it."

"That's all bullshit, and you know it."

I walk out of the garage bay, intent on going back to Elizabeth's house and telling her everything.

"Just take a minute and think before you make things worse."

I stop and scowl at him, and it's then that I notice his cut lip.

"I'm on your side. I confronted him last night. We got into a fight. But I also listened to him explain everything to me. Ry, man, he is torn up about it. He knows he fucked up, but he panicked. All he could think about was Liz not being in his life anymore because she would be with you, and he freaked out. You remember how he reacted last night. He was scared out of his mind."

Dad walks back in with an ice pack and hands it to me.

"Put this on your hand."

Julien doesn't wait for Dad to go before saying, "Do you love her enough to let her go? Will you be able to forgive Jay for his weakness for loving her, too?"

Julien cuffs my neck and touches his forehead to mine, then leaves me alone to think about the things he just said.

Chapter Fourteen

ELIZABETH

WHAT A GODAWFUL MESS, and it's all my fault. I hate myself for what happened. I hate that I'm weak when it comes to my feelings for Jayson and Ryder. I wish I knew what to do to fix it.

Freda dragged Jayson home to clean him up and call his father. Mom sent Hailey up to her room and told her to stay there until she called her because she wanted to talk with me in private. I had to rehash the past twelve hours to Mom—I left out the part where Jayson came through my window, and we made out for hours after he declared he loved me. Yeah, I didn't think that would go over well.

Mom was quite understanding about everything, her parting words before I asked her permission to check on Jayson being, "It's about time that boy made his move," followed by, "Your dad is going to have a fit that his little girl is dating now."

She laughed about that one. I didn't. Dad was going to kill me.

So, here I am, standing on the front porch next door, wringing my hands together, wondering what happens next.

"Hey, Lizzie," Freda greets me as she opens the front door to let me in. "Jay is upstairs in his room where he will be grounded for the next week until we leave for our trip. But you are more than welcome to come in. I was just about to make some soup and bring it up to him."

Freda could lay down the law, but she did it in the nicest way possible.

"How's he doing?"

"He's pretty banged up, but he'll live. Nothing some ibuprofen and an ice pack won't take care of." She smiles, but it's not reassuring. "Jay told me what happened. How are you feeling about things, sweetheart?"

"What do you mean?"

"Jayson said he asked you out."

He did a lot more than ask me out.

"I'm assuming that was what the fight was about. But from my perspective, it seems as if you have been thrown in the middle of a tug-of-war between those two boys."

This is getting awkward. I nod my head.

"I know you have your mom and dad and Hailey, but if you ever need someone else to talk to, I'm here too, sweetie."

"Thanks, Mrs. Jameson. Is Julien upstairs with Jayson?"

"He left a few minutes ago. Go on up, honey. I know Jay would love to see you."

I take my time walking down the hallway to the twins' bedroom, examining the pictures Freda has hung all along the wall. One in particular catches my attention. It's a photograph of me and the boys last Christmas, standing beside the six-foot snowman we built. Jayson is carrying me piggyback style, Julien has his arm slung around Ryder, and Ryder has his pinkie looped with mine. Will things ever be the same for us again?

I stop in front of the bedroom door and give a soft knock

before opening it. Jayson is lying in bed, phone in his hands. He's changed clothes and looks like he also took a shower.

"Hey you."

I close the bedroom door behind me. He smiles when he sees me, or at least he tries to. His cheek has swollen to the size of an orange, and he has a black eye.

"Oh, Jayson." I rush over to his bedside, but he pats the bed for me to sit beside him. "I'm so sorry. This is all my fault."

"Liz, what are you talking about? Nothing is your fault. If it's anyone's fault, it's mine."

Tears fall unbidden and soak into the comforter on his bed. "But what happened with Ryder—I have never seen him that angry before. It scared the crap out of me. You wouldn't be fighting if it weren't for me."

I suddenly find myself on my back with Jayson on top of me. The shock of us in this position abruptly dries my tears. He puts his weight on his forearms, clasping his hands around the nape of my neck.

"Ry is my best friend. I will do whatever it takes to make things right...well, anything but give you up."

"Jayson—"

"Please trust me."

My heart wars with itself.

"I do trust you."

Gazing up at him, my heart swells with empathy as I press gentle fingers to his battered face. Wanting to offer him whatever comfort I can, I raise up and brush my lips over his, careful of the cut on the corner of his mouth. His scent fills my senses, a blend of woody cedar and spicy notes that intoxicate me. My hands tremble with the overwhelming desire to touch him, to feel the warmth of his fragrant skin against mine. It becomes an irresistible urge.

I explore the rough texture of his stubbled cheek as I trace the contours of his jawline with trembling fingertips.

"I like how this feels," I tell him, giving myself permission to continue.

Intimacy is new to me, but I feel safe with him. Not many girls get to experience first love with one of their best friends.

Jayson's hand moves down my torso. The slow glide of his knuckles down the curvature of my rib cage is exhilarating. Once he gets to the hem of my tank top, he slips underneath. His calloused palm glides up my chest to the under swell of my breast before skimming lower to rest flat against my stomach.

His touch makes me tremble, and I'm battered with new sensations I've never felt before. I shift underneath him, and that's when I feel a hardness dig into my pelvis. Without my permission, my legs fall open and wrap around his waist. I clutch the front of his shirt, gripping the cotton fabric in a fist.

He grinds his erection into my core, and I *moan* at how good it feels. Eyes wide, we look at each other, afraid to take it further but also not able to stop.

He does it again, closely watching my reaction.

"Does that feel good?"

"God, yes," I whimper when he rocks into me, wanting it more than anything even though I have no idea what *it* is.

Freda taps on the bedroom door. "Lunchtime."

Jayson and I fly apart at lightning speed. By the time she pushes it open, we're sitting on opposite ends of his bed.

He adjusts the pillow over his lap, and I duck my head to hide my red face.

Thankfully clueless to what we were doing, she hands him two pills. "Take these and eat your soup. Lizzie, I know you said you weren't hungry, but I brought extra just in case." She places the tray down on the bed between us. "Your dad wants to talk to you after you finish eating."

Jayson's face blanches. "How mad is he?"

She kisses the top of his head. "Pretty mad."

Brushing my hair off a shoulder, she says, "You can come back tomorrow to visit, but he's grounded for the next six days." She pauses at the door. "Oh, and an open-door policy is in effect from now on when Lizzie is in your room."

"Mom! Oh my god."

We hear Freda chuckling all the way down the hall.

Chapter Fifteen

RYDER

I'VE BEEN KEEPING to myself the past few days, mulling over Julien's words, still angry at Jayson, missing Elizabeth like crazy. It breaks my heart when I see her name light up my phone before I hit decline. She's been calling and texting constantly, begging me to talk to her. I'm hurting her with my silence, but I'm not ready to face her yet. Because I know I will have to face *him* as well.

Dad and I have been talking a lot while I hang with him at the garage. He's an old romantic at heart. Told me that if Elizabeth was *the one*, then I should be patient and give her time to explore her feelings, that we were young and things would change as we grew older.

I know he had good intentions but fuck that. I'd been waiting for seven goddamn years already. We'll be leaving for the beach in a few days, and I'm going to be forced to wear a false happy face while I watch Elizabeth and Jayson together. It's going to be utter hell.

I run my hand along the side of my new Hellcat. Dad

surprised me with it yesterday. Just drove it into the bay and tossed me the keys.

It's a gorgeous car, and I am itching to begin working on it. I know exactly what I want to do, down to the paint color and interior. I plan to take this bad boy out to the Fields as soon as I'm done. After days of feeling like shit, it's nice to have something to work toward to pass the time.

I'm looking over the car, clipboard in hand, making notes of the things I want to change, replace, or modify. I don't know how long he's been standing there, hands pushed deep in his back pockets, shoulders hunched, when I notice him.

"What the fuck do you want?"

Jayson flinches at my asperity. "Liz has been trying to get in touch with you. She's worried. She doesn't know I'm here."

"She's not my problem anymore."

I don't mean it and hate that I said it.

"That's a fucking stupid thing to say. Her heart is breaking because she misses her best friend, and I promised her that I would fix it."

"Get out of here, Jay. I've had enough of your bullshit."

I give my back to him and ignore his stupid ass.

Running around me, he plants himself in my way. "I fucked up. I'm sorry."

Flinging my clipboard down, I throw my arms up in exasperation.

"What more do you want from me? I came to you and Julien. I looked you dead in the eye and told you how I felt about her and what I was going to do about it. And you ran as fast as you could over to her house and laid claim. You didn't care about how I would feel. You didn't care how much that would hurt me. You took our friendship and stomped all over it."

Fed up with him, I storm off, not wanting to hear anything else that comes out of his mouth.

"She loves you."

I stop in my tracks.

Exhale.

Dammit.

I turn around.

Jayson pulls out a metal stool and sits down on it like he has no more energy to stand, the heaviness of our situation taking its toll on him. He leans forward and rests his elbows on his knees, the pose of a humbled man.

"She loves you, and it kills me knowing that. Liz has been my universe since the day I gazed into her gorgeous green eyes. God, I remember that day like it was yesterday." He looks over at me. "I know she loves me, too, but I'm terrified that maybe, just maybe, she loves you a little bit more."

Hearing it doesn't lessen the hurt, but I understand.

"You should have told me that instead of bolting."

"I panicked, and I'm sorry. I'm so sorry for all of it. I wish I could go back and do things differently."

Not believing that for a second, I snap, "Do you?"

Of course, he doesn't answer because he knows it's a lie.

Rising to his feet, he swipes a hand through his hair. "Liz needs you in her life. *I* need you in my life. You're my best friend. Is there any way you can forgive me? I will do anything to make this right."

I want to shout, *"Then give her up!"* but I keep quiet and think about what Julien asked me. Do I love her enough to let her go and find happiness, even if it's not with me?

"I'm not saying that I forgive you. It's going to take time for me to even want to be in the same room as you. You broke that trust. You're going to have to earn it back. But this is not Elizabeth's fault. She shouldn't have to suffer because of us."

I offer him my hand. No fist bump. This time we shake hands like men.

Chapter Sixteen

ELIZABETH

JAYSON SAID he had to run out for a bit and would be back later. We're officially going on our first date tonight. Since he's still grounded, I wonder exactly where he thinks we'll be going. The fact that his mom even let him out of the house to run an errand is a miracle of its own.

The swelling on his face has disappeared, and all that remains is a faded yellowish bruise on his cheek and a purple crescent under his eye. It doesn't bother me because all I see is Jayson. What does bother me was seeing Ryder and Jayson fighting, a scene that keeps playing out in my nightmares every time I close my eyes.

Hailey hands me a chilled water bottle, the condensation cool against my fingers, before settling back into her lounge chair. We're enjoying a rare moment of quiet on the back patio. I've got my earbuds in, music playing softly, and a book open on my tablet, but it's hard to focus under the sun's oppressive rays. The summer swelter arrived early this year, the air thick and sticky with humidity as the thermometer hovers in the upper nineties. Sweat drips from my skin, and the occasional hot breeze does little to offer relief.

A text message pops up on my tablet from Hailey, even though she's sitting less than a foot away.

> Hales: Ryder can't ignore you at the beach. Captive audience. Brea has this plan...

I stop reading and pull out my earbuds.

"Can you not talk to me like a normal person?"

I twist off the cap of the water bottle and tip it back, the cold liquid blissfully soothing my parched throat—until I choke at her next message.

> Hales: No because Ryder is here.

I barely manage to cover my mouth as I force the water down. Slowly, I glance up. Ryder is standing right in front of me.

"I'm going to head back inside now."

Very subtle, Hales.

I wait until she slides the door shut behind her, and in that instant, something in me snaps. The sadness that's been weighing me down ignites into ire.

"Unless your phone was abducted by aliens, you've been ignoring me for days."

"I know. I needed some space."

Space. Away from me. Because I'm the reason everything's falling apart—why Jayson and Ryder are at each other's throats. And there's nothing I can do to fix it without shattering Jayson's heart in the process.

"Ryder, I'm so sorry."

"No. I'm sorry." His amber gaze drops to the ground, his voice thick with regret. "I shouldn't have hit Jay. That was a despicable thing for me to do in front of you. I—" He swallows hard, his eyes darting back to mine. "I didn't hurt you, did I?"

He looks terrified that I might say yes.

"No, I'm fine," I assure him. "But I'm worried about *you*. Please don't hate me."

He should. I deserve it. Every ounce of his anger. Why does everything feel so impossible? Why am I like this? The feelings twisting inside me, pulling me in two directions at once—it's not normal. *I'm* not normal. The feelings I have for two guys are *not* normal.

"I don't hate you, Elizabeth. Jay, um, actually came by the garage today and apologized."

"He did?"

A spark of hope flares inside me, only to flicker out when Ryder continues.

"I can't promise that we'll ever be friends like we used to be."

His words hit me like a punch to the gut. I ruined them. I broke us.

"But I can promise you this—I'm not going anywhere. You still have me, if you want me...as a friend."

Friend. It feels like the tiniest of lifelines, but I'll grab onto anything he'll offer, any scrap of himself that he'll give me.

"Absolutely! Yes! Best friend?"

"Best friend," he replies with a small smile.

Relief surges through me, so intense it knocks me off balance. Without thinking, I leap from the lounger and throw myself into his arms. For a moment, he stiffens, his body rigid with hesitation. But then his arms wrap around me, pulling me in tight. His embrace is fierce, strong, like he's holding on just as hard as I am.

"Thank you."

"You'll always have me, Elizabeth."

A throat clears behind us. Without turning around, I know it's Jayson.

Ryder releases me and steps away. Suddenly, a few inches feel like a vast ocean between us.

"I was just leaving." Ryder brings his hand to my cheek, his thumb a whisper across my cheekbone. "I'll see you around."

All I can do is nod. I watch him walk down the back patio steps and disappear around the corner of the house, taking half my heart with him. How do you split a heart in two and still feel whole? The ache is unbearable.

"So," Jayson says.

I turn around and face the boy who owns the other half of my heart. I can't keep wishing for things that are impossible. Those hopes are a child's fantasy. I'm almost seventeen, on the cusp of being an adult. I can't hold on to the selfish whims of youth where I get everything I want. Time to grow up and be the girlfriend Jayson deserves.

"Thank you for keeping your promise."

"Always, Princess."

"Where are we going on our date tonight?" I ask, changing the subject.

"Not telling. It's a surprise." He reaches for me, and I go willingly. "Have I told you lately that you are fucking gorgeous?"

I blush, not used to him saying things like that to me.

"Wait. Isn't that the new bikini top you bought the other day?" Jayson's eyes heat, and I feel his smoldering look right down to my toes.

"Yeah, why?"

"Oh, Princess, I think I need to show you what happens to naughty girlfriends who send sexy pics on their phone."

Giggling, I ask, "What happens?"

I yelp when Jayson lifts me and hoists me over his shoulder.

"What are you doing? I'm too heavy!" I exclaim, laughing, my efforts to wiggle out of his hold useless. "Freda will ground you for another month if she finds out you're here."

"Will be totally worth it," he says and marches us inside the house to kiss me breathless.

Chapter Seventeen

ELIZABETH

MY NERVES GET the better of me, and I wind up pacing back and forth while I wait. Jayson told me to stay in my room, and he would pick me up. How? He's still grounded, and it's almost ten. Where the heck does he expect to take me for our date?

Like any typical sixteen-year-old girl going on her first date, it took me over an hour to pick out the perfect outfit after trying on everything in my closet—and Hailey's—and then another hour to make sure my hair looked perfect. Jayson loves it when I wear it down, so I added some corkscrew curls to my long blonde locks.

A little mascara, some lip gloss and blush, and a spritz of my favorite jasmine perfume, and I'm ready.

Just as my bedside clock turns ten, Jayson appears outside my bedroom window. I should have known.

"Oh, my gosh," I gush when he holds out a small bouquet of wilting flowers.

Taking them, I hold them to my nose and sniff.

"I may have stolen them from Mom's garden. Hope you like them."

Aw. So freaking sweet.

"Liz, you look beautiful."

My heart soars that he notices the effort I put in to look good for him tonight, so I repay the compliment.

"You look very handsome as well."

And he does. He changed out his usual tee and basketball shorts for a polo and chinos.

We take a minute to absorb what feels like a significant moment before he reaches for my hand and bows at the waist, all gentleman-like.

"Princess Elizabeth, I am here to escort you to your date."

I want to say something silly like, *I thought my date was already here*, but I don't want to ruin the romance of what's happening with jokes. I place my hand in his, and he raises it to his lips, placing a tender kiss on my wrist. I don't know if I'm going to survive the night if he keeps this up. I'm already melting into a puddle of goo at his feet.

Jayson waggles his eyebrows. "Follow me," he says and pulls me to the window.

My first thought is, he's going to make me climb down a tree. My second thought is, I'm glad I decided not to wear a dress.

Jayson, Julien, and I have gotten very good at climbing up and down the old oak tree between our houses. We've been doing it since third grade.

Jayson helps me out of my window and carefully guides me down to a lower branch, one that's sturdy and thick.

Clasping his hand like a vise, I lower to straddle the branch with my back to the trunk. He sits down facing me and takes out a small remote from his pocket. My eyebrows raise in curiosity.

"Wait for it," he says in a hushed whisper and presses a button.

Hundreds of tiny white fairy lights come to life around us. When did he do this, and how did I not notice?

I touch a small bulb. "Jayson, this is amazing. It's like that time when we were camping."

It's one of my favorite memories. The site where we pitched our tents would glow with thousands of fireflies every night. It was magical.

"As a first date goes, how am I doing so far?"

I'm filled with wonder for this boy, for all the ways he shows me that I am special. He built me a starry fairy light universe. He truly does treat me like a princess.

"Really good."

He reaches into his other pocket and brings out a small item wrapped in tissue paper.

"This is for you."

"You got me a gift?" I ask in disbelief.

"I hope you like it. Jamie helped me make it."

I pull off the tape, being careful not to tear the tissue paper. I want to preserve it in a scrapbook, one I will make to commemorate all of Jayson's and my firsts. I carefully pull back the last corner. Nestled inside is a necklace. But it's not just any necklace. There's a charm hanging from a thin leather cord. It's the rose quartz heart Jayson found in the creek and gave to me when we were younger. He must've stolen it from my rock jar.

"I love it."

They're inadequate words to express how I feel right now.

"As first dates go, you knocked it out of the park. And you're definitely telling me later how you were able to do all of this without me seeing. But for now, I just want you to kiss me."

He feathers his nose across my cheek. "*That* I can absolutely do."

Chapter Eighteen

JULIEN

July 2
Secrets and Confessions

THE LEAD up to our beach trip was rife with restrained drama. Things have been...tense between Jay and Ry, and that's a blatant understatement. How all this will play out once we graduate high school and go to college—once we grow up and become adults—only time will tell. Life has a funny way of throwing you curveballs when you least expect them.

Liz's laughter floats in my direction, shaking me back to reality and away from my thoughts. I watch as she and Jayson jump the three-foot breakers that grow and collapse as they reach the shoreline. We've been out on the beach all day, boogie boarding, swimming, playing volleyball. We even made a kick-ass sandcastle like we used to do when we were kids.

Dipping my toes into the water one last time, I walk up the sandy shoreline and join our parents under the shade of the canopy. Ryder takes two bags of chips out of the cooler and offers me one.

"Jayson Patrick Jameson!" Liz shouts before he launches them both under the breakers.

Without directly looking at him, I know Ryder is watching them. Unrequited love and heartbreak are two emotions I'm becoming very familiar with.

"Want to toss the football?" I ask him.

"I think I'm going to head on in and take a shower."

"Want some company?"

He punches my arm.

"Not what I meant, dickhead," I clarify, and he barks out a laugh.

"I knew what you meant. Still funny though."

He pops a chip into his mouth and glances over to where Jayson and Liz are bobbing in the swells. He sighs, and I physically feel his disappointment.

Tossing the half-eaten bag of chips back inside the cooler, he says, "I need a break. I'll probably walk over to the arcade and play a few games. Want to join me there?"

"Sure."

It's been hard for me to step back and watch the Jay-Ryder-Liz love triangle from hell go down. To not take sides. But no matter which way I look at it, I'm stuck in the middle regardless.

At least Jay did the right thing and apologized. I'm proud of my brother for that alone. I still don't agree with what he did, but I'm glad he and Ry are putting their personal issues aside for Liz. She feels a fuck-ton of guilt over their fight. The four of us may have a very screwed-up, unconventional kind of friendship, but it's one worth fighting for.

Later that evening, I find myself alone on the beach, enjoying the stillness of the night. Reposed on my elbows in the cool sand with my legs bent up at the knees, I take a moment to languidly scan the water's edge as a warm land breeze blows in from behind. I peer over my shoulder when I hear the swish of soft footsteps.

"Hey you," Liz says, sitting down beside me.

She rests her head on my sunburned shoulder. Her presence is exactly what I need right now.

"Where's our boy?" I ask.

"Believe it or not, he and Ryder are playing video games together inside. Other than when we eat, it's the first time they've stayed in the same room with one another for more than two seconds. I tiptoed out of there like a silent ninja," she replies with a grin.

Jayson and Ryder were in the same room, and it didn't come to blows or get bloody? I call that progress.

"I'm really happy to hear that."

"I know everything is so weird between all of us right now. Seeing them together like old times gives me hope."

"They both love you and want you to be happy."

Her response is automatic. "I love them, too. That's why this" —she gestures around at nothing in particular—"is so hard."

"I'm here if you want to talk."

"You've been so great with all of it. Thanks for that and for not making me feel worse than I already do."

She kisses my shoulder and wraps her hands around my upper arm, snuggling into my side.

Liz and I sit in silence for a while, watching the night sky and listening to the rhythmic pounding of the waves against the shore. The lights from a night trawler glimmer along the horizon as a ghost crab scuttles past our feet across the sand. One of our favorite nighttime beach activities is to come out with flashlights and search for ghost crabs as they pop out of their holes. There are so many of them scattered along the shoreline, it's like watching a game of whack-a-mole.

"Julien, what's going on with you?"

"What do you mean?"

"Just like I know those two boys inside, I also know you. You've been quiet the entire week."

This girl has been my heart since the day I met her. My love for her is a profound type of love. A love of deep friendship. The type of love where I know I can trust her with my deepest secrets. Everyone thinks that because Jayson and I are twins, we have an unbreakable bond. Don't get me wrong—we do. But there are some secrets I can't tell him. Secrets that scare me.

I take Liz's hand and link our fingers. "It's complicated."

She chuckles. "Have you seen my life recently?"

I release a dejected laugh. She's right. This past week has been a shitshow of massive proportions.

Five minutes go by as our gazes remain locked on the dark horizon illuminated by a half moon. That's how long it takes for me to finally build up enough courage to tell her.

"I like Elijah," I whoosh out.

Liz angles her head and smiles at me. "The two of you have been hanging out with each other a lot lately. He's a good guy."

"No, Liz. I *like* Elijah."

The euphoric feeling of finally, *finally*, being able to voice those words has a freeing effect on me. Like the weight of the world just got released from my shoulders because I'm able to tell her the one secret I've been too afraid to acknowledge to anyone, even to myself.

I anxiously wait for her to say something. I can see every emotion flash across her expressive face. I can also see when understanding hits her.

"Oh. *Oh!*"

I pick up some sand with my left hand and let it sift through my fingers, counting how long it takes for all the grains to fall, like an hourglass counting down time.

"Are you...does he...does he like you back?"

"He asked me out on a date."

"Julien, that's wonderful."

"I told him I wasn't ready, and we could only be friends."

Her face falls with disappointment.

"It's so stupid. I'm stupid," I groan, letting my head fall back on my neck.

Liz reaches around my shoulders and pulls me to her side. "You are *not* stupid."

"I am. Can I tell you something?"

"Of course."

"I think I first realized I was...well, the way that I am, that day at Jay's swim meet. Remember that day when he went up against Elijah for the first time, and then afterward when Elijah came over to congratulate him?"

Before then, I had been too young to understand my feelings. My childhood crush on Ryder should have been my first clue.

She kicks sand at my feet. "Do you mean that time he asked for my number but the three of you scared him away? Or later, when you all treated me like I was a baby and lectured me on why I wasn't allowed to date anyone? Oh, yeah, I remember *that* day."

I wince at her rightful indignation, but I love how she can lighten the most somber mood.

"Not our finest moment. What Ry said was funny as shit though."

Liz purses her lips. "Let's agree to disagree."

"I was actually a little jealous of you," I confess, shamed at having had such a petty feeling toward her.

"Jealous? Of me?" she asks, surprised. "Why?"

"I thought Elijah was the most handsome boy I had ever seen. But then he started talking to you, not me. My feelings scared me —a lot. How could I like girls and him at the same time?"

"You know what they say about denial not only being a river in Egypt," she says, referencing the overused idiom. "So, um, are you saying that you're bi?"

As we talk, I create a picture in the sand out of broken pieces of seashells. "Maybe. I don't know. I guess it would make sense. I mean, you're the only girl I've ever truly been interested in. And, yeah, I like Elijah, too. I have dreams about me and him kissing. When we were younger, I had a crush on Ry."

"You know it's okay to be confused, and it's okay to have questions." She takes my chin in her fingers and turns my face to hers. "It's okay to like Elijah. You're allowed to like and have feelings about whomever you want, Julien. Guys or girls—it doesn't matter."

"It should," I argue.

"Well, it doesn't," she argues back. "Have you talked to Jayson about how you feel?"

I shake my head, that familiar lick of panic blooming inside me. "No. No one knows. You're the first person I've told."

She gapes in shock. "I'm honored. Thank you, Julien."

My breath releases in a torrent at her kindness and understanding. Why did I think she would react any differently than she's doing now? *Because you're an idiot*. Liz has always supported me in everything I do. She's my biggest cheerleader. And I'm ashamed that I've kept things bottled up for so long. I should have opened up to her sooner.

"Do you plan on telling Jayson?" she asks. "Or your parents? I'll be there with you, no matter when, or where, or how. Whatever you need, I'll do it. Just say the word."

Liz would walk through fire for me. I'm so damn grateful to have her in my life. Her capacity to love is overwhelming.

"I don't think I'm ready for that yet. It's been hard enough trying to figure out what's in my head. I've always felt different in some way."

"You're not different, Julien. Don't ever think that. You're strong and kind and honest. You put others before yourself. You're genuine and wonderful. I don't know what I would do if you weren't in my life. Your parents, Jayson, and Ryder will support you no matter what. They won't abandon you. Being gay or bi doesn't change who you are," she passionately asserts, placing her hand over my heart. "You must know that, right?"

"I know things are better today than they used to be. But there's still a lot of hate and prejudice out there. I don't know if I'm ready to face all of that if I decide to start dating Elijah. Especially when we go back to school."

"Those small-minded people can go fuck themselves," she voices vehemently.

I'm not used to hearing the f-word come out of Liz's mouth.

"Anyone wants to mess with you, they'll have to get through me first. I mean it, Julien. No matter what, you need me, and I'm there."

"I love you, Liz."

"I love you, too."

The hug she gives me is like coming home.

Chapter Nineteen

JAYSON

July 4
Making Our Own Fireworks

I GLANCE OVER AT RYDER. I understood Liz's intentions last night when she silently slipped out of the room, leaving me and Ryder alone for the first time since our fight. But I also understand that the rift between us will take a lot of long, hard work on my part before it mends. I've asked myself a million times if I would've done things differently if given the chance. Yes and no. Having Liz as mine? Fuck no. No regrets. Not a damn one.

Overhead, bright flashes of red, gold, green, and blue explode across the evening sky and reflect upon the ocean's surface. Sitting between the vee of my legs, Liz leans back and watches the barrage of fireworks put on a dazzling show. From our spot on the southern end of Topsail Island, we can also see fireworks going off in Wilmington and Wrightsville located miles away. The boom and thunder of each explosion reverberate like a heavy drumbeat, and Liz makes a little gasp every time one detonates.

"Oh, I love that one," she voices in wonder and points to the cascade of golden sparkles showering down like a waterfall.

Figuring we have another twenty minutes before the big finale, an idea takes root. Between the morning parade, the cookout, and now fireworks, I haven't had one minute alone with her. Not to mention she's currently wearing that damn bikini top, and I'm at the point where I will lose my ever-loving mind if I don't get my hands on her soon.

"Come with me," I whisper in her ear.

She tips her head back and cocks an eyebrow.

"Come on, Princess," I urge in a hushed voice, standing up and bringing her with me.

I look around to make sure no one's watching, and luckily for us, all attention is still on the fireworks. Holding hands, we crouch down and race behind the dunes until the coast is clear.

"What are you up to Jayson Jameson?" she asks, clearly suspicious.

I pull her along between the dunes to a secluded spot I found earlier this week when Julien and I were out exploring.

Thankful that I had the presence of mind to grab a towel before we snuck off, I spread it out on the sand.

"I figured we could make our own fireworks," I tell her with a cheeky grin.

Liz makes an indelicate snort. "I think that's probably the cheesiest thing I've ever heard."

"You ain't seen nothing yet, baby."

She tries to come up with some clever comeback, but I don't give her the chance because my mouth greedily takes hers. I couldn't wait another second. Liz's response is immediate, and her lips part for me.

We haven't done much more than kiss, and the need to take things further has been building between us. I know it's merely a matter of time when we'll need to have *the talk* and decide how far and how fast we want to go. But not tonight.

Lips melded together, we sink to our knees onto the towel. Liz lifts the hem of my T-shirt up and runs her hands over my back and up to my shoulders.

"I love how your body feels," she whispers.

A loud bang of a nearby firework goes off but we don't notice, our focus on each other so intense it blots out the rest of the world.

Gently lowering her onto her back, I position myself between her bent knees, running both hands up her smooth thighs, her torso, and then around to finger the strings of her bikini top. How my shaking fingers are able to untie the back bow, I don't know.

I see in Liz's gorgeous green eyes when the sensual fog begins to clear, and reality comes crashing in.

Her hands clutch my shoulders and push. "What if someone sees?"

I raise my head to look around. Another firework explodes. We're surrounded on all sides by tall dunes and far enough from the houses and the road that no one will be able to see us unless they walk right on top of us.

"We're good. No one can see."

"Are you sure?" She looks doubtful.

I kiss the hollow of her bare shoulder where her pulse pounds a fast beat and hum my answer against her soft skin. My lips trail a path down her neck to her clavicle, her little moans of pleasure lighting the way. She arches her hips and instinct takes over, telling my good intentions that say to take it slow to take a hike.

"You're so beautiful."

I slide her bikini top to the side to expose her breasts to my eyes for the first time. My cock goes rock hard in an instant and pride swells inside my chest. I'm the first guy to see her like this.

I take a moment to look at her, wanting to memorize every detail. Her skin, kissed by the sun this week, is flushed and glistening. Her nipples are a pale pink, the tips tightening into puckered buds. *I'm the first to touch her like this,* I think, as I circle my fingers around her nipples. *I'm the first to taste her like this.* My tongue mimics what my fingers are doing, and I close my mouth around a taut peak. The breathy moan Liz lets out drives me to devour her.

"*Oh, god,* Jayson."

Liz's hands are everywhere, frantic as she claws my back, then lower. Lower. I jolt when I feel her hand cup my hardness and squeeze, and every fiber of me wants to rip off our clothes and sink into her. Luckily, there's a sliver of my good conscious still working that tells me our first time together can't be on a towel outside in the middle of some sand dunes.

"Liz, we need to stop." I reach down between us and bring her hand away from my crotch and place it over my pounding heart. "Not here, Princess. We need to stop."

Her knees tighten around my prone position. "Jayson, I ache. I don't know what's happening, but I ache. Please, *please,*" she begs.

I may not be sexually active, but I'm a guy who hangs around a bunch of other guys, so I know enough about sex to understand what she's talking about. And yeah, I admit it, I've watched my share of online porn, so I know what she needs and how to fix it.

I suck a nipple into my mouth and slither a hand down her stomach to tease the top of her shorts. Her eyes flutter closed as a round of fireworks go off in the distance, casting a rainbow of colors over her face. Liz's breath falters when I pop the button of her shorts and ease the zipper down. I can feel the heat of her, the first tickle of her pubic hairs against my fingers.

I kiss her slowly, my hand slipping lower to find her wet and swollen.

With only touch to go by, my fingers stroke her hot softness. My mind takes a mental snapshot that I'll be using the next time I jerk off in the shower. I find the little knot of her clit and tease light circles over it with my thumb.

Liz's eyes pop open, an endless sea of green, and just as the finale of the fireworks begins, her muscles lock, and she moans out my name, her cries of pleasure drown out by the cacophony detonating above us.

The most gorgeous smile spreads across her face. "You were right," she sighs, coming down from her very first orgasm, one that I gave her.

I roll us over on the towel and hold her in my arms. "Right about what, baby?"

"We did make our own fireworks."

I chuckle and kiss the tip of her nose.

"What about you?" she asks.

"What about me?"

"I, um, you didn't get to..." Her voice trails off.

"Yeah, I did."

"You did?"

"Yeah."

The stickiness of my release dampens my underwear. I'll need to take a shower as soon as we get back to the beach house. Totally worth it.

"Oh." She sounds dejected.

"What's wrong?"

"It's just that I...I wanted to make you do that."

"Liz, it's not like I could help it. It just happened. Seeing you, hearing you moan—you were so goddamn beautiful."

That seems to make her happy.

"Oh, okay." She hooks her leg over me, scooting closer, our joined hands between us. "Next time?"

The hopeful look in her eyes lights another fire in me, but I tamp it down, knowing we need to go back soon. Everyone must be wondering where the hell we got off to.

"We have years and years, Princess. So many years of next times."

Chapter Twenty

ELIZABETH

End of Summer
My New Normal

I HATE how fast the summer flew by, but I did get to experience my very own summer romance, thanks to Jayson. He took me on picnics, we sat under the stars and watched a production of Shakespeare in the Park, and he gave me many more clandestine nighttime dates in our tree.

Jayson would leave me small presents on my windowsill to find when I woke in the morning. Little trinkets like polished pebbles from the creek, wildflowers from his mom's garden, paper butterflies, and stars with little love notes written in them.

And like he promised, we've had many more next times. I blush as memories of this summer play in a loop. We've experimented and fooled around, tried out different ways we can bring each other pleasure without going all the way.

We decided we wanted to take it slow, not rush into sex, and let things work themselves out organically. Just enjoy each other and exist in the moment. It makes each time we touch, every kiss, every spoken word of love, that much more special.

Since we returned from our beach trip, Jayson has been working hard to rebuild his relationship with Ryder. Several days during the week, he goes to Randy's garage to help Ryder work on his new car. Jayson says that they don't talk much, just quietly work side by side.

Ryder has been coming around more often, mostly to hang with Julien, but he no longer leaves the room when Jayson walks in.

"Ow!" Hailey yelps, sucking her thumb into her mouth. "I hate camping! Stupid tent!"

We're currently trying, unsuccessfully I might add, to pitch our tents for tonight's backyard campout.

I pick up the pole Hailey threw to the ground. "You're going to break all the poles in half. It's not like it's rocket science," I reply, trying to bend it through a fabric loop and not eat my words. It really is harder than it looks.

Jayson comes up behind me and places a kiss on my shoulder.

"Need a man to help you out?" he murmurs suggestively, squeezing my hips.

My thighs clench, making it difficult to get out of his way. "Be my guest."

After ten minutes of enjoying watching him struggle to put our tent up and failing, I smirk at him.

"Oh, poor baby," I mock. "Need a woman to finish the job?"

Jayson lunges for me and tickles my ribs. "I always finish the job."

"Not always," I playfully reply, trying to wriggle away from him.

"Oh, now you're really going to get it," he declares, and I run for my life. "Julien, save me from your brother!" I shout and dash over to him, throwing myself behind his back for protection.

Out of nowhere, a blast of water hurls across the backyard and drenches us. Hailey and Elijah laugh hysterically as they douse us with their water guns. And then pandemonium ensues.

Water droplets glisten in the air as we dart around the backyard, trying to outmaneuver their aim. Ryder leaps into the fray, armed with a super soaker that towers over his shoulder. With a mischievous grin, he turns the nozzle toward Hailey and Elijah, and they scatter like leaves in the wind, ducking to avoid the deluge.

For just a moment, time seems to stand still as we revel in the simple pleasure of being together, caught up in a carefree moment of happy silliness.

"Liz, catch!" Julien says and tosses me a foam water cannon.

"Hey!" Jayson protests when he doesn't get one.

"I'll protect you, baby," I tell him and go straight for my sister. Payback is a bitch.

"Brea, a little assist here!" Hailey squeals as she narrowly avoids a direct hit, her flip-flops kicking up grass as she sprints toward the safety of the back patio where Mom is sitting.

"Fend for yourself," Brea shouts, chasing after Ryder.

Elijah attempts a daring maneuver, leaping behind a tent to take cover. But Julien is relentless in his pursuit, determined to soak him to the bone.

The grass beneath my feet is slick with water, adding an element of slippery chaos to the game.

I turn my water cannon and aim at Jayson.

"Don't do it," he warns when he sees the playful defiance glinting in my eyes.

I let out a dramatic sigh, pretending to be wounded. "So untrusting." I spray him directly in the face. "Oops."

He tackles me to the ground and sits on top of me.

"I surrender!" I giggle-snort when his fingers dig into my ribs where he knows I'm ticklish.

He grins down at me. "Thought so."

Breathless and soaked from head to toe, Ryder collapses on the grass next to us.

"That was fun."

I reach for his hand and hook our pinkies, so happy that I could burst.

This is the first time in a long time that everything feels normal again. That we're *us* again.

"Yes, it was."

It's too late in the summer for fireflies to be out, but the cicadas have emerged and are creating quite a racket. I look around at all my friends, and a feeling of contentment washes over me. Jayson is sitting beside me, holding my hand on his thigh, while everyone else is sitting in lawn chairs, talking.

The sun has long dipped below the horizon. The sky is an inky blue, deepening toward twilight, and the moon hangs low and full, illuminating the scene with a silvery sheen. The stars are just starting to twinkle, barely visible through the light haze of humidity.

The late summer evening is still unbearably warm, the kind where the heat of the day lingers oppressively in the air, softened only a smidge by a light breeze. It's too late in the season for fireflies to dance among us, but the cicadas have emerged, their loud, rhythmic song blending with the murmur of conversation.

A deep sense of contentment washes over me as I feel Jayson's hand resting on my thigh, his fingers gently intertwined with mine. The world feels peaceful, suspended in this perfect moment.

Someone taps me on my shoulder, and I turn to see Ryder holding my acoustic guitar. He smiles at me with a crooked grin.

"Play for us?"

I haven't played in front of a group since the cookout at Ryder's house years ago. I usually just play with my dad or sometimes with Ryder. Dad has been giving Ryder guitar lessons, but he refuses to play for anyone other than me.

I'm immediately greeted with chants of "Sing!"

When I take my guitar, Ryder pulls me out of my chair and into the middle of our circle.

"Ladies and gentlemen, please welcome Fallen Brook's very own Elizabeth Fairchild."

An embarrassed blush scorches my cheeks when everyone claps.

"Okay, here's one," I say and wink at Jayson.

He's not the only one who can be romantic. My fingers tenderly pluck at the strings, lightly strumming the music for "The First Time I Ever Saw Your Face" by Roberta Flack. My voice starts soft and low, then grows with intensity and power as I belt out the words about a woman who experiences her first kiss, her first touch, her first all-consuming love with the man she desires.

Even though we're surrounded by our friends, Jayson and I are the only two who exist as I sing the ballad just to him. His chest rises and falls with deep inhalations, and his eyes change from silver to black, reminiscent of the night he came to my room and kissed me for the first time. By the end of the song, when my voice drifts off into the summer air, no one makes a sound.

"Jesus, Liz," Jayson breathes.

He gives me such a heated look, my heart skips a beat, and my legs go weak.

We stay up for another few hours before everyone retires to their tents. Hailey decides to sleep in Brea's tent, but I don't plan to sleep in our tent either.

Waiting feels like forever, but it doesn't take long before the sounds of light snoring can be heard. I've been on the verge of a panic attack for the past half hour, trying to decide when will be a good time to sneak out and hope like hell that no one wakes up or needs to go to the bathroom at the wrong moment.

Knowing tent zippers are loud, I left my tent door open. As soundlessly as I can, I poke my head out to make sure the coast is clear.

It's not.

I silently slip out and sneak up on Julien.

"Where are you off to, Julien Jameson?" I whisper.

He startles and glowers at me. "Liz, what the hell?" he whisper-hisses.

I try not to laugh.

"Wait. Where are *you* going?" he says.

"I'm being naughty. What about you?"

His glances at Elijah's tent.

"*Ohmygod, ohmygod, ohmygod*! You finally said yes, didn't you?" I dance around in a circle, my happiness uncontainable.

He frantically shushes me. "Yes. Be quiet."

I throw my arms around him and rejoice in his ear. "I'm so happy for you. You better tell me everything tomorrow."

He smirks, but the smile that lights up his face speaks volumes.

I kiss him full on the mouth. "Give that to Elijah."

He rolls his eyes. "Good night, Liz."

I wait for him to disappear inside Elijah's tent before tiptoeing to Jayson's.

"About damn time," I hear him sleepily say in the dark.

But sleep is the furthest thing on our minds when he pulls me down onto the sleeping bag, takes off my shorts, and buries his face between my legs.

Best. Night. Ever.

Chapter Twenty-One

ELIZABETH

Eleventh Grade

Ryder: Where u at?

Me: At the library.

Ryder: Meet me out front in 5.

I TURN off my phone's screen and hand my application over to the head librarian. After talking with my parents about getting a job, we decided that something part-time after school would be appropriate. They're worried anything more will interfere with my studies. I love books and have volunteered off and on at our local library for years, so me working here is basically a given. I just have to go through the formalities of an application and background check first.

"Before I finalize next week's schedule, is Monday, Wednesday, and Friday, from four to six still good with you?"

"Yes, ma'am. Thank you," I tell Mrs. Peters.

"Sorry about all the paperwork."

"It's not a problem. I understand. I'm excited that I actually get to work here now. I love this place."

Mrs. Peters chuckles. "I still remember you in pigtails when your mom would bring you and Hailey in for story time."

The loud rumble of a car engine draws our attention to the double glass doors, and my mouth drops open.

When I see who the driver is, I tell Mrs. Peters goodbye and hurriedly rush outside.

"Oh my god, Ryder! You finished your car!" I run over and place my hands on the open passenger side window. "This is the most unbelievably kick-ass car I have ever seen!"

Without further invitation, I open the door and hop inside. Ryder waits for me to buckle up, then shifts into first gear and roars out of the parking lot.

"What do you think?"

I take in the black leather bucket seats with red stripes down the middle and red trim, the swirled stainless steel of the dashboard, and the high-end sound system. The car is a sleek, glossy black with a red stripe painted down the middle of the hood to match the interior. I know he must have done some serious work with the engine because it sounds incredible and vibrates powerfully when idling. If this car was a boy, I would be drooling.

"You did this?"

He nods.

"You really did it?"

He nods again, an ear-to-ear grin splitting his face.

"It's gorgeous. I want to marry it." Feeling giddy, I glide my hands all over the soft buttery leather.

"Good grief, woman. Stop molesting my car," he teases.

I point at the radio. "Do you mind?"

"Go right ahead."

He hands me his phone. I open his music app that he's already linked to his sound system and go through several songs before finding the one I want. Selecting it, I turn up the volume to blast out "Alive" by P.O.D.

"Can it go any faster?" I ask, my voice dampened by the roar of the engine.

Ryder's grin widens as he presses the accelerator, and the world blurs around us. The G-force slams me back into my seat, a thrill tightening in my chest. Wind tears at my hair, sending it flying in wild tangles. I reach my hand out the window and let the air rush between my fingers. The sensation is electrifying. The hum of the engine, the pulse of speed—it feels like we're flying.

This is freedom.

"Where are we headed?"

"You're the first to get a ride in her. Where do you want to go?" he asks, his copper eyes sparkling with pride.

"I'm the first? Not even your dad?"

"Nope. I wanted it to be you. I knew you'd appreciate her."

"If it's a her, you just destroyed my dreams of marrying it." I run my hand over the dashboard, smooth and warm under my palm. "Okay, maybe not. She is gorgeous. Aren't you just a beauty, Stella?" I coo, patting the car affectionately.

"Stella?" His eyebrow kicks up with amusement.

"Yeah, Stella. A sexy name for a sexy car," I reply, dead serious.

We drive for a while, the road unwinding ahead of us in a blur of asphalt and countryside. When I notice that we're near the Fields, I bounce excitedly in my seat.

"Seriously?"

I catch Ryder's grin, and without a word, he veers left onto the dirt road that leads to the track. Dust kicks up around the tires, the car gliding over the uneven terrain as though it's weightless.

"I can't wait to see you race Stella here," I say.

"Who says you have to wait?"

He pulls the Hellcat into position at the start of the track, his hands steady on the wheel. The engine purrs low and dangerous. Ryder revs it a few times, wiggling his eyebrows to the rhythm of the growl, making me burst into laughter. Before I can brace myself, he releases the clutch, and we're off—thrust into motion so fast my breath catches in my throat.

Adrenaline surges through me. The open windows funnel the wind, wild and warm, as Ryder drifts around the first corner. Lap after lap, he maneuvers Stella with precision—speeding, sliding, the tires juddering as they grip the dirt on every turn. God, I love this. I never want it to end.

He shifts down and comes to a stop. "Your turn."

I literally stop breathing. "I'm sorry, what?"

"Your turn," he says, putting the car into neutral and getting out.

Is he out of his mind?

"No, Ryder. I can't!"

He pulls my door open. "Yes, you can."

"Are you crazy? I'll probably drive it off into a tree!"

"No, you won't."

"Yes, I will."

"Elizabeth, get into the driver's seat."

"Nuh-uh. Nope. No way. You can't make me."

I cross my arms, petulantly shaking my head.

Before I know what's happening, Ryder has my seat belt unfastened with me hoisted over his shoulder.

"What is it with you guys always carrying me around like a

sack of potatoes!" I grab onto the back of his shirt—which causes me to notice the hard muscles underneath.

Then it hits me. Something buried deep. Something potent and alive, wanting desperately to claw to the surface. Something that causes my heart to constrict. Something I should not be feeling because I forced it into lockdown when I chose Jayson.

Everything stills.

"Ryder, put me down, please," my words a low timbre.

Ryder stops. His arm, the one banded around my thighs, tightens before slowly relaxing. He takes my hips and moves me down his body until I am standing on my own two feet. My hands press flat against the muscular plain of his chest, his fingers still gripping my waist. I inhale—his clean, masculine scent perforating my overstimulated senses. I keep my head bowed, looking at our feet.

"Ryder, we can't."

"I know."

He steps impossibly closer.

We stand motionless like that for several minutes.

"I'm sorry."

"I know, Elizabeth."

Our arms reach around each other at the same time, bringing our bodies together in a hug. It's an embrace of two friends, two best friends who could have been more if things were different.

Ryder is the first to pull away. He tips my chin up with a finger and gives me one of his captivating smiles, letting me know we're going to be all right.

"You're still driving."

"No, I'm not."

Yes, I did, and it was awesome.

Chapter Twenty-Two

RYDER

ABOUT A YEAR AGO, the senior class at Highland High started throwing bonfire parties. The location of each bonfire event is kept secret until the last minute when a mass text is sent out, giving the GPS location for where to show up. Tonight, we're headed to an abandoned warehouse an hour north of Fallen Brook.

Julien drums his fingers to the beat of the music playing over the radio and looks out at the scenery flying by as we drive down an old county road. In my rearview mirror, I can see Elizabeth in the front seat of Jay's truck, Jay at the wheel, and Hailey and Maria behind them in the back.

"How's your leg feeling?" I ask Julien. I noticed earlier that he was limping as he walked.

Last week during a game of pick up at the park, Marshall, an asshole who plays on Highland High's soccer team, got a little aggressive and drove his spiked shoe into Julien's calf. It ripped about six inches of skin off his leg. We had to take him to the hospital. If rumors are to be believed, Elijah beat the shit out of Marshall the next day.

Julien stretches his leg out as far as it can go in the footwell. "It doesn't look as bad as it did a week ago, and it seems to be healing quicker than the doctors expected. I'll have a scar."

"You can impress the girls with stories about how you got it. Say it was a shark attack or something."

Julien chuckles. "Yeah, like that scene in *Jaws*, where they're sitting around shooting the shit and comparing wounds." Julien looks at his phone. "The warehouse should be right up ahead."

I can already see cars and trucks lined up all along the sides of the road. The glow of the bonfire creates a halo in the distance. I pull over to park behind an SUV, and Jay parks behind me.

I hear Maria as soon as I open my car door.

"Holy shit! This place is packed."

Julien doesn't wait for anybody and starts walking, or rather limping. His leg must be bothering him more than he lets on. I'll make sure to keep an eye on him tonight, but for now, my attention is solely fixed on the beautiful blonde emerging from Jay's truck.

Black skinny jeans, black knee-high leather boots, and a green blouse that leaves little to the imagination. Her hair is plaited in some kind of fancy braid that wraps around her neck and falls over a shoulder. I watch as Jay pushes her up against the side of his truck and kisses her neck, sending her into a fit of giggles. My jaw clamps down hard. Seeing them together never gets any easier.

Maria approaches with a wide smile. "Hey tall, dark, and handsome. Aren't you coming?"

Tearing my gaze away from the girl who still owns my heart, I sigh. "Yeah."

"I can be your wingman tonight. You know, my Goose to your Maverick," she says, referring to the *Top Gun* movie.

"As long as I don't have to sing."

Her brown eyes go comically big. "What? You haven't lost that loving feeling?"

"Nope."

"Don't you feel the need for speed?"

"Already drive a Dodge Hellcat, so I'm good."

"Wanna buzz the tower?" Maria hip bumps me to get me going.

"You're a riot, Goose."

"I have my special talents, Mav," she says, clicking her tongue and making finger guns.

I find myself laughing at her antics. "You're corny as hell."

"A hell of a lot of fun," she replies, hooking her arm through mine as we walk to catch up with the others.

Elizabeth glances back at us, a frown on her face.

"It's my first time at a bonfire party, and I'm in the mood to try my first beer. You can be my DDB."

"DDB?"

"Designated Drinking Buddy. Keep up," she teases. Spying the row of open coolers, she asks, "Want one?"

I hadn't planned on drinking tonight since I drove.

"I'm good."

"Hell yeah, you made it!" Fallon shouts.

He's with a few other guys from Highland High. Fallon and I have been friends for a long time, but you wouldn't know it. Not even Jay, Julien, and Elizabeth really know. We have a complicated history.

Walking over, we tap fists. "Hey, man."

"Where were you last night?"

I didn't go to the Friday night races because Dad needed my help with inventory.

"Garage."

I do a double take when Jacinda suctions herself to his side and licks up his neck. He reaches around her back and casually cups her breast beneath the strap of her tank top. My gaze drops briefly to her chest, because, well, shit, I'm a guy. Jacinda notices me looking and smiles.

"Hey, Fallon," Julien says when he joins us.

He ignores Jacinda. He can't stand her. She has a thing for Jayson and hasn't been the nicest person to Elizabeth.

"Heard about what happened. How're you doing?" Fallon asks.

Julien shifts his center of gravity to take pressure off his injured leg. "Better."

"Marshall is a prick. He deserved that beatdown from Elijah."

"Wouldn't know," Julien replies.

Fallon grins. "Uh-huh. Speak of the devil," Fallon says when Elijah arrives. "Just talking about the fight."

"Don't know what you're talking about," is all Elijah says, but none of us miss the bandage he has around his right hand.

Julien slaps my back. "Going to get wasted. I've earned it. I promise not to throw up in your car."

"Thanks," I reply, not amused.

He and Elijah peel off, lost in their own conversation.

Fallon looks past me. "I see that kitten's here."

I have no clue when he started calling Elizabeth 'kitten,' or why for that matter.

Someone yells his name, and he lifts his middle finger.

"Party calls. Text me later. I bought something that I want you to check out."

"What happened to the Brabham?"

The guy seems to buy a new car every month. I enjoy the benefit of being the person who gets to work on them. Other than my dad, he doesn't trust anyone else to touch his precious car collection.

Fallon's ice-blue eyes twinkle under the light of the bonfire. "Still have it. Wanted something new."

"There's an orphanage somewhere that would love some of that money you like to waste."

He laughs. I'm glad I love the guy. Fallon may pretend to be a narcissistic rich prick, but underneath his façade of false assholery is a man with a huge heart. He cares. Deeply. And he'll burn the world to the ground to protect those he loves. He's the antithesis of his upbringing. His father is an abusive sadist, and his mother... she deserves a special place in hell.

Jacinda peers back at me as Fallon drags her away. "See you around."

Jayson shoves a beer I don't want into my hand.

"She's trouble," he says and takes a long pull of his drink, guzzling over half of it.

My gaze naturally drifts in Elizabeth's direction. "Not interested, so it doesn't matter."

"She seemed *very* interested," he replies. "Maybe you should—"

Maria runs over. "I'm going to get drunk tonight and hump some legs!"

This girl has zero filter.

"That's not something you want to announce to everyone," Elizabeth says as several boys' heads turn our way with interest.

Since it's Maria's first bonfire party, I give her a couple of important tips. "Okay, Goose. There are two rules to remember."

"What, like don't talk about fight club, or what happens in Vegas, stays in Vegas?"

"Close." I hold up one finger. "Rule number one: Don't accept a drink from anyone." I lift a second finger. "And rule number two: Just say no to drugs."

Maria snorts and pulls the fingers I'm holding up, bringing them to her forehead and giving me a mock salute.

"Yes, sir!"

Elizabeth watches our exchange, a fresh scowl on her face.

Close to the bonfire, a guy pops the trunk of his Monte Carlo, revealing a huge sub-woofer. The air vibrates to the bass beat of the music blasting out.

Maria spins in a circle, arms above her head. "Hell yeah! Wanna dance, handsome?"

"Pass." There's no way in hell I'm dancing.

"Your loss." She gyrates her ass over to the bonfire, Hailey trailing behind her.

"Lizzie! Get your butt over here!" Maria shouts.

Jay kisses her shoulder. "Baby, go have some fun."

"I'm not in the mood." She takes a sip of her bottled water.

We both know she's dying to get out there. Her hips are already moving to the beat of the music. A girl passes in front of us carrying four beers. Jayson reaches out and snags two of them.

"Asshole!" the girl yelps before she sees that it's Jayson. Then, she goes "Oh!" and blushes bright red. "Hey, Jayson. Hi, Ryder."

Elizabeth frowns. She's been doing that a lot tonight.

"Thanks for the beer." He turns around, completely ignoring her.

"Lizzie! Come on!" Hailey calls.

"Elizabeth, seriously. Go dance," I tell her.

She glances warily at Jay when he pops the top off one of the bottles he stole and downs that one just like the first.

She'll be nursing Jay's inebriated ass later at the rate he's going. And he isn't a fun drunk either.

"Go, Elizabeth. I've got him," I assure her.

She hooks her pinkie with mine and squeezes before leaving to join the girls.

Once she's out of earshot, I tell Jay, "You need to slow down."

"Whatever. I don't need a babysitter," he slurs slightly, somewhat buzzed and heading toward tipsy fast.

"Suit yourself."

Something stirs inside me when I hear Elizabeth's voice belt out the lyrics to the song she's dancing to. I love hearing her sing.

"She's so fucking sexy," Jay groans.

I couldn't agree more.

"You should hit up Maria."

For the second time in as many minutes, I reply, "Not interested."

He throws down his empty bottle. "Be right back."

Stalking over, he grabs Elizabeth and smashes his mouth down on hers.

I know I should turn around and leave. Why torture myself? But that's exactly what I do. I watch him kiss her. I watch him grab her ass and lift her up. I watch her legs wrap around him. I watch his lips suck on her neck. I stand there like a lovesick idiot and watch it all, wanting to be him, jealous that I'm not. Jayson stumbles off with her, and I watch that, too.

"Hey." Jacinda slides in next to me, holding out a bottle.

I take it.

Bad decisions are always made when heartbreak and beer are involved.

Chapter Twenty-Three

JAYSON

AS SOON AS Liz steps out of my truck, she's distracted, and that distraction is Ryder and Maria. Maria has always been a bit odd, but tonight she and Ry appear to be hitting it off. I'm happy for him. I want him to move on. He's a great guy and deserves to be with a great girl—unfortunately, the great girl he wants is mine.

Ry and I have been slowly putting our friendship back together. It's almost like old times between him, me, and Julien, and it feels good to have my friend back. Doesn't mean that I'm going to let my guard down when it comes to him and Liz. He still loves her. I see the look he gets on his face when he watches her. It's the same look she gives him. She'd never cheat on me. I know she loves me. It's a complicated fuck of a mess. I just hope, given enough time, those feelings between them will simmer and die, and I can have her love all to myself.

Perhaps I can help push his attention elsewhere, and Maria seems as good as any for me to use to start that push.

I kiss Liz's neck right where I know she's most ticklish, and she laughs, no longer paying attention to them. Good.

When Ry and Maria eventually catch up to us, Liz pulls her aside. "What was that all about?"

I take that opportunity to go get us drinks, but I can still hear them talking as I stroll over to a cooler sitting in the dirt.

"What was *what* all about?" Maria asks.

"You and Ryder."

"What about me and Ryder?"

My evening takes a turn when I see Fallon. I hate that pompous asshole. Rich prick syndrome, more like it. I'll never understand how he and Ryder are friends.

"She's trouble," I warn Ry.

Jacinda looks back, eye-fucking Ryder right in front of Fallon.

"Not interested, so doesn't matter."

My irritation rises when I see him looking at Liz.

"She seemed *very* interested. Maybe you should—"

Liz and the girls join us, cutting me off, and I see Liz frowning once again as she watches Jacinda. My mood suddenly sours. I gulp down my first beer, hoping it will help alleviate the ache in my chest, decide it isn't enough, and start guzzling my second. Those old fears decide to rear their ugly heads. The only way I'm going to get through tonight is to get hammered.

When Maria shouts, "I'm going to get drunk tonight and hump some legs!" I tip my bottle back in absolute agreement with the first part of what she said.

Things start to go a little fuzzy as the quick infusion of alcohol settles warmly in my blood. A girl walks past with more beer, and I steal two of them. My brain is on autopilot, my mouth moving to say things I don't pay much attention to. The nice buzz I've got going helps take the edge off my compulsion to punch Ryder in the face because he can't stop looking at Liz.

Jealousy is a dangerous, pernicious thing that can make the smartest person do the stupidest things.

"She's so fucking sexy," I groan.

Ryder's attention doesn't stray from Liz.

I tap his arm with my beer bottle. "You should hit up Maria."

"Not interested," he replies.

No shit.

Time to show him who Liz belongs to.

"Be right back."

I weave a crooked path to my girl and grab her, claiming her lips and kissing her deeply. *Mine.* Not his.

Liz startles before realizing it's me.

"Jayson, what—"

Nope. No talking. Only kissing.

I groan into her mouth and lift her up in my arms. She wraps those gorgeously long, toned legs around me, her skin glistening with sweat from dancing around the bonfire.

"Your body is so goddamn lethal," I grunt.

My footsteps are unsteady when I carry her off to a more secluded spot.

Liz braces her hands on my shoulders. "What are you doing?"

"Kissing my girlfriend."

Pressing her up against the nearest tree, I lift her green blouse and shove her bra aside, my hand taking her breast. Fuck, she's soft.

A tiny whimper leaves her. *Hell, yeah.*

"Not here," she says.

I use my weight to pin her in place. I can't wait another damn second to get my mouth on her. I pinch her nipple until it hardens, and then take the tight bud into my mouth.

"Jayson, stop."

"I need you," my tipsy brain says.

Liz and I decided a while ago not to rush into having sex. Do I want to? Hell, yes. Every damn minute of every hour of every day.

She walks in a room, and I get hard. When I'm in my bedroom and can hear her voice from her open window, I get hard. I wake up every morning after dreaming of her, and I am hard as a rock. The fact that she and I breathe the same air makes me hard. I love this girl so fucking much. But I know she's not ready to take that next big step. But right now, my drunk mind doesn't care. My insecurities are high. Old fears about her and Ryder wage a war inside my head.

I nip her breast one last time before I step back, allowing her legs to drop from around my waist.

"Jayson," she says my name again. My name, not his.

My hands immediately go to the zipper of her jeans.

"I said no."

I don't listen. I tug on the metal pull—my need to claim her, to make her want me like I want her—drive my impulses.

With a strength that belies her petite size, she firmly grasps both my wrists.

"I said no," she calmly repeats.

Shame begins to seep through the haze of alcohol.

"We're in the middle of the woods, and you're drunk."

I struggle to focus on what she's saying, but comprehension alludes me, the four beers I practically inhaled in minutes showing their effects.

"Let's go find Julien and sober you up."

All I can manage is a nod as I rest my dizzy head against her chest. God, she smells good. Like jasmine and sunshine.

"Hold on to me."

Liz throws my arm over her shoulders and takes most of my weight as we stumble back toward the bonfire.

Beer sloshes around my insides in a tidal wave of nausea. I should have eaten something before we came.

Liz suddenly halts in her tracks, and the sudden jostle makes my stomach heave. Through the white noise filling my ears, I hear her pained, confused gasp.

"Ryder?"

And then I throw up all over her.

Chapter Twenty-Four

RYDER

JAYSON CARRIES ELIZABETH OFF, and I'm powerless to do anything. Why can't I move on from her? Why am I still so obsessed? I sit by and pine away, waiting for her to notice how I continue to hold out my heart to her, pleading for her to take it.

She's still my best friend. She still loves me. I know she does. Shouldn't that be enough?

Thoughts of what they're doing right now cut me like a thousand jagged shards of glass. Have they had sex yet? Are they having sex now? Has she given her body and her innocence to him, like she's given him her kisses?

Jacinda slides her hand across my stomach.

"You're not here with anyone tonight, and I'm not with Fallon."

My eyebrows raise in question. She smiles and slips her hand lower.

"Want to get out of here?"

Part of me is desperate to move on, to try and find a semblance of happiness with someone else, even if it's not with Elizabeth.

She's with Jayson. She's happy. Me? I want one goddamn minute to not live in my pathetic self-imposed seclusion. I want to feel alive like I do when I'm with *her*. Feel the rush like I do when I race. Just one minute to forget.

Fuck it.

I take Jacinda's hand and lead her toward the warehouse.

She giggles. I don't want to hear her voice. It's not the voice I crave. I just want to forget. I know that I'm being a bastard. I'm about to use a girl who I couldn't care less about just so I can escape my need for the girl I want but can't have.

I justify what I'm about to do by telling myself that Jacinda freely offered. She was the one to approach me, to come on to me, to make the first move.

I pull her around the side of the building, out of sight of the bonfire where darkness can shroud us. She tries to kiss me, but I turn my head and maneuver my lips to her neck. Jacinda moans loudly. I close my eyes and imagine a different scene playing out, a different girl. I'm an asshole.

Getting disgusted with myself, I pull away from her, but she spins me around and pushes me up against the cold steel metal of the warehouse.

Jacinda drops to her knees in front of me and hastily unzips my jeans. I squeeze my eyes shut and give in, let it happen.

Elizabeth, Elizabeth, Elizabeth, I chant, as Jacinda pulls my cock out and immediately takes me in her mouth.

I don't remember much of what happens next, but I know it doesn't take long for me to come down her throat. I should feel sated, but all I feel is dirty. Hollow. Empty.

And then my worst nightmare happens. A gasp. A voice I would know anywhere because it haunts my dreams.

"Ryder?"

Jacinda stands up and licks her lips, a smirk spreading across her face when she sees Elizabeth.

I can't tuck myself in fast enough. I zip up my pants, humiliation dousing me like gasoline and Elizabeth is the match ready to burn me to the ground.

A strained silence full of regret and remorse hangs over me as the crickets chirp, and the voices of partiers drift over from the bonfire.

Before I can say anything or beg Elizabeth to forgive me, Jayson vomits all over her shoes.

Chapter Twenty-Five

ELIZABETH

Valentine's Day

VALENTINE'S DAY. A day of hearts and flowers and romance. Jayson is taking me to Anaïs, a very exclusive restaurant located in the next town over. Maria and I went dress shopping last weekend, and I found a gorgeous dark blue V-neck chiffon A-line midi dress to wear tonight.

Pulling the plastic protective covering off the hanger, I hook it over the bathroom door. Cranking up the music I have playing, I shake my butt to the beat as I finish straightening my hair with the flat iron.

My phone chimes.

> Maria: What do you think? Too much?

She attaches a selfie of herself standing in front of a full-length mirror. Maria is wearing the yellow cocktail dress she bought. It looks good against her tanned skin and dark hair. She's paired it with gold T-strap five-inch heels. Her hair is twisted up on top of her head with loose tendrils curling around her ears and neck. She looks stunning.

She and Ryder started dating a month ago, and I'm trying not to act weird about it around her. She's so smitten, and I just want him to be happy.

Me: You look beautiful.

Maria: I'm so nervous.

Me: You will break hearts tonight. Have fun.

Maria: OMG! He's here! Got 2 go xxoo

I go back to the bathroom mirror and pick up my tube of mascara, needing to hurry because Jayson will be here in ten minutes. My hand shakes as I bring the wand to my eyelashes. *Dammit.* I toss it aside and brace my hands on my bathroom vanity. In the mirror, I take in my reflection, but I don't recognize the girl staring back at me anymore. I used to.

My phone chimes again.

Julien: Our boy is about to climb the walls waiting to come get you.

Me: I'm almost done getting ready.

Julien: Hold on...

My phone goes off, and I see Julien's name requesting a video call. I swipe to accept.

"Hey, sexy girl," Julien says as soon as his face comes up on the screen.

I squint at the grainy image. Julien's face is hard to make out.

"Where are you? It's really dark."

"I had to hide in the laundry room so Jay couldn't hear me. You look gorgeous, Liz."

I snort. I'm still wearing my unicorn bathrobe. "Yeah, right. Are you about ready to head out?"

"Yeah. I'm going to wait for you guys to leave first, just in case. And I want to see what happens."

"What's going to happen?"

"You'll see." His grin is a mile wide.

Even though he's full of teasing right now, I know Julien is apprehensive about his date tonight. I'm the only one who knows about it, and he has sworn me to secrecy. He still hasn't come out to his parents, or to Jayson and Ryder. I feel guilty about keeping secrets from Jayson, but it's not my secret to tell, and I will not betray Julien or his trust.

"Did you and Elijah decide on a restaurant?"

"We thought it would be safer if we drove to Fayetteville. No one should know us or recognize us there."

When Julien first told me he liked Elijah, I was worried. Not because of anything he said, but because I didn't want Elijah to break his heart. Come to find out, Elijah had been crushing on Julien since the first time they met. When Elijah would show up to the races at the Fields or the parties we went to, it wasn't to see me. He was there for Julien. I was merely an excuse—even the first time he asked for my number.

It took Julien a while to accept his feelings for Elijah, but once he did, the two of them have been inseparable. But I've been sworn to secrecy because Julien isn't ready to tell his family. He's scared of what will happen. Terrified at how his parents or Jayson will react to learn that he's bi. It guts me to think that Julien feels that way, because I know in my heart that they will accept his bisexuality with open arms. They love him. He deserves to be happy without having to live his life in fear or feel shame because of who he is. Because to me, he's perfect.

"Julien, Fayetteville's like over an hour away."

"Better to be safe than sorry," he replies. "Liz, hold on. I think I just heard Jay leave the house."

I haven't even put my dress on.

"Got to go. Love you!" I blow him a kiss and end the video call.

Mom shouts my name from downstairs, and I rush to shimmy into my chiffon dress, hastily step into my yellow strappy heels, spritz on some perfume, and dash downstairs. If I wasn't holding onto the stair banister, I would have tripped.

Because waiting for me at the bottom of the stairs is a very handsome, well-dressed Jayson. I haven't once seen him wear anything fancier than khaki slacks and a dinner jacket. Tonight, however, he's dressed in a dark charcoal suit, a blue dress shirt, and a dark tie with blue and silver accents. He even styled his hair.

Leaning a shoulder against the wall and one hand casually draped in the pocket of his slacks, Jayson looks every bit as dashing as a GQ model. His intense silver gaze rakes up my body in slow increments from my strappy heels to the panels of my dress that seem to float around my knees to the deep V of the dress's bodice.

"Liz...Jesus..."

The butterflies in my stomach wake the hell up and flutter their wings.

"Hi." I smile.

When I get to him, Jayson offers me his hand.

"Hi back."

Careful of my hair, he reaches one hand around my neck and spreads his other hand across the dip of my spine, pulling me in. He holds me like that, gray eyes traveling over my face, before inching in and capturing my lips in a kiss that makes my toes curl.

"If I didn't have to make the reservation months in advance, I would take you upstairs right now and eat you for dessert," he whispers in my ear.

Mom loudly clears her throat.

Awkward.

"Picture time," she says, camera in her hand, with Dad right beside her.

"Is this how it's going to be at prom next year?" Dad asks her.

She pats his arm. "Oh, much worse, I'm afraid."

He groans.

Jayson and I stand for what seems like hundreds of pictures because once Mom is done, Hailey jumps in with her phone to take more.

"Sorry, fam, but we need to go," Jayson apologizes.

He guides me outside, his hand placed possessively at my back. On our way to his truck, I stop when I see bright twinkling lights. Our oak tree is decorated from top to bottom with fairy lights and silver origami stars, and an old-fashioned swing hangs from the bottom branch. I take it all in. It's the most wondrous thing I have ever seen.

"It's beautiful."

Jayson threads his fingers with mine and brings my hand to his lips for a reverent kiss on my wrist. He leads me over to the swing and holds it steady for me to sit down.

"Aren't we going to be late for dinner?" I ask.

"I planned ahead."

He smiles, waiting behind me as I smooth down my dress and gently lower to sit on the polished wood board of the swing. Once I'm settled, he gives me a small push.

"You keep surprising me," I say, tilting my head back to look up at him.

"I used to daydream about doing this when we were younger."

"Your dream was to push me in a swing?"

"Actually, yeah. You would be wearing your blue princess dress, the one you wore the first day we met, and that plastic tiara."

"Don't remind me."

Looking back, that whole outfit was embarrassing.

I straighten my legs, feeling the wind rush up my dress every time I pendulum forward.

"I liked that tiara. And stop interrupting. I'm trying to be romantic."

"Oh, by all means, please continue."

He playfully narrows his eyes. "Like I was saying, I would picture you in the swing like this, and every time I gave you a push, your hair would whip back, all beautiful and shit. You'd smile at me and laugh, telling me to push you higher so you could swing into the sky to catch the stars."

He lifts a hand and plucks one of the silver origami stars down from its string.

"Open it."

I place my feet on the ground to stop the swing from swaying and carefully unfold the paper. Inside, he wrote, *"a daughter who has your eyes and your smile."*

Curious, I ask him, "What does it mean?"

Jayson bends down to my upturned face and says, "Inside every star is a wish."

My brows scrunch together before understanding hits me. His wish is for a daughter—*our* daughter. Tears spring to my eyes, the emotions I feel so intense, it would set the world on fire.

"Every star on our tree is filled with a wish. Wishes that I want to share with you. Spend the rest of my life giving to you. All you have to do, Liz, is reach for the stars, and I will give them all to you. I love you so fucking much."

He kisses my ear, my neck, my bare shoulder, then my lips.

"Jayson, I don't know what to say." I'm so enamored with this boy. "I love you, too. So much."

A single tear slips down my cheek, one that he captures with his finger and brushes across his lips.

The mood is completely shattered when Hailey shrieks feet away from us.

"That's the most romantic thing I have ever seen!" She picks up her phone and snaps picture after picture of us and the tree. "Brea won't believe this."

Jayson groans against my shoulder.

Chapter Twenty-Six

ELIZABETH

IT'S past midnight when we get back, and I am ecstatic to see the tree is still lit. I expected Mom and Dad to still be up waiting for me, but the windows are dark, and the curtains closed.

"Thank you for a wonderful dinner."

Jayson leans over the console and kisses me. "Our night isn't over yet."

After helping me down from the truck, he opens the passenger door and grabs something from the back seat.

"What's that for?" I ask when I see the swirled hand-blown glass jar.

"We're going to capture some stars."

"But there are no fireflies," I reply, clearly misunderstanding.

He walks to our tree and plucks one of the origami stars from its string.

"For your jar collection. Every day, you can open one up and read it."

"A daughter who has your eyes and your smile."

I run my hand across the flat of my stomach, a sudden burst of love for that future unknown child consuming me.

We take our time picking off the paper stars from the branches and placing them inside the jar. Since I'm wearing a dress, Jayson retrieves the ones that are higher up. Once we finish and the jar is full, he takes my hand and leads me into the backyard.

"Where are we going?"

"Patience."

We enter the forest where we used to play. The sliver of moon casts faint light through the canopy of deciduous trees, but not enough for me to see more than a few inches ahead.

"This isn't going to turn into some lame B-horror movie where clueless teenagers go out in the middle of the woods to make out and are attacked by a chainsaw-wielding mass murderer with a hook for his hand, is it?"

He grins. "Who says we're making out?"

We stop at our old fort, the one Hailey and I built but belonged to me and my two princes. Memories of our days playing out here coalesce in my mind like a slideshow, one image after another.

Jayson uses the flashlight on his phone to light the rest of the way, and I immediately notice that something is different. New plyboard has been put up in place of the old fence boards that used to make up the walls of the fort.

"Stay right there." He pulls aside a heavy tarp covering the entrance and disappears inside.

The inside of the fort starts to glow, and he says, "All right. Come in."

Strands of fairy lights crisscross from wall to wall, like a sky full of stars, just like on our tree.

Amazed, I turn in a slow circle. "When did you do all of this?"

"Julien helped. I hope you like it."

"I absolutely love it. But you may have put yourself at a disadvantage."

He pulls me in for a slow dance. "How so?"

With our cheeks pressed together, we dance to the music of our heartbeats.

"How can you possibly top this?"

"I'll show you."

He slowly brings his hands to my face, tipping my chin up, thumbs rubbing gentle circles over my cheeks. The heated look in his eyes sends my pulse skyrocketing, but the way he kisses me has my core throbbing painfully with unfulfilled need.

I cling to his biceps and hold on for dear life, needing him to anchor me in the maelstrom assaulting my senses by his seduction.

Jayson touches his forehead to mine, his breath wispy puffs across my face.

"I love you so much."

His mouth reclaims mine, his tongue sweeping inside.

This kiss is different than his others. Dangerous.

My body starts to float, lifted high on euphoric pulses of desire. I give myself over to the boy I have loved since I was six years old. I want to savor each second because I know what this is. A claiming. A promise of something more. Childhood best friends who are transitioning into lovers.

My hands latch on to the front of his shirt as my hunger grows like a wildfire out of control, and there is nothing to stop it. The feel of his hard body, muscles conditioned by years of swimming, has me eagerly pushing his suit jacket down his arms, fingers already at the buttons of his dress shirt.

One button, two, three, four, until I have released them all.

We break apart and clash back together. The smooth skin of his chest sends tingles through my fingertips as my hands roam his body with delight. Planting soft kisses as I go, my touch is demanding as I explore every inch of him. I lick my lips, tasting the saltiness of his skin. I take my time and relish my newfound exploration. Jayson remains motionless; the only movement is his chest heaving in and out with heavy, deep breaths.

"I love the way you look at me," I say and nudge the straps of my bodice aside—first the right, then the left—letting him know without words that I want him. That every single part of me now belongs to him.

Jayson suddenly comes back to life, and without hesitation, spins me around and roughly pulls me flush to his bare chest. He slides the zipper of my dress down, trailing his fingertips along my spine. What takes just seconds seems like forever.

With a flick of his wrist, my dress falls to the ground and pools at my feet. Jayson presses his mouth to the juncture where my neck meets my shoulder and lightly bites down, like he's hungry for me. Craves me.

His hands knead my skin as they move up my stomach to my breasts. My stomach muscles quiver, and I whimper when he treats my aching breasts with the same seductive massage.

Shadows move around the fort, creating a dreamlike ambience. He undoes my bra, then eases the straps, first one, then the other, down my arms. When it falls to the ground, I turn my head and seek his lips.

As our kiss consumes me, he trails feathery touches along the seam of my underwear, sliding a finger back and forth. Back and forth. Arousal trickles down my legs, followed by an explosion of goose bumps that scatters stardust everywhere he touches.

"Jayson," I pant.

He turns me in his arms and drops to his knees, nuzzling my soft belly.

Jayson licks me from my pubis to my navel.

"Princess," he murmurs against my skin.

My legs buckle when he slides down my underwear, puts his mouth on me, and consumes me.

I was already teetering on the edge of release, and it doesn't take long for his tongue to bring me to orgasm. He drinks my release, my moans, drawing out every shudder. As if I weigh nothing, he lifts me in his arms and gently lowers me onto a blanket he must have laid out earlier. Too enthralled with the fairy lights, I hadn't noticed it when I came in.

Raising to his full height, Jayson towers over me, his eyes worshipping my naked body sprawled out on the blanket, my long blonde hair fanning out like a halo around me.

"You are so goddamn gorgeous," he proclaims, a fine tremor making his hands shake.

He removes his shoes and socks, then his trousers and underwear. I watch every piece of clothing come off, impatient to see his body.

Tanned skin kissed by hours spent in the sun every day, moonlight eyes, sexily tousled dark mahogany hair, and a chiseled physique that makes my damn mouth water.

I suck in a sharp breath when he fists his hard cock. Not letting the opportunity pass me by, I go to my knees and remove his hand so I can take over. My fingers curl around the thick girth of his cock. Jayson makes a guttural moan when I slowly drag my tongue up his length to the tip where a bead of liquid appears at the slit. I lick it off, tasting him, and go back for more.

"Jesus, fuck, wait," he hisses, stepping out of reach.

Picking up his trousers, he fishes out a condom from his wallet.

"Not going to come in your mouth, baby. Tonight, I'm coming inside you."

Joining me on the blanket, he pushes me onto my back and takes my face between his hands, staring into my eyes one last time before he brings our lips back together in a needy kiss. My legs open to accommodate him, and once I feel his hardness pressing against my pelvis, I wrap my legs around his hips.

When he tongues my breast, my back arches up for him, desperate for more. His hands are everywhere, pulling and pushing, guiding my body where he wants it, giving me pleasure wherever he touches. Every part of me is so overstimulated at this point, I'm a writhing, needy mess.

"Now. Please. Jayson," I beg, digging my fingernails into his back.

Jayson lifts off me to grab the condom, and I whimper out a protest at the loss of him. He rips open the foil wrapper with his teeth and quickly rolls it on before dropping back down, arms on either side of my head, biceps flexing. I can see the vein in his neck throbbing, feel his heart pound against his chest in tune with my own. He reaches down between us and slides one finger inside me, testing my readiness for him.

"I love you, Liz."

I brace for him, ready to invite him inside me and fill me completely.

He whispers to me, words fused with love that I don't understand because my sole focus is on him. I throw my arms around his neck as he thrusts inside me, taking my innocence. There's a pinch of pain, then a massive pressure at being invaded and stretched for the first time.

Jayson slowly rocks back and forth, his cock thrusting deeper, inch by excruciating inch.

"You feel so fucking good," he groans between clenched teeth, sweat beading along his forehead.

"I need you to move," I urge him as a sudden bolt of pleasure ignites my core when he slowly pulls out, then pushes back in.

"I don't know how long I'm going to last, Liz. This feels too good."

"We'll have many more next times," I tell him, using the words he said to me that Fourth of July after he gave me my first orgasm under the fireworks. "Don't hold back."

I open my legs wider and hook my ankles together, holding on tight for what I hope will be a rough ride. Screw slow and soft. I want hard.

Jayson takes my cue and pounds into me, punishing me with thrust after thrust. My eyes roll back, and I moan so loudly, I'm afraid the neighbors might hear us.

I always thought our first time would be gentle and sweet with quiet kisses and lazy touches. This is nothing like that. It's rough and dirty and perfect.

His hard thrusts propel me higher and higher, catapulting me closer to that precipice I need to fall over so badly. Our mouths ravage each other, our kisses sloppy and wet. The sounds of our grunts and moans punctuate the night air as our bodies claim total possession over each other.

And then I detonate.

I watch in fascination as Jayson orgasms, groaning loudly. When he collapses on top of me, I bury my nose against his neck and brush kisses against his damp skin.

"Give me about ten minutes to recover," he murmurs, his voice muffled against my hair.

I giggle, and he tugs the lobe of my ear with his teeth.

When he tries to roll off me, I pull him back.

"Don't you dare move, Jayson Jameson. I want to feel you against me a little while longer."

I don't tell him my legs won't work, and I wouldn't be able to move right now if my life depended on it. I already feel sore in so many places, and it brings a smile to my face.

He smooths back my hair and kisses me tenderly—once, twice, three times, like he so often does.

I reach up to trace his eyebrows. "I'll never look at this fort the same way again."

He laughs, and the vibrations alert me that we're still intimately connected.

"I need to get rid of this."

He reluctantly pulls out and disposes of the condom.

We spend a few more hours in our forest fort, my promise of many more next times coming true before we make our way home just as the sun rises.

Chapter Twenty-Seven

ELIZABETH

AN INCESSANT NOISE pulls me out of an exhausted sleep. At first, I think it's my alarm for school. But then I remember that it's Saturday. Intending to fall back asleep, I flip over and snuggle into my body pillow.

The noise stops, only to start up again.

I'm going to kill whoever keeps texting me at—I squint to focus on my bedside digital clock—ten in the morning on a weekend.

Stretching, I groan at the severe stiffness of my aching muscles. Why am I so sore?

Last night.

Jayson.

I had sex.

It really happened. Jayson and I really happened.

A smile spreads across my face. Oh, yes, it definitely happened.

The bathroom door clicks open, and Hailey peeks in.

"Thought I heard you moving around."

I pull back the covers for her to join me, and she belly flops onto the bed.

"So?" Hailey grins, propping her chin to her closed fist.

I don't know if I'm ready to tell her about last night. I buy myself some time by deflecting.

"How was your Valentine's evening?"

Hailey gives me a knowing look but replies, "Brea and I just hung out and watched cheesy Hallmark movies. We also tried out your new swing. Hope you don't mind."

"Of course not."

My phone chimes again, but I ignore it.

"Are you really going to make me pull it out of you?"

"Pull what out of me?" I ask innocently.

"Fine, have it your way. I heard you and Jayson come in here at six this morning. Mind telling me what my big sister was doing out all night?"

I cringe. Were we that loud sneaking in? Did Mom and Dad hear us?

"Dinner at Anaïs was fabulous."

"Not what I'm talking about, and you know it. Dinner doesn't take twelve hours."

Hailey tickles me, her fingers attacking my rib cage and under my knees where she knows I'm most vulnerable.

"Okay! Uncle! Uncle!" I capitulate.

"Spill the beans or I go for your feet."

When I hesitate to answer, she makes a grab for my foot, and I jerk it away.

"After dinner, Jayson took me to our old fort."

She waggles her fingers as she waits for me to continue. "And?" she prods, inching her hands closer.

"And it was *everything*," I exhale, picturing Jayson's face hovering above me, his eyes boring into mine as we made love for the first time.

Hailey jumps on top of me with a fierce hug. "I knew it! Oh, Lizzie. Oh, I'm going to cry."

Slightly bewildered, I push her off and sit up. "Why are you going to cry?"

"Happy tears. I'm so happy for you. Are you okay? You did use protection, right? How do you feel?"

For some unknown reason, I remember the words Mom said to me when I was little about crying love tears. I get it now.

"I feel good." I falter, trying to find the right words. "Changed. Different."

"That's all I need to know. I don't need any details. I just wanted to make sure you were happy about it."

"I am."

"Mom left some breakfast for you. They don't know you stayed out all night. I covered for you."

"Thanks, Hales."

"And take a shower. You smell like Jayson's cologne."

I toss my pillow at her as she exits through my bedroom door.

"Heading to Brea's," she yells.

Unlocking my phone, there are several texts from Jayson, Maria, and Julien. I read Julien's first. He sent me a picture of him and Elijah at their dinner in Fayetteville. Julien has his arm behind Elijah, and Elijah is leaning into his side. They look so happy together. I hope they had a good time last night and didn't run into any problems.

> Me: Love the pic you sent. How did it go?

While I wait for Julien to respond, I read Jayson's texts.

Jayson: Wanted to be the first to tell you good morning. Love you, Princess.

Jayson: Thank u for giving me the best gift last night. I will cherish our first time forever.

Jayson: I'll drop by later. Check your windowsill.

Jayson: Many more next times to come.

I look over and see an origami star on my windowsill and get up to grab it just as Julien texts me back.

Julien: We had a great time. Stayed at a hotel after.

Me: And?

Julien: No 'and.' Don't want to jinx it. But what did happen was nice. Very nice. Not one to kiss and tell <wink emoji>

Me: So happy for you both. Really. Give E a huge kiss from me. Love you. Always.

Julien: Love you too.

He sends me another photo, this one of him and Elijah at a table drinking coffee.

Julien: Don't forget to delete our convo.

Me: On it. xxxooo

I delete our entire chat and the two pictures he sent. Since Jayson and Hailey know the password to my phone, Julien asked me to erase any text or picture that included him and Elijah. I wish he would talk to his brother, especially since things seem to be getting serious with Elijah. I remind myself that it's Julien's story to tell when he's ready to tell it.

I should read Maria's texts next, but I can't seem to do it. I don't want to hear about her date with Ryder last night.

What if they took things to the next level like Jayson and I did?

Okay, that's extremely hypocritical. I shouldn't be jealous over the possibility that Maria may or may not have had sex with Ryder, and I hate myself for it as much as I can't help feeling that way.

Sitting down on my bedroom floor, I open the paper star Jayson left for me. Inside is a quote: "*You aren't just a star to me, you are my whole damn sky.*"

I press the paper to my chest. Once I feel more settled, I gather the courage to read Maria's texts.

Maria: Text me as soon as you get up.

Maria: It's past 8! You never sleep past 7. Text me asap!

Me: Just woke up. Didn't get home until late. How about you?

Maria: Normal time.

Normal time? I bite my lip and ask myself if I really want to know.

Screw it. I do.

Me: No sleep overs?

Maria: Nope. Ryder took me to dinner and brought me home after.

Maria: I did try to attack him in the car. He looked so f'ing hot last night.

Me: And?

My heart is thrumming.

Maria: Said he wanted to go slow. Wasn't ready for that yet. <frowny face emoji>

Relief pours through me.

Maria: U and Jay do the dirty?

Me: You are so crass <vomit emoji>

And this is where I lie to my friend, something I have never done before. I'm not ashamed of what Jayson and I did last night, but I *do not* want even a hint of it to get back to Ryder. So, I lie.

Maria: That doesn't answer my question.

Me: Nothing major to tell. Jayson was very romantic. Lit our tree up with lights and hung paper stars with love notes in them. Made me a tree swing. Dinner was nice. Then came home.

Maria: Guess we both struck out.

Me: Jayson is coming over. Need to get ready.

Maria: Ryder said he had to help his dad today so I'm going back to bed.

Me: Hugs. Sweet dreams.

The need to go pound out some of this pent-up energy suddenly hits me. I take a quick shower and decide that banging on the drums would do me good. Maybe Dad will join me, but when I get downstairs, he isn't there. Mom is gone, too.

I grab the toast she left out for me and head to the music room. Taking a seat behind Dad's Yamaha drum set that he uses to practice with, I twirl the sticks between my fingers, trying to decide on what to play. Scrolling through my phone, I select the Foo Fighters' "My Hero."

As soon as I hear the first beats at the beginning of the song, I quickly join in and lose myself in the tribal pounding of the drums. My arms and legs work in synchronicity, and I can feel sweat already trickling down the hollow of my spine from exertion.

I'm so connected to what I'm doing, I almost lose the rhythm when an electric guitar joins in. Ryder stands in front of me, riffing the chords like a pro. We grin at each other like fools, never once breaking eye contact as we play. I'm breathless by the time the song ends.

I fan my face. "That was awesome."

He stopped doing lessons with Dad after...

I don't go there. Not a trip down memory lane I want to take right now.

"Want to do one more?"

"Absolutely. Your pick. Fast or slow?"

Ryder scratches the side of his jaw with the guitar pick. "Another fast one. How about some Fall Out Boy? 'Sugar, We're Going Down.'"

I select the song on my phone and hit play. Ryder cues into the music with his guitar, and I can't help but stare at him. He really is gorgeous. Dark hair that's more black than brown, and those eyes, such a unique color that resembles amber when the sun hits them.

There are also some subtle changes that have occurred over the past year. His shoulders and chest are wider, his hair a tad longer, his arms thicker with muscle. Jayson is taller, his body more streamlined from swimming, whereas Ryder is more muscular.

Ryder catches me checking him out, and my face burns a fire-engine red. Totally busted.

Jayson and Dad appear in the doorway, as Ryder and I finish the song.

Dad walks in and picks up his bass guitar. "You guys sound good together. Mind if your old man joins in?"

"Sure."

"What's up?" Jayson says.

"Not much. Keeping busy," Ryder replies.

Jayson gives me a short, sweet kiss.

"Hey, baby."

I tap a drumstick against his butt. "Do you mind waiting while we play?"

"Not at all," he replies, kissing me one more time, and pulls up a stool.

"What do you want to play?" I ask Dad.

"Do you guys remember 'Come Closer?'"

"Oh! I love that one."

He wrote it for Mom.

Ryder strums the first three measures of the song to refresh his memory. "I think I got it."

I tap my drumstick against Jayson's knee to get his attention. "Would you mind videoing us?"

I want to treasure this rare moment—me, Dad, and Ryder playing together like old times, and Jayson with us.

We play a few songs together, and when we finish, Dad lifts me up in a great big bear hug.

"Love you, Pumpkin."

I squeeze him harder. "Love you more."

I'll be leaving for college in a little over a year and will miss getting my favorite daddy hugs. I want to pack as many in as I can, especially since he'll be gone again for a six-city tour in a few weeks.

When Dad leaves, Ryder goes to the minifridge in the corner and takes out three waters, handing me one and tossing the other to Jayson.

"That felt really good. It's been a while since I picked up a guitar."

I miss playing with him. Just one more thing I lost when things...changed.

"We should do it more often."

Jayson hooks his arm around my waist. "What brings you by?"

I give him a perplexed look. Ryder has a key like everyone else and can come over whenever he wants to. He doesn't anymore, but that's beside the point.

"Taking a break before I have to head back to the garage."

"Maria said you guys had a good time last night," my mouth blurts before I can stop it.

"Yep," is his one-word reply, then, "Saw the video of the tree." A flash of sadness briefly flickers across his face before disappearing. "I need to head back."

Jayson surprises me when he suggests, "If you have time, why don't you come to Ruby's with us. Liz and I were going to grab some lunch in town."

Ryder hesitates, so I push. "You'll come? Please?"

He glances over his shoulder before replying, "Sure. Yeah. I'll come. Thanks for asking. Mind if I meet you guys there?"

"Half hour?" Jayson asks.

"I'll be there."

Jayson waits until he hears the front door close.

I'm abruptly lifted and pressed against the adjoining wall, and I only have a second to blink when he lands a hard kiss on my lips.

"I couldn't wait another second to get my hands on you. One of these days, I plan on fucking you while you're draped across your piano."

I'm hefted higher when he wedges a leg between my thighs.

"Get yourself off."

He doesn't wait and grabs my waist, grinding me on his thigh. The ease at which he takes me from zero to sixty is ridiculous.

Sealing his mouth over mine, he captures my moan when I climax. That was fast.

Jayson shuts and locks the door.

"What are you—"

"Your dad is still in the house, and I don't want him to kick my ass if he finds me defiling his daughter."

He turns me and pushes me face-forward against the wall.

"Arms up," he commands, and I obey without question.

He sneaks clever fingers under my shirt and plays with my nipple, while his other hand slinks underneath the waistband of my yoga pants.

"Be very quiet," he whispers in my ear, sending a cascade of goose bumps down my arms.

I nod yes, lost in the sparks of pleasure he reignites when he plays with my swollen clit, still vibrating from the first orgasm.

"You're soaking."

He slips one finger inside me and groans. I love that he finds pleasure in touching me.

My back arches, begging for more. A second finger joins the first, and he finger-fucks me to another embarrassingly quick orgasm. I bite my lower lip to stifle my moan of release. Lips kiss all along my neck until my tremors die down and my legs stop shaking.

He pulls his hand out of my pants and twists me back around. With a wicked grin, he sucks his fingers clean.

"You are so dirty."

"And you love it," he replies smugly and unlocks the door.

He checks to make sure the coast is clear. No dad in sight.

"Ready for lunch?"

"Dad!" I yell.

"Yeah?" he answers from upstairs.

"Going to Ruby's with Jayson and Ryder. I'll be back later."

"Okay, hon."

My legs are still wobbly, and Jayson laughs the entire way to his truck. He helps me up and buckles me in, then comes around to hop into the driver's seat.

"That was a really nice thing you did, inviting Ryder to join us."

"Anything for you, Princess."

He reaches for my hand and places it on top of his thigh as he backs out of the driveway.

"How are you feeling this morning?" A hint of nervousness creeps into his voice.

"Good. A bit sore."

"I could tell. You flinched a little when I fingered you. How do you feel about last night? About what happened between us?"

Is he worried that I regret being with him?

"Jayson, pull over."

"Why?"

"Just pull over."

He slows the truck and eases onto the grassy shoulder. Once he puts the truck in park, I release my seat belt and climb over the console to straddle his lap. I cup his face and press soft kisses on the corners of his mouth.

"Last night was the most incredible night of my life. Do not ever think that I regret what happened between us for one single second. You made it beautiful." I peck his nose. "*'You aren't just a star to me, you are my whole damn sky.'*"

A whoosh of relieved breath tumbles out. "I needed to hear that so badly."

"Many more next times, remember?"

Chapter Twenty-Eight

ELIZABETH

SITTING in our favorite booth at Ruby's, I listen to the guys talk, their voices weaving together like the familiar hum of a favorite song. The scent of burgers sizzling on the grill and the faint sweetness of apple pie meld together, mixing with the warmth of the diner's red vinyl seats beneath me. I soak it all in like parched earth after a hard rain, every laugh, every inside joke, filling the cracks of something I had broken without meaning to.

It's been so long since the four of us sat together like this—just talking and being silly. The kind of easy, carefree moments that used to come naturally before things got...complicated. I can still remember the way we'd all pile into this very booth on Friday nights after the Fields, legs tangled under the table, elbows brushing as we shared secrets and stole fries off each other's plates.

I glance at the guys—Ryder grins at Jayson's sarcastic quip, and Julien rolls his eyes, pretending not to be amused.

It's weird to feel like an outsider looking in, grasping for something that slipped through my fingers when I started dating Jayson. There was a time when nothing else mattered but being together. Four best friends against the world.

Balancing a large round tray in one hand, our waitress brings our food to the table. I haven't had anything to eat today other than the piece of toast Mom left out for me, and I'm ravenous.

"Pass me the mustard, please."

Jayson grimaces and hands me the squeeze bottle. I have an addiction to mustard and fries. I'll even put mustard on my potato chips. It grosses Jayson out every time.

Because he's making a face, I slather my fry in the yellow condiment and pop it into my mouth.

"*Mmm*. So delicious."

"Don't expect me to kiss you after that."

I coat two fries with a hefty amount of mustard and eat them in one bite. "I can live with that."

Jayson is quick and snags my next fry, but Ryder steals it and dips it into my mustard.

"You know, this shit is actually pretty good."

"Thank you, Ryder. See?" I stick out my tongue.

"I stand by what I said. Now mayo, that's the thing."

Julien gags. "If you start dipping your fries in mayo, I'm going to lose my lunch."

He holds his straw up and fires a wad of paper at Jayson. The tiny ball hits him on the forehead and falls into his lap.

"It's so on, brother."

Our lunch dissolves into a spitball war, and our waitress is none too happy about it based on the scowls she throws our way. We clean up our mess and finish eating our burgers.

"I'm pretty sure we're going to Hawaii this year for summer vacation," I tell them.

Ryder reaches over the booth and picks a paper ball out of my hair.

Thank you, I mouth.

His foot touches mine under the table.

"No, shit. Seriously? That would be so fucking awesome," Jayson says.

"I may have eavesdropped the other night when she was video chatting with Freda and Faith. Sounds like we'll be heading to the Big Island in June."

"Hell yeah!" Julien high fives Jayson across the table. "The waves in Hawaii are so much bigger than here."

Thinking out loud, I say, "I'll see if Maria wants to help me shop for some new bathing suits."

Twin groans erupt from Jayson and Ryder.

"What?"

Jayson pulls me to his side and leans in close to my ear. "Don't forget what happened the last time you wore your bikini top."

He ignores the eye flare I send him when he drops his hand beneath the table and slides it between my legs. My thighs squeeze tightly together before he can do what I think he's about to do.

Julien looks at his phone. "Elijah said there's a party at Fallon's tonight."

"I may hate the guy, but his parties are wild. Want to go?" Jayson asks me.

Not really.

"I don't—"

"Please. Pretty please."

Those big gray eyes get me every time.

As usual, I give in too easily. "I guess."

I'm not comfortable with the idea of going to one of Fallon's parties. They are notorious for being drugged-up, sexed-up, and completely debauched.

"Elijah will be there. We can hang with him," Julien says, code for *please help me distract my brother, so I can spend some time with my boyfriend.*

Looks like I'm going to Fallon's party.

"Are you and Maria coming?" I ask Ryder.

I have a feeling that I'll need backup with Jayson. For once, I would like to enjoy at least one party without having to spend the entire night babysitting my boyfriend over the toilet.

"I'll text her later and see if she's up for it. Anyway, thanks for lunch. I need to head back to the garage," Ryder says, getting up.

I clamber over Jayson to get out of the booth, so I can give Ryder a hug. "I'm sorry we kept you out so long. I'm glad you joined us."

"Me, too. Jules, want a ride to Fallon's tonight?"

"Sounds good. You guys carpooling with us?"

Jayson takes my hips and pulls me down into his lap.

"I'll bring Liz in the truck. We'll meet you there. Text me Fallon's address."

Three phones go off at the same time.

When we leave, we make sure to tip the waitress extra. She deserves it for putting up with us.

Chapter Twenty-Nine

ELIZABETH

THE MONTGOMERY ESTATE IS HUGE. Luxury mansion huge. Most of the kids that go to Highland High are from wealthy families, but good grief, this house is a mini palace. We had to pass through a grand palisade before driving up a half mile private road to get to it.

Cars are lined up on either side as far as the eye can see. Jayson manages to find a place to park his truck, and we get out to walk. A large five-tiered fountain sits in the middle of a wide circular drive and cascades water into a reflection pond that is about the size of a normal backyard swimming pool. If this is what the driveway looks like, I'm afraid to see the inside.

"This is crazy," Jayson shouts, but I can barely hear him over the thumping music blasting out from inside the house.

I avoid getting trampled by a group of drunk girls and spot Ryder, Julien, and Maria waiting for us in front of the steps.

"This is insane."

I slip my arm through Maria's. "What?"

"I said, this is insane!" she repeats louder.

"Let's find the beer," Jayson tells the guys.

I bite my tongue. Not worth the argument.

"Where's Elijah?" I ask Julien.

He checks his phone. "He's here. Will find him once we get inside."

"Hey, Elizabeth."

I look up at Ryder. "Hey!"

Maria jerks on my arm. "Come on."

We walk up the stone steps and enter the house through the open double doors. The stench of cheap beer and what I think is pot hangs thick and acrid in the air. I assume Fallon's parents are out of town, because who in their right mind would let their kid throw a party like this?

To be insanely rich and not give a damn—would be nice to know how that felt.

Once we walk into the expansive foyer, we collide with guys and scantily clothed girls, some dancing and others drinking from plastic red cups. I'm pretty sure the two people on the stairs are having sex, and another girl is giving a blow job to some guy in the alcove next to us. What the hell have we walked into?

I let go of Maria and cling to Jayson's hand. I'm not a prude, but scenes like this make me very uncomfortable. I will never understand why people think drunken depravity equals fun. Okay, maybe I *am* a prude.

"This party is off the charts!"

I have an utterly different opinion from Maria's.

She glues herself to Ryder's side. "Let's go get something to drink."

He sidesteps out of the way when two guys run past. Naked. Can't unsee that.

"I'm good here."

She tugs on his shirt sleeve. "This is a party. Let's go have some fun."

"I'm good," he snaps at her.

She glances from him to me, a frown growing.

"I'll go with you," Jayson offers and lets go of my hand. "You guys want anything?"

"No," Ryder and I say at the same time.

"Hey, there you are!" Elijah shoves some drunk people out of his way to get to us.

"E, where's the beer?" Jayson asks.

"There's a keg set up next to the bar and some coolers with other stuff beside it. Straight ahead and make a right into the kitchen."

Elijah points the way, and Jayson and Maria disappear into the sea of writhing bodies.

Thumbing over his shoulder, Elijah raises his voice so we can hear him over the music.

"Follow me. We'll head out back to the patio. It's quieter and less crowded."

We follow him through the throng of people. One guy we pass reaches out and grabs my ass.

"Hey!" I smack his hand off me.

"Fuck off," Ryder tells him and shoves the guy away from me.

I try to find where Jayson and Maria are but don't see them anywhere.

Moving me in front of him, Ryder places his hands on my hips and walks us through the dining room and out the door to the back patio.

"You okay, Liz?"

Julien sits down on the plush patio sofa and pulls me down next to him.

"Just a drunk guy getting grabby. I'm fine."

There are groups scattered around the patio and in the backyard, but Elijah was right—it's much quieter out here.

Elijah sits down across from us. "I should have texted you or Julien after I got here to let you know how crazy it was. Fallon throws some big parties, but this is insane."

"We're here. It's all good. I'll just stick to staying outside. I promise I won't ruin anyone's good time."

Julien squeezes the back of my neck, and I go limp like a wet noodle.

"I'd rather be out here with you guys than in there."

"Ditto what he said," Ryder agrees.

Using Julien as a back support, I look up at the stars and listen to the frogs sing their evening musicals. The guys talk about the upcoming race at the Fields, but I block them out as I search out different constellations in the night sky. I find Cassiopeia and the big and little dippers.

Conversation trails off when Julien checks his watch. "It's been almost twenty minutes. I wonder what's taking them so long."

"I can go in there and find—"

"Look who came to the party."

Julien and Elijah's postures stiffen when they hear Marshall's voice. And he's not alone. Three other guys are with him.

"Not tonight, Marshall," Elijah says.

Marshall is the guy who messed up Julien's leg. He's also conceited and a major jackass.

Marshall's leering gaze lands on me. "Damn girl. You fucking both brothers now? Or do you swap one for the other since they look the same?"

Indignation has me standing up and replying, "Want to repeat that?"

I may be a girl, and he may be twice my size, but no one talks to me that way.

Julien gently pushes me toward Ryder. He tucks me behind him and reaches back, finding my hand and holding it to keep me in place.

Marshall decides to pick on Julien. "How's the leg feeling?"

Elijah checks Julien with an outstretched arm.

"It feels like it wants to kick your sorry ass," Julien warns him.

Marshall's grin widens when he sees me holding Ryder's hand.

"Guess the rumors really are true. What's it like fucking the three of them?" His gaze returns to Julien. "Does one take each hole?"

"Watch your fucking mouth!" Ryder roars, and it's my turn to hold him back.

"Or what, motherfucker?"

"Or I'll make you," Ryder threatens.

"He's not worth it," I tell him.

I've seen him fight Jayson. Not something I want to experience again, even if Marshall deserves it.

"I think I hit a nerve. You." He points at Elijah. "We have unfinished business. I owe you a beat down."

I don't like how the guys with Marshall fan out, or the way Marshall smiles like he's claiming victory over a fight that hasn't happened yet.

Ryder backs me up. "Go inside."

"No."

"Shit's about to get serious. Get inside now."

My heart feels like it's about to tear open my chest and hurl itself across the backyard. I'm scared out of my mind. Where the hell is Jayson?

I steel my courage and stand my ground. "I'm not leaving any of you out here."

If having three guys as your best friends has taught me one thing, it's how to protect myself. They wanted to make sure I knew what to do to future assholes who thought they could put their hands on me without my permission, or from guys who didn't listen to the word no. I've only kneed one guy in the balls before, but I'll happily do it again to this asshole.

"You may want to listen to her. I'll gladly take your whore and give her the ride of her life once we finish with you three pussies."

I jump when a large blur flies past and slams into Marshall, taking him to the ground. They tumble off the patio and onto the grass in a heap of punches and grunts.

Someone in the yard shouts *"Fight!"* and all hell breaks loose.

Ryder slips from my grasp and runs into the vicious melee when Marshall's friends go after Elijah. It's a free-for-all of violence and chaos as fists make contact with flesh.

Maria appears out of nowhere. "What's going on?"

"Where's Jayson?"

I get my answer when I hear his rage-filled bellow. "Piece. Of. Shit!"

Jayson sits on Marshall's chest, pounding his face, blow after blow after blow, unrelenting in his attack.

My mind has trouble processing everything. It's total carnage, and I don't know what to do or how to help. Ryder steps away from the guy he just took down with one punch and goes to help Julien. Jayson continues to pound Marshall, even though he's no longer moving. He's clearly unconscious, but Jayson doesn't stop wailing on him.

The partiers from inside spill out onto the patio, screaming encouraging words for the fight to continue.

"Someone get Fallon!" I shout.

As soon as I say it, Fallon walks outside, Jacinda and Samantha with him.

"Goddamn, what a mess," Fallon says, pushing through the crowd of onlookers. "Get that fucker off my lawn and take him to one of the guest rooms."

Five guys immediately do as he says, and it takes three of them to pull Jayson off Marshall.

When Marshall moans and rolls over, I breathe a sigh of relief. Not for him, but for Jayson. He could face serious repercussions if Marshall decides to press charges.

"You guys just took out three of our defensive linemen." Fallon chuckles in amusement and slings an arm around Ryder's shoulders. "I think this deserves a drink, don't you?"

Ryder searches the crowd until he finds me, but my sights are locked on Fallon. There is nothing funny about what just happened.

His smile falls when he sees me looking.

"Let's get you cleaned up," Fallon says, dragging Jayson up the patio steps.

Before I can get to him, Jacinda is there.

"He's with me," she says and slips her arms around Jayson. They disappear together through the french doors.

Are you kidding me? He gets into a fight and goes inside with Jacinda hanging all over him, leaving me out here all alone. What the actual hell?

"Jayson!"

Maria stops me, and I become livid.

"Leave him alone and let him cool down."

Screw that.

"Liz, are you and Maria all right?" Julien asks.

He wipes blood off his cut knuckles and curses. I reach for his hand and inspect the damage.

"Just a scratch," he says.

"Just a scratch, my ass. You need to clean this and put some antibiotic ointment on the cuts."

Lifting my chin, he forces me to look up at him.

"I'm good, Liz. Don't worry about me. Where did Jay go?"

My angry eyes slice over to the patio door, hoping to see Jayson, hoping he came back out to get me.

"He went inside with *Jacinda*."

Ryder rests his hand on my lower back. "Let's go find him, yeah?"

"Jesus, Ryder. She doesn't need you to babysit her all the damn time," Maria snips.

"Not fucking now, Maria."

I don't want to be the cause of another fight tonight. I'm pissed, and I'm tired, and I just want to go home.

I walk into the house, a woman on a mission, and scour the crowd, but the mansion is massive, and I have no clue where I'm going.

With a gentle nudge on my back, Ryder steers me through a labyrinth of rooms.

"You know he wouldn't intentionally leave you and walk off with some other girl, especially Jacinda. We'll find him, don't worry."

His words of reassurance don't lessen the queasy, uneasy feeling I have in my stomach.

It's impossible to take more than five steps at a time because we keep getting stopped by people wanting to congratulate him on the fight. He brushes off their platitudes and keeps walking, carving a path through the crowd.

My worry elevates when we unsuccessfully search the first floor of the house for over half an hour and don't see Jayson anywhere. Eventually, we spot Fallon in the kitchen, smoking a joint with a few seniors from our school.

"Where's Jay?" Ryder asks him.

Fallon takes a drag from his blunt and dangles it from his bottom lip.

"Hey, kitten."

I glare at him.

"Fallon, we need to find Jay. Have you seen him?" Ryder asks again.

"No."

He walks off. What an asshole.

"Holy shit! Look at this." Maria holds up her phone.

Someone posted a video of the fight. *Dammit*. The boys could get into real trouble—legal trouble, especially Jayson.

We head upstairs, opening each door we come across.

"Jayson? Shit, sorry." I quickly shut the bedroom door.

Gross. I'll need to bleach my eyes after seeing that.

Maria replays the video a few times. "It's too dark to make out who anyone is. You can't see faces, only their backs."

"That might not be the only video, Mar. A lot of people had their phones out. This is so messed up."

Ryder checks the room to the left. I already feel lost with all the rooms and hallways that look the same.

"We'll cross that bridge when we get to it," he says and heads to the end of the hall.

He opens the door. Maria and I slam into his back.

"Maria, take Elizabeth to the car and wait for me."

I try to wriggle past him. "What's going on? Move, Ryder. Is Jayson in there?"

Ryder tries to block me, but I duck under his arm.

Everything grinds to a standstill.

My heart, my lungs, my brain, all sounds around me.

I blink.

One by one, my senses click back on. My breathing returns, my mind runs rampant, and my heart breaks.

Sitting on the end of the bed is Jayson. He's hunched over, elbows resting atop his knees, face blank, eyes staring straight ahead like he's in a trance. And he's shirtless. What happened to his shirt? But that's not what fills me with a rage unlike any I have ever felt. My hands curl into tight fists, and my eyes narrow on who is wrapped around Jayson from behind, tonguing his neck and writhing all over him half naked.

Jacinda Blanchard.

At least she left some of her clothes on, if I count the red push-up bra and panties.

Maria sucks in a gasp. "*Ho-ly shit!*"

"If you don't get your skanky-ass hands off my boyfriend right *now*, I'm going to rip every fucking piece of hair off your whore head, you conniving bitch!"

The sound of my voice seems to break Jayson from whatever suspended stupor he's in. He looks up at me, and for a second, a smile spreads across his face, like he's happy to see me. His loopy smile disappears when he notices Ryder and Maria. It gets better, almost comical, when Jayson looks down at his chest and the feminine hands running across it. He looks back at me and leaps off the bed, trips, then stumbles into a chest of drawers.

I can't watch anymore. The hurt and betrayal flaying me alive almost bring me to my knees.

"Ryder, please take me home."

I've seen all I can handle tonight.

I won't allow myself to cry, not in front of Jacinda. She doesn't get to see me break.

Maria threads her arm through mine, and I allow her to walk me downstairs.

Jayson shouts my name, but I'm done. This party has been one giant nightmare.

I vaguely remember texting Julien as soon as I step outside. I don't remember much after he arrives and walks me to Ryder's car.

I stare straight ahead the entire drive home, my heart completely shattered by the boy who said that he loved me.

Chapter Thirty

JAYSON

"LIZ! ELIZABETH!"

I fumble and try to push past Ryder but am stopped when a wave of nausea hits me hard.

Ryder shoves me back, making it worse.

"Get out of my way!"

Why am I slurring?

"You need to calm your shit before you make matters worse."

Jacinda palms my ass. "Let me know if you want to pick up where we left off."

"Fuck you."

"Oh, you were about to, baby," she taunts. "Here's your shirt."

She dangles it in front of me, and it takes me a few grabs before I get it from her. I clumsily shove it over my head.

"Don't you think that you've caused enough trouble?" Ryder says.

She runs her hands up his chest. "If you want a repeat of the bonfire party, come find me."

I stumble over my feet and fall back onto the bed. "I still can't believe you let her suck you off."

Why the hell does my voice sound so weird? It's like my brain knows what it wants to say but my mouth is refusing to say it.

"Yeah, well, I was having a bad night. Not as bad as the one you're having," Ryder replies, his tone full of disappointment.

"Liz. I need to find Liz."

I don't know what she thought she saw, but I need to explain to her that nothing happened. *Fuck*, I don't even know what *did* happen. I drag my hands over my face and into my hair and pull.

"What the hell is going on?"

He closes the door to the bedroom to give us privacy and crosses his arms over his chest.

"I think that's a question you need to answer."

I stare up at the revolving ceiling. Oh, god. I'm going to puke.

"I feel weird, and I'm nauseous as hell. And dizzy."

"How much did you drink tonight?"

How much did I drink? I had that one cup, and then maybe another...

Why can't I remember?

"I don't know."

"Then tell me what you *do* know."

I shake my head on the bedspread, trying to clear some of the cobwebs, and rub my temples to stave away the headache I feel coming. It takes a moment for my tongue to work.

"We all got here. Maria and I went to get beer. Jacinda and Samantha were at the keg and handed me two drinks. Fallon told me to fuck off when I asked him where you were. I fucking hate that guy. Why are you friends with him again?"

"Focus, Jay."

"Yeah, yeah. Okay. He told me to check outside. I started

feeling bad, like woozy and lightheaded. I heard Marshall say something about Liz. And then things get fuzzy from there."

Two of Ryder lean over me. "Back up. I can barely understand what you're saying. You said Samantha and Jacinda handed you drinks? Are you sure you're not drunk?"

"No. Yeah."

"Bottles?"

His two faces blur into a blob. "Huh?"

"Did they give you a bottle or an open cup?"

I try to lift my arm. It feels heavy. "Red cup."

"Did you drink any of it?"

I nod.

Ryder braces over me, getting in my face. "Did Maria drink hers?"

"No. I did."

His face disappears.

"You stupid jackass. Someone slipped something in the drinks."

"Nooo." No way.

"Do you remember beating Marshall until he passed out?"

I did that? Good. The guy's a prick.

"No."

"Know how you got up here? How Jacinda got here? How you both lost your shirts and ended up in bed together?"

I fly off the bed, wanting to punch him for even insinuating I would cheat on Liz. Never in a million years would that ever be a possibility.

A wave of dizziness hits me hard, and I sink to the floor.

"Oh god, my head is killing me." I lunge to the side and grab the waste basket next to the dresser just in time. I think I'm dying.

Ryder pulls his phone from his back pocket and texts someone. I throw up a second time.

"I think we need to get you to the hospital and get your stomach pumped."

I vigorously shake my head but stop when it makes me want to puke again.

"No hospital. I need to talk to Liz. I need to explain."

What have I done? What must Liz be thinking? My sweet girl. I just want to find her and wrap my arms around her and never let go. Tell her I'm sorry. Tell her I love her.

There's a light knock before Elijah walks into the room. "Jesus, Jay, what did you do?"

I stare at him with bleak, red eyes. "Is Liz okay? Where is she?"

"Why is he talking funny?"

"Liz in the car?" Ry asks.

"She's with Maria and Julien."

Ryder hands Elijah his car keys. "Give these to Jules. I'll handle Jay."

"On it. Hey, Jay?" When I see Elijah's concerned expression, my stomach churns again. "She's torn up. She just zoned out and won't talk, but we're taking care of her. She's in good hands. You take care of you now."

"Come on. I'm taking you to the hospital just to make sure."

Ryder helps me off the bed, and I lean on him as we walk downstairs and out to my truck. Everyone looks at us, whispers, laughs. They can all go fuck themselves.

Ryder fishes my keys out of my pocket and opens the back passenger door. He none too gently shoves me inside.

"I think it may be better if you lay down."

"My parents are going to kill me."

"That may not be the worst of it. I'll explain later, after we get you checked out by a doctor."

Ryder gets into the driver's seat and turns the engine. I take out my phone.

His eyes find me in the rearview mirror. "I don't think that's a good idea."

"She needs to know I love her and that I didn't cheat on her. She needs to know. I can't lose her."

Great. I'm all weepy on top of everything else.

"We'll figure out what happened. You won't lose her. I'll make sure of it."

I drop the phone when the truck hits a pothole. Bile rushes up my esophagus, and I swallow it down.

"Why would you do that for me, after what I did to you?"

Ryder slows down to stop at a light and twists around to look down at me in the back seat. "Because I love her, and she chose you."

The light turns green, and we drive in silence until we get to the ER. Ryder walks me inside, and after he tells the check-in nurse that I may have unknowingly ingested a date rape drug, they immediately get a doctor and rush me back into a room. After the nurses take several vials of blood and a urine sample, I'm hooked up to an IV. Then I pass the hell out.

"How are you feeling?" Ry asks.

I groan when my eyes crack open, only to be blinded by harsh fluorescent lights. It takes me a long minute to remember where I am.

"Like crap. What's going on?"

"Just waiting for the doctor to come back with the lab results."

More lucid and able to think clearly, I tell him, "Thanks for staying with me."

His loyalty compounds my shitty mood because his support and friendship are just two more things I don't deserve.

"Can I have my phone?"

"You sure that's wise?" But he hands it to me anyway. "I called your parents."

That's a conversation I'm glad not to have overheard.

I check my messages, hoping to see a text from Liz. Nothing.

I adjust my position on the bed and the IV line tugs on my hand. I hiss at the sting it creates and stop moving. The automatic blood pressure cuff attached to my arm decides to turn on and squeeze the life out of me.

"Why is it taking so long?" I complain, sounding like a whiny bitch. I can't help it because that's exactly how I feel right now. "Did Jules say anything about Liz? Has she asked about me? Does she know I'm here?"

I'd give anything to see her beautiful face walk through my hospital room door.

Ryder drags a chair to the side of the bed and sits down.

"He said she fell asleep in the car, and he didn't want to wake her. He carried her upstairs to her room. Her parents were out, but Hailey was home and will keep an eye on her."

My hope deflates like a popped balloon. She doesn't know. She's not coming.

"Are you going to finally fill me in on what the hell happened at the party?" I ask.

"Are you sure you're ready to hear it?"

I nod yes, even though my mind screams no.

I listen as Ryder tells me what went down outside when I was inside with Maria. When he describes how that sleazy bastard kept taunting Liz to get a reaction from Julien, my blood rages and causes the heart rate monitor to rapidly beep. A nurse is in my room a minute later to check on me. I want Ryder to be able to get everything out before my parents arrive, so I focus on calming down. I don't want any more interruptions from the hospital staff thinking I'm having a heart attack.

As soon as the nurse leaves, I ask, "What happened next?"

"You came charging out and knocked Marshall to the ground. We didn't know what was going on at first because it all happened so fast. As soon as we realized it was you, we jumped in. But fuck, man. You wouldn't stop. You beat on Marshall until he was no longer moving, and you still didn't stop."

I cringe. "I don't remember."

I look down at my hands. The nurses cleaned them up and bandaged them. Why can't I remember what I did?

"That may not be the worst of it." Ryder hands me his phone. "Hit play."

I watch the video, and even though it's dark and you can't make out who is who, I know what I'm seeing. An obscured form sits on top of a body on the ground, assailing it with punch after punch. *Jesus.*

Once the video ends, I hand Ry back his phone.

"They could press charges. Marshall's family could sue you. This may get worse before it gets better."

I release a disgusted laugh. That's not the half of it. If colleges and scouts see me on the video, I can kiss my chances of getting a swim scholarship goodbye. I could face jail time and have a permanent record if they charge me as an adult.

"I know what you're thinking. Don't jump to any conclusions. I've already spoken to Fallon, and he assures me that he'll take care of it. Marshall and everyone at the party won't go against Fallon. They know he'll fuck them up if they say anything."

I'm sure Ryder's right. As much as I can't stand the guy, no one in their right mind wants to be on Fallon's shit list. He just doesn't go after you, he'll go after your family and friends, too. He has enough money and resources to ruin you in every way possible. It's why I stay out of his way and hate him from afar.

Our conversation ends when we hear the sounds of heavy footfalls outside in the corridor, followed by Mom's voice. There is nothing worse than facing the wrath of my mom when she's angry, and as sure as I am that the sun will rise, she's going to be very, *very* angry.

My hospital room door flies open, and Mom rushes inside, followed thirty seconds later by Dad, Julien, and a doctor.

Mom runs her hands over my face and shoulders, making sure I'm in one piece.

"What happened?"

"Are you Mr. Jameson's parents?" the doctor asks, electronic tablet in hand and stethoscope draped around his neck.

Dumb question. Of course they are.

"Yes, and this is his brother, Julien," Dad says. "Ryder, thank you for calling us. Can you please tell us what happened?"

The doctor clears his throat, and all eyes turn to him. "My name is Dr. Dukovny. I'm the doctor assigned to your son's case."

He sets the tablet down and shines a thin flashlight in my eyes to check my pupils. Next, he listens to my heart and checks the IV drip line. Once he's satisfied, he sits down on a rolling stool next to my bed.

"Your vitals look good. The lab work did find trace amounts of GHB in your system."

Mom's hands fly over her mouth in horror.

"But I only had one drink." I think.

"If you had waited to come in, it wouldn't have showed up at all, so be glad that your friend brought you in when he did. From the timeline you both gave the medical staff and your symptoms, along with the blood results, it's safe to say you didn't ingest a large amount. You should recover quickly. We'll keep you on a drip overnight to continue to flush your system and rehydrate you just to make sure. Any questions?"

"Shouldn't my son report this to the police?" Mom asks. "If someone put it in his drink without his knowledge, isn't that against the law or something?"

"The hospital is not required to report instances such as this. It's up to your son if he would like to speak with the authorities regarding this matter."

"No police."

"Jayson! Why?"

"No police, Mom."

"I'll leave you to discuss matters privately. Mr. Jameson, if you need anything, just press the call button. I'll come back and check on you again before my shift is over."

As soon as Dr. Dukovny exits the room, four sets of eyes turn toward me.

"I can't believe you were drinking alcohol. You're eighteen years old!" Mom shouts.

"Freda, honey, I don't think yelling at him is going to help the situation." Dad wraps his arm around Mom. "Let's let him explain."

Julien comes to my bedside. He places his hand on my arm in a show of support.

"Yes, Mom, we drink. We party. We have sex."

My parents' eyes bug out like it's the most shocking thing to hear that their sons are having sex.

Oh, hell. Now they know that Liz and I are having sex. Fucking fantastic.

"We use protection, we don't do drugs, we would never drink and drive, and we always have someone as a designated driver. We try to be responsible and look after one another. It's not Jay's fault that someone slipped him something without him knowing.

What is his fault"—he stares me down—"is that you took an open drink. You know better."

He's right. There is nothing I can say to refute that.

"Wait a minute. You were with Lizzie tonight. Where's Lizzie? Oh, dear, is she here, too? Did anything happen to her?"

Mom frantically rummages through her purse to find her phone.

Julien stays her hand. "Don't call Ann. Liz is fine. She doesn't drink. I drove her home, and she's fast asleep, safe in her bed. Hailey's with her."

I tap the bed railing to get Ry's attention. "Can you go check on her for me?"

He looks down at his shoes. "I can do that."

"Tell her that I love her. Tell her—"

"I know. I'll take care of it. Just rest. I'll see if she'll come back with me before you're discharged tomorrow."

Mom launches herself at Ryder and fiercely hugs him. "Thank you. Thank you for bringing Jay here and thank you for looking out for him."

She kisses his cheek. Dad is next and gives him a quick hug and a handshake, and then Ryder leaves to go talk to my girl.

Chapter Thirty-One

RYDER

IT'S after two in the morning when I arrive at Elizabeth's. Knowing better than to use my key and walk inside, I go around the side of the house and peer up at her window.

Her light is on, so I take a chance that she's awake, even though she hasn't responded to any of my texts.

I carefully examine the tree that sits between her house and the Jameson's. Only way up is to climb.

Jay and Julien do it. Hell, even Elizabeth climbs up and down the damn thing.

Here goes nothing. I take a few steps back and leap off the ground. My fingers grasp one of the rough, low-hanging branches, and I use it to pull myself up. The tree sways slightly under my weight, but surprisingly, it's not as difficult as I expected—so long as I don't look down.

When I finally reach Elizabeth's window, I pluck a small acorn from a nearby branch and toss it at the glass, the soft *thunk* barely audible. I throw another for good measure. *Please be up.*

After what feels like an eternity, the curtains part, Elizabeth's wide, shocked eyes gape at me.

She fumbles with the latch and slides the window open. "Are you out of your mind?"

"Can you wait to yell at me until I get inside?"

My gaze slips, just for a second, and I catch sight of the ground far below. Definitely not my brightest idea.

"Aren't you afraid of heights?"

"Yep," I croak, feeling ridiculous.

She leans out the window, arm outstretched. "Grab my hand and move a little closer."

I breathe a sigh of relief when my feet hit her bedroom floor, and I fold like an accordion, sliding down the wall until I land on my butt.

Elizabeth crouches in front of me and vigorously rubs my arms. "You okay?"

"I don't have hypothermia."

"I can't believe you did that."

"You do it all the time."

"I also don't have acrophobia."

I have no comeback for that.

Sitting cross-legged on the floor in front of me, her fingers stroke over my busted knuckles. Without saying a word, she gets up and goes into her bathroom. I hear Hailey's voice before a door closes. Elizabeth comes back out with a first aid kit and sits back down, grabbing my right hand.

"Let me take a look."

She ever so gently feathers her fingers across the scabs that have formed over my middle three knuckles.

"This may sting a little," she says, tearing open an alcohol wipe.

Elizabeth takes her time wiping away the old blood and applies some ointment. She repeats it all over again with my other hand.

"Do I get a lollipop for being a good patient?"

Her light green eyes trail up to my face. Lifting my hand to her lips, she brushes a soft kiss over each knuckle, then blows. All the blood suddenly rushes southward.

"I'm out of lollipops. Will that do?"

No.

I shift farther back against the wall, needing the extra space between us before I do something stupid to make this shitty night go from bad to worse.

"I came here to see how you were doing and to tell you about Jay. Why didn't you text me back?"

A flicker of pain crosses her expressive face. "I turned my phone off. And we're not talking about him right now."

"You don't understand, Eliza—"

"We are not talking about him right now!" she snaps and then immediately backs down, exhaling loudly. "Sorry. I'm not mad at you."

"I really need to tell you—"

She slaps her hand over my mouth to shut me up. "I said no, Ryder."

When I nod yes, she drops her hand.

In a whirl of frantic movement, she springs to her feet and paces back and forth in front of me. "I think I made a mistake."

"What mistake?" I ask, not understanding. She didn't do anything wrong tonight.

Her blonde hair swirls around her face as she pivots sharply on her heel.

"It's something I think about all the time. Something I couldn't stop thinking about tonight. God, this is so crazy. My thoughts are a mess, and I'm angry."

Her words spill out in disjointed bursts, as if they're fighting to be heard before she can stop them.

"Elizabeth, you're not making any sense. And I really do—"

She halts mid-step, turning to face me. "What if it was you that came through my window that night?" she says at the same time I finish saying, "—need to talk to you."

"What?" we say at the same time.

"That's what I think about," she continues, her voice dropping to a near-whisper, like a confession she's been holding back for far too long. "I think about you. What if it was you that night? There's always a part of me that wonders...'what if.'"

What she says hits me with the subtly of a freight train, and for a moment, the world seems to blur around the edges. My mind stutters, trying to process the gravitas of its meaning.

I need to tell her about Jay, how he was drugged and is in the hospital. How he needs her there with him. But I can't because my mouth won't cooperate with what my brain is telling it to do.

"There's a part of me that knows that no matter what, no matter how much I love him, I will always love you, too."

Her words are like jagged slivers of glass, each one cutting deeper.

She loves me. *Holy shit.* She said it. Out loud. *She loves me.*

"He ripped my heart out tonight, Ryder. I gave him everything. I chose him over you, and he destroyed me. It hurts so much." Huge, silent tears trace down her face.

Elizabeth's liquid, verdant eyes beg me to ease her pain, make it go away, give her promises that I know I won't be able to give and still live with myself without a heavy burden of guilt weighing me down. I decide to once again be the better man, even though it kills me to do so.

I go to her and take her in my arms. It's a beautiful torture to hold her like this, knowing that I'm about to let her go once again to be with him.

"I know you're upset, and angry, and confused. I know you're hurt and want that hurt to go away. I wish I could be the one to give that to you. I wish things were different. But they aren't. I told you that I'm not going anywhere. Perhaps, one day, we'll get our chance. *Fuck*, I wish that with everything in me. But today..." I kiss her temple. "Today, you need to be with Jayson."

"I'm so sorry," she cries into my chest, shoulders shaking, her hands gripping the front of my shirt now wet with her tears. "You must hate me for saying these things to you. I'm screwed up. I'm selfish. I want things that I shouldn't."

"Not selfish, Elizabeth," I tell her. "Just wishing for something that's not possible right now. Maybe someday, just not right now. And after you truly understand what happened, you would hate yourself if we allowed things to happen between us tonight."

I need to see her eyes, knowing my next words will inevitably make her go back to him.

"Jayson is in the hospital. He needs you, Elizabeth. I came here to bring you to him."

Her voice cracks with grief. "What? How? Why?"

"I think we need to sit down for this."

I pull her to sit on the side of her bed. She and I will forever be tied together, just like she is with Jayson and Julien. I meant what I said, believing the words my dad told me the day my world fell apart, and I lost her to Jay. She needs to experience life and love, the good parts and the bad. And I will hold out hope that one day she will be free for me to love. Hope that all of this, the things we feel and do and say right now, will be worth it in the end.

"He didn't do it, Elizabeth. He told you the truth."

"How do you know for sure? We saw the same thing. He and..." She swallows hard. "They were half naked on a bed together. I know what I saw!"

"He was drugged. He didn't know what he was doing."

"What?" she almost shouts before lowering her voice. "How do you know?"

I fill her in on everything. As I explain to her what happened after she left, she goes from worried to furious to murderous.

"The bloodwork confirmed it. He had GHB in his system. I looked it up and everything he did, the over-the-top way he went after Marshall, the dizziness and vomiting, not remembering stuff."

Elizabeth grabs her tablet and looks GHB up on the CDC website to confirm what I'm telling her.

"How can we be sure that he didn't take it willingly?"

I also had the same question.

"I texted Maria on my way over here. He was never out of her sight, even when she went to grab the bottles of water. She saw Jacinda and Samantha give him the red cups. She said that was the only thing he drank."

Elizabeth curses Jacinda's name.

"It's not his fault, Elizabeth. You also didn't see him after. He's torn up that he hurt you. He's blaming himself. Can you forgive him? He really needs you. Will you let me take you to see him in the morning?"

She worries her bottom lip and slowly nods.

"I'll pick you up at seven. If everything's good overnight, they'll discharge him in the morning." I stand up and wipe my hands on my jeans. "Is it all right with you if I exit through your front door and not the window?"

"Will you stay with me? Or just hold me until I fall asleep?"

I hesitate for only a second. "Elizabeth, I would do anything for you."

I remove my shoes and climb on top of her comforter, leaning back against her headboard with my legs outstretched. She joins me and snuggles into my side, resting her head in the crook of my shoulder, and closes her eyes. The smell of her jasmine body lotion envelops me. She always smells like flowers.

"Would you rather," she begins in a soft cadence, her voice husky with sleep. "Would you rather be rich and feel somewhat content, or poor and be extremely happy?"

"That's easy," I say. "I'd rather be poor and happy."

"Me too," she replies, eyes fluttering closed with exhaustion. She's had a very long, hard night. "You make me happy, Ryder."

"You make me happy, too," I murmur back, kissing the top of her head, but she's already asleep.

Chapter Thirty-Two

JAYSON

MOM, Dad, and Julien just left to go home and take showers. The doctor on rotation came in not long ago and said I should be discharged later this morning after they do one more blood draw to make sure things look good. The hospital staff have been nice, but the food is atrocious. I check my phone again. Still no word from Ryder or Liz. I text Julien.

> Me: Bring me back two sausage biscuits. Hospital food sucks. I'm starving.

> Julien: See you in an hour.

To pass the time because I'm bored out of my mind, I play a game on my phone. I don't look up when my hospital door opens because it's more than likely a nurse coming in to check on me. At least the blood pressure cuff isn't going off every fifteen minutes anymore.

"Hey," a soft voice says from the door.

My head whips up so fast I see flashing lights behind my eyes.

Or maybe they are caused by the sight of Liz standing in front of me looking like a gorgeous fairy princess in a rose blouse and brown skirt, her long platinum hair hanging loose around her shoulders. She is a fucking sight to behold, and my gaze devours every inch of her.

Ryder steps up behind her. "Hey, man. How are you this morning?"

I don't care how he did it, but she's here. She's really here.

"I feel fine. They're letting me go home today."

I lick my lips, which have suddenly gone dry as a desert, and reach for the cup of water on the side table.

"Does she know?" I ask because she looks apprehensive as hell.

"Yeah, she knows. I told her everything."

"Baby, I'm so sorry."

I reach for her, wanting her to come to me, but she steps back and drops her head. That familiar panic rises. She's decided she doesn't want me anymore. We're done. She's leaving me. It's all my fault.

I watch helplessly as Ryder backs out of the room and closes the door, leaving me alone, not knowing what to do or what to say to Liz to make things right with her. The room is so silent, only the sound of the hospital equipment and the tiny rhythmic plops like raindrops hitting the floor can be heard. I look down and see little puddles of tears at Liz's feet, and my heart drops.

"God, baby, don't cry. Please don't cry," I choke up.

"Did you have sex with her?" she asks, her voice broken and barely audible.

My answer is loud and strong, leaving no doubt. Ryder said that I still had my jeans on when they found me in the room with Jacinda.

"No. I would never do that to you. I would never want to."

"Did you kiss her? Touch her?"

I wish I could say no with absolute certitude, but I honestly don't remember. I pray that I didn't. Wish it with all my heart. The only girl I want is her. No one else. Only her.

"I love you so fucking much. So much, Liz. Please come here. I need you to come here. Please let me hold you," I beg.

She wipes under her eyes and shakes her head.

"Liz, please, baby. I love you. I need you. Please."

She looks at my outstretched hand, then at me. Finally, she takes it.

As soon as her hand is in mine, I pull her on top of me in the hospital bed. I shower kisses all over her wet face, drinking up her tears. She wraps her arms around my neck, and it doesn't take long for her to kiss me back.

"I'm so goddamn sorry."

She sniffles.

"They say make-up sex is the best sex."

My heart soars when I feel her lips curve against my skin.

Liz pulls back, no longer amused. "Did Jacinda drug your drink?"

"I don't know. She handed me the drinks. Maybe that shit was meant for her or Samantha. Maybe it was a prank. Who the fuck knows?"

Liz grows solemn. "I hate her guts, but I hope no one tried to spike her drink on purpose. What about the fight? Ryder explained on the way here that Marshall could bring assault charges against you."

I roll her to my side and allow her to get comfortable, which is hard in this tiny as fuck bed, but I'm not letting her go.

"We'll just have to wait and see and hope for the best. If it comes down to it, I have the bloodwork that proves someone slipped me a roofie."

She plays with one of the strings of my hospital gown. “We'll get through this together.”

“We will?” I sound like a pussy asking it.

“We will,” she replies.

I feel a huge weight being lifted, releasing the stranglehold on my heart, allowing me to breathe again.

“I promise I won't be that stupid ever again. You have my word.”

“I'm just glad you're okay. I'm having a hard time wrapping my head around what happened. When I saw you and...her...”

“I love you, Princess. I would never do something like that to you.”

I hold my girl, and no more words are spoken. By the time Julien and my parents come back, I'm finally discharged.

Figuring I won't see him for the rest of the day, I text Ry a heartfelt thank you for bringing Liz back to me.

So, imagine my surprise when I see him, his parents and sisters, along with Liz's mom and Hailey, sitting in our living room when we get home.

“Mom?” Liz questions, her confusion apparent.

“Please come sit,” Ann says, patting the spot on the sofa next to her and Hailey.

Julien stops beside me under the entryway of the living room. “What's going on?”

“No clue.”

My mom begins. “In light of everything that happened and everything we learned about last night, we thought it best for all of us to sit down and talk.”

“Talk about what?” I ask.

“Drinking. Drugs. Sex.”

Did not see that coming.

"Boys, please have a seat," Dad says, and we immediately do as he asks, knowing now is not the time to argue.

I lower to the armrest of the couch next to Liz, and Ryder and Julien sit on the floor. Brea and Jamie occupy the armchairs on either side of us. I reach over to take Liz's hand, and at first, she pulls away. Her avoidance of my touch breaks my heart all over again.

The room grows tense as we wait.

"I think it's safe to say that we are very disappointed in you."

Jamie fires off, "Wait a minute! I didn't do anything. I was at work."

"For brevity's sake," Faith responds to her oldest daughter, "we will be using the 'royal we.' It doesn't matter if you were at the party last night or not, we feel that what we discuss today is important for all of you to hear."

Faith motions for my mom to continue.

"Like I said, we are disappointed. To find out our children are attending parties where there's underage drinking and drugs concerns us greatly. It also scares the hell out of us. Look what happened." She aims her silver gaze directly at me. "We are so thankful that you are all right, but things could have turned out much, much differently."

Liz's mom's breath audibly catches. It could have been Liz that got slipped the date rape drug. John is out of town on tour, and my guilt skyrockets a thousandfold knowing Ann is having to deal with this all on her own.

Over the next two hours, we have a serious discussion about what our parents expect from us, including the always dreaded sex talk. They ask us questions about Fallon's party and talk to us about the dangers of underage drinking and drug use. Ann and Faith have a conversation with their daughters about date rape.

Those were two of the most excruciating hours of my life. Not because of what our parents said, but because I broke my parents' trust. I broke Liz's trust. And I have a feeling that the rift I created may be impossible for me to mend.

It took a few months for our parents to ease up on their worry whenever we left the house to go out. Once again, I was grounded —this time for an entire month. I didn't mind. Liz and I took that time to focus on mending our relationship. The months following the party fiasco flew by and before we knew it, another school year had ended. Ryder was right. Fallon's threats worked, and no charges were brought against us for the fight. No other videos were posted either, and the one that did pop up was taken down and disappeared within a day after it had been posted. I hate knowing that I now owe Fallon.

Our families took the trip to Hawaii for summer vacation, and it was fucking awesome. My favorite memory? Liz and I got to fulfill number three on my Hawaii bucket list. I fucked her on the black sand beach under a full moon. Best night ever. It was her fault for wearing that damn bikini again.

Things between all of us were good. Better than good. Our unit was tight, our friendships were solid. We went into our senior year looking ahead to the future, planning to spend it together. I would later regret those words.

Chapter Thirty-Three

ELIZABETH

Senior Year

IT'S our first day of our senior year, and I'm sitting on Julien's bed waiting for Jayson to get out of the shower. I swear, Jayson's worse than a girl when it comes to getting ready. He takes for-*freaking*-ever. I get dressed in about fifteen minutes. The irony is not lost on me.

"Yeah, we're getting ready to leave in a few," Julien tells Elijah and turns his phone toward me. "Say hi and bye to E, Liz."

Elijah's grinning face greets me on the screen. "Morning, Liz!"

I put down my tablet and take the phone.

"Hey, handsome. Are you coming with?"

"No can do. It would take too long to drive there and back. Would be easier if we all went to the same school."

The shower turns off, and Julien plops down beside me so that both of us can be seen on the video screen.

"Babe, I got to go. Love you."

"Love you, too. And you too, Liz," he adds when I pout.

Shutting off his phone, Julien sits up.

"You two are so cute."

"Sexy, not cute. No one wants to be called cute."

He kisses me on the nose and clambers off the bed when Jayson enters, a towel wrapped around his waist, steam billowing out behind him from the bathroom. Seeing him wet and half naked causes heat to race up my legs and settle between my thighs.

"Keep looking at me like that, Princess, and I can't be held responsible for what happens."

Julien takes that as his cue to leave.

"Don't need to see that. I'll meet you guys downstairs. Ryder said he was on his way, so no hanky-panky because we've got to go. You have ten minutes."

He walks backward out of the room, doing that double finger to eye thing.

Jayson laughs and shuts the door in his face. With a flick of the lock, he turns around and stalks toward me. My heartbeat picks up with excitement at his possessive smirk.

"He said ten minutes. I only need five."

He grabs me before I can dash to the door and hauls me against his still-damp body. Jayson's towel falls away when he picks me up and carries me into the bathroom. He sets me down on the bathroom vanity and hikes up my skirt. Teasing a hand under my panties, I moan when his fingers slick through my arousal.

"We need to be quick."

He rips my panties out of the way and lines himself up. Last summer, we decided that I would go on the pill, and he's been taking me bare ever since.

Gripping my neck, he jerks me forward for a blistering kiss, moaning into my mouth when he plunges into me with one hard thrust. Jayson kisses me the same way he fucks me. Carnally. Brutally. My fingers curl over the lip of the vanity, and I throw my head back when my orgasm hits me hard. He buries his face between my breasts and grunts his release before easing out of me.

"One day, I'm putting a baby in you"—he trails a fingertip through the wetness between my legs and shoves his cum back inside me—"and my ring on your finger."

He's been saying things like that a lot to me lately, and for some reason, it instills a feeling of apprehension when he does. He keeps making all these big plans for us. College. Living together. Marriage. Children. Don't I get a say about what I want for my future?

He strolls out of the bathroom and returns with his discarded towel. With gentle care, he cleans me, then tosses the towel into the wicker laundry basket. Figuring there is nothing I can do to fix the state of my underwear, I ball them up and shove them inside my backpack on the floor.

"I'm going to have a hard-on all day at school, knowing you aren't wearing any panties."

"Then stop destroying them."

Mom probably thinks I have an underwear fetish with the amount I'm forced to order every month because Jayson keeps ripping them.

At least my skirt is long enough that I should be fine, provided that a strong wind doesn't suddenly blow out of nowhere.

"Blue or black?" He holds up two shirts.

I point to the blue one. Putting it on, he zips up his shorts and sits on the end of the bed to lace his sneakers. I smooth down my hair and adjust my clothes. I give myself a once-over in the bathroom mirror and decide I look presentable enough. Thoroughly fucked, but presentable.

Julien is standing at the bottom of the stairs, waiting for us. "Nine minutes. I'm impressed."

Ryder passes me the yellow packets of sweetener, and I rip two of them open and dump their contents into my coffee.

"Coach told me there would be a couple of scouts at the game."

Varsity soccer season is several months away, not until next year at the beginning of February, but it's tradition for Fallen Brook and Highland High to play a scrimmage match at the start of the school year.

"There's no doubt in my mind that you and Jay will get a full ride to college," Ryder comments, shoveling a ham biscuit in his mouth.

I nibble on my scone to allow time for my coffee to cool down. Jayson rests his arm along the back of our booth and plays with the ends of my hair.

"You know, we should apply for early admission to CU."

That was a pact we made a long time ago. Jayson and Julien are CU or bust. CU obsessed is more like it. I should count myself lucky that Jayson let me have his favorite CU T-shirt, which I kind of stole and refuse to give back to him. I like to sleep in it.

Ryder doesn't care one way or another which college he goes to since his future is certain. He's going to take over his dad's garage, but plans to get an MBA. Me? I haven't figured that part out. I guess where they go, I go.

Julien throws a sugar packet at his brother.

"There's no rush. We have several more months before we need to start sending in applications."

The waitress drops our check on the table, and Jayson pulls out his wallet.

"On me today. We need to head on out if we want to make it

before the first bell." He slides out of the booth and reaches for me. "Jules, you with us or Ry?"

"I'll ride with Ry."

I hug Julien and Ryder goodbye, and Jayson opens the passenger side door of his truck for me to get in. It's not like I won't see them again today. Julien, Jayson, and Ryder are taking two AP courses with me, first period being one of them, and I'll see them again for lunch.

Once we get to school, we park in the senior lot. Maria is already waiting next to the walkway that leads from the lot to the school building. She runs over to Ryder's car when he pulls in and jumps him as soon as he gets out. He subtly pushes her away. If I wasn't watching so closely, I would have missed the exchange. I wonder what's going on.

I jump out of Jayson's truck before he has a chance to come around to open the door for me.

"Maria!"

She saunters over. Jayson places a quick peck on my lips and joins the guys.

"Ready for senior year?" I sling my backpack over a shoulder and walk with her.

"I can't wait to get out of this place."

Maria wants to live in a big city. I never want to leave Fallen Brook.

When we get to the quad, she says, "Skanky bitch alert."

Jacinda hears her and turns around. It's not like Maria was being quiet.

"Who are you calling a bitch, *la puta*?"

Samantha and a few other girls from the cheerleading squad gather around Jacinda.

"Whore, really? That's the best you can come up with? At least I don't have to drug guys to get them to have sex with me."

Did Maria really go there? She knows how touchy I am with what happened at Fallon's party between Jacinda and Jayson.

"Maria, let's go."

I try to get her to move, but she isn't budging.

Jacinda smiles a wicked grin. "Your boyfriend won't even touch you. I got to touch him all over."

She puts her finger in her mouth, moving it in and out to imitate a blow job. Another shitty night I'd rather forget.

Fed up with *Mean Girls* bullshit, I snap, "Do you always have to be such a vapid bitch?"

Samantha pops her hip and throws her long ponytail over her shoulder. "Don't even get me started on you."

Her eyes flick to something behind me.

"Do I need to tell Fallon that you're messing with Elizabeth?" Ryder says.

Apparently, that works because Jacinda and her crew skulk off without saying another word.

Ryder touches Maria's arm. "Come on. I'll walk you to class."

Without saying bye to me, Maria follows Ryder into school.

Looking at Jayson, I ask, "What did he mean about Fallon?"

"No clue and don't care. Come on or we're going to be late."

"Julien?"

"Nope."

I huff. "Seriously?"

I'm met with silence.

Chapter Thirty-Four

ELIZABETH

Ryder: Jamie's car broke down. I'll try to meet up with you guys at the party. Tell Jules I'm sorry I missed the game.

Me: He's doing great. Already scored 2 goals. Haven't seen Marshall. Not that I'm complaining.

NO REPLY. I slide my phone into my pocket.

"Ryder will probably miss the entire game," I tell Hailey and Jayson.

They're seated on either side of me on the bleachers. Not that Jayson is paying any attention. He's been closely watching the scouts sitting three rows down from us.

"They haven't taken their eyes off Julien the entire game," he says excitedly, most of that excitement coming from the fact that he found out one of the scouts was from Carolina University.

Hailey leans forward to get a better look. "Want me to go sit behind them and cheer loudly for Julien, scream how awesome he is?"

"Please don't," I say as Jayson says, "Yes."

"Absolutely not, Jayson Jameson. Julien would be mortified if you did that. And you, troublemaker of a sister." I poke her in the side. "Don't—"

Hailey flinches in pain and jerks away from me.

"I'm so sorry, Hales. Did I hurt you?"

She drops her hand quickly from her side. "I'm fine. It's nothing," she replies, her eyes avoiding me.

I try to lift the side of her shirt, but she slaps my hand away.

"I said I'm fine, Lizzie. Geesh, stop mothering me."

I can't believe she just smacked me.

She rolls her eyes. "If you must know, I ran into the door this morning and have a bruise. No biggie. Nothing to worry about. Um, I need to go to the restroom. Be right back."

"What's up with your sister?" Jayson asks and then jumps up, shouting at the ref, when Julien is tripped by one of the opposing team members.

Jayson sits back down and pulls me over into his lap, burying his nose in my hair.

"His leg still bothers him. If he gets injured again..."

No college wants a player who can't play to their full potential.

"Julien's got this. See?" I say when Julien picks himself back up and jogs into position.

After ten minutes and no sign of Hailey, I text her.

Me: Where are u?

Another five minutes and no response.

I get up. Jayson pulls me back down.

"Where are you going?"

"To look for Hailey."

"Game's about over."

"I'll be quick."

"I'll come with you."

Slightly exasperated, I reply, "I am capable of surviving for five minutes on my own."

"Still coming with you."

Once we pass through the stadium gates, we walk across the grass to the school building. A bunch of students congregate around the unlocked entrance to the gymnasium where the restrooms are located.

"What's up, Henry?" Jayson says and fist bumps one of our school's resource officers.

While they're talking, I slip inside to check the women's restroom. Two girls I know from class are primping in the mirror.

"Hey, Beth. Hey, Celeste."

"S'up, Lizzie," Beth exclaims and gives me a big hug. "Should have figured you'd be here watching Julien."

Celeste reaches around for a hug. "Where's your boy? I'm surprised he let you out of his sight for more than a second."

"He's not that bad."

She gives me a look.

Beth applies lip gloss in the mirror. "You and Jayson are like Ross and Rachel. Or Bennifer."

Celeste flaps her hands. "Oh! Lizzie and Jayson. You can be Jizzie."

We burst out laughing.

"I don't think so." I check under the stalls for feet. "Have you seen Hailey? She's disappeared on me, and the game's almost over."

"Didn't we see her with that guy earlier?" Beth says.

Guy?

"What guy?"

Celeste nods. "Yeah, she was with some older guy in the hallway. Didn't recognize him, so he must not go here. They looked like they were arguing."

Hailey has got some explaining to do when I find her.

"Do you mind showing me where you saw them?"

"Yeah, no prob."

I follow them out of the restroom and around the corner of the hallway. The metal accordion gate is down and locked. No sign of Hailey.

"This is where we saw her."

My phone vibrates, and I pull it out.

Hailey: Met up with a friend.

Me: Where r u?

Hailey: Already left.

What is going on with her? I don't know whether to be mad or concerned.

Me: We'll be at the truck. Meet us there.

Hailey: Not going to the party. Doing something else. Don't wait up.

I tap my phone to my chin, then type: **Who's the guy?**

I wait for her response. Nothing. Instead of texting, I phone her. It goes to voicemail.

"Everything okay?" Celeste asks.

I honestly don't know.

"Yeah. Thanks. Are you going to the party?"

"Right after the game," Beth replies.

"See you both there," I tell them and head out to find Jayson.

He's right where I left him, talking with Henry.

"There's my girl." He smiles and slides an arm around me.

I check my phone as we walk to the truck.

"Hailey bailed on us."

Jayson shrugs. "Then I get you all to myself."

Groups of people stream past. I guess the game is over.

We get stopped by some of Jayson's friends. After the third time, I break off and pop the tailgate to the truck. The sun is about to set, and I lie back, looking up at the sky. A few free-tailed bats zip above me, catching their early evening meals.

"Sorry about that," Jayson says, gripping my thighs and moving to stand between them. He pulls me to sit up and kisses me.

I run my hands over the expanse of his muscular shoulders and down his arms. I love how his body feels, so hard and strong and smooth. Jayson turns and sits down, wrapping my legs around his waist. I circle my arms around his neck and rest my chin on his shoulder. He makes a low humming noise of contentment, the vibrations tickling my fingertips.

"There's something I wanted to tell you," he tells me in a low murmur. He twists around so he can see me better. "I want us to move in together when we go to CU. Find a place off campus just for the two of us. What do you think?"

I'm not ready for that. Once again, he's making decisions about us without asking me first.

"When did you decide this?"

He doesn't catch the sarcasm in my tone.

"College will be our first real chance for it just to be about us. I know Jules and Ryder will be there too, but it'll be different, you know? I want us to have our own space that we don't have to share. You and me forever."

I cover my uneasiness with levity.

"No more climbing through my window."

The thought of losing that tradition makes me sad. I have all these wonderful, precious memories of growing up next door to him and Julien. Of our tree, our forest fort, my swing, my paper stars. Once I leave home, those things will be relegated to a mental box labeled good memories.

I remind myself that no matter where we go or where we end up, Jayson, Julien, and Ryder will give me new memories just as special. It's scary, though. In many ways, I still feel like a kid. I don't think I'm ready to start adulting.

Jayson reaches over his shoulder to touch my cheek. "You are my forever, Liz. I want us to make a life together."

That greasy coil of uneasiness churns in my gut again when he mentions our future and forever. He's making choices and decisions for us, not once asking if it's what I want. He just assumes it is.

Julien jogs over, hair damp from the shower he must have taken after the game.

"Mind if we grab something on the way? I'm starving."

I untangle my legs from around Jayson and leap off the tailgate into Julien's arms.

"The scouts couldn't tear their eyes off you."

Julien keeps me locked in his arms. I can tell something is up by the ear-to-ear grin plastered across his face.

"That's why I'm late coming out. I got the offer."

A happiness bomb explodes inside me.

"Are you serious?"

Julien's smile broadens. "Full ride to CU if I want it."

Jayson grabs his brother, and I get squished between two very enthusiastic men.

"Holy shit! That's so fucking awesome. We need to tell Mom and Dad."

"Guys." I laugh. "Put me down. I can't breathe."

"They'll send everything over to Coach next week, and he wants Mom and Dad to join us for the meeting. Honestly, if everything looks good, I think I'll go ahead and accept. I don't care what other offers I get. CU has been my dream, so why wait, you know?"

"I'm over the moon for you," I tell him.

This is something he has dreamed about, and I'm so happy for him.

Jayson clutches Julien in a tight hug. "So proud of you. I love you."

"Thanks," Julien replies, not able to stop smiling. "Now, let's go celebrate."

"Couldn't ask for a better night to party."

The party is at Curtis Matthews's house. He's on the swim team with Jayson. I've been to his place once before. His family owns a small plot of land near Mr. Jacoby's farm. After the nightmare that was Fallon's last party, I haven't gone to another one. This will be my first since then.

Me: Game's over. We are heading to Curtis's now. What's your ETA?

Ryder: OMW.

Me: Have some great news to share. See u there.

Ryder: Have some news too. Be there soon.

Chapter Thirty-Five

ELIZABETH

YEP, it's official. I still hate parties.

My nerves are frayed, and there's this raw, buzzing tension coiling tighter inside my chest with each passing second. The heavy thrum of bass vibrates the windows, while shouted conversations become a relentless pounding inside my head. I watch everyone around me with suspicion, half-expecting someone to try to drop a roofie into our drinks or for Marshall to suddenly materialize out of nowhere with his three friends.

I can tell that Jayson is getting irritated with me because I keep nagging him about how much he's drinking. I need to get a grip, but it's hard to do when the edges of the room feel like they're closing in.

Curtis's party is nothing like Fallon's. It's quieter, less chaotic. But it doesn't matter. The same overwhelming urge to escape gnaws at me, clawing up my spine like a phantom hand. I wonder if I'll ever be able to handle crowded rooms again without this panic chipping away at my sanity. I thought I was over the events of Fallon's party. I was wrong. At least Jacinda isn't here.

"Jayson, can you take me home?"

"Hold up, man," he tells Curtis and peers down at me. "Why do you want to leave? We haven't been here that long."

"I've got a headache."

Someone bumps into me from behind. A girl stumbles by, her giggle slurring out an unsteady "sorry" as she weaves across the room.

"I don't want to ditch Jules. Ryder should be here soon."

I glance toward the living room, where Julien is celebrating way too hard. He went from buzzed to completely trashed about half an hour ago. With Elijah out of town, Ryder has the distinct pleasure of babysitting him tonight. Normally, I'd step in and help out, but Jayson's already on his fifth beer.

"I need some fresh air. Come find me when he gets here."

Another person rams into me, and I stumble forward. For fuck's sake. I locate the nearest door that leads outside and burst through it. Finding myself on the front porch, I breathe in the humid night air, hoping to clear my head.

Spotting the porch swing, I take a seat, lean my head back, and close my eyes...only to open them again when I hear, "Hey, kitten."

Speak of the devil and he shall appear.

Fallon emerges from the darkness, a joint hanging from his mouth. He pinches the end off and tosses it into a nearby bush, then pockets the remaining piece.

"You here alone?"

He climbs over the porch railing, and I'm immediately on alert. I don't know why he has that effect on me. It's like a fight-or-flight reaction that always skews toward flight. Fallon has an air of recklessness and danger about him that attracts girls like moths to a flame. I seem to be the outlier. He scares the shit out of me.

"Jayson and Julien are inside."

He makes a humming noise and stares at me with those unnerving, glacial-blue eyes.

Since I'm always running in the other direction whenever he's around, I've never really spoken to him.

"Fallon, can I ask you a question?"

He cocks his head in an almost predatory manner. "Depends on the question."

I might not get another chance to talk to him like this, so I need to get it all out now, before I lose my nerve.

"Did you do anything to Marshall or the other guys to keep them quiet about Jayson? Did you tell Jacinda and Samantha to back off?"

He chuckles and swipes a hand through his artfully tousled blond hair. "That's two questions, not one."

"Would you mind answering both?"

His eyes gleam as he slides off the porch railing with catlike grace and settles beside me on the swing. The bench creaks under our combined weight, and the sharp, acrid stench of marijuana clings to him, burning my nose and making my eyes sting. I try to create space between us, but he closes the gap effortlessly, his smirk growing.

"What's in it for me?" he asks, a challenge hidden beneath the question.

"Absolutely nothing," I reply, taking offense.

I tense as he nudges the swing into motion with the toe of his shoe, the gentle sway doing nothing to ease the tension coiling between my shoulder blades.

He leans in closer, his breath warm against my skin, and murmurs, "Secret for a secret."

"What does that even mean?"

His lips curl into a slow, dangerous smile. "I'll answer one of your questions for every secret you tell me."

Is he serious?

"This isn't a game. Besides, I have no secrets to tell."

"First of all," he says, his voice dripping with amusement, "everyone has secrets. Second, everything is a game. It just depends on how you play. And tonight..." He pauses, eyes locking with mine, his tone darkening. "I want to play with you."

Before I can react, he reaches out and curls a strand of my hair around his finger. His touch is too intimate, too invasive. I smack his hand away, and he laughs—a deep, unbothered sound that makes me angry.

"Kitten has claws."

"Stop calling me kitten, Fallon."

"Make me, Elizabeth."

I only wanted some answers to my questions—questions that none of the boys would answer. But something tells me this is not a game I want to play with him because I would lose.

And why is he even here at a high school party? He graduated in May.

Fed up, I abruptly stand. "Fuck you, Fallon."

He's faster than I give him credit for, especially in the doped-up state he's in. His hands snake out and grab me by my hips.

"Oh, Elizabeth, those are dangerous words."

A deep voice booms behind me, and I jump. "Get your hands off my girl, Fallon."

My girl. And it's not Jayson.

Fallon releases me and gets to his feet, the squeaking of the chains as loud as the thrashing of my heart.

"Kitten and I were just talking."

He takes out the half joint, lights it, and walks back around the side of the house into the darkness.

"What the hell was that about?"

I really don't know.

"Nothing. You know how he is," I reply, hoping Ryder will drop it, but of course, I'm not that lucky.

"Be careful around him, Elizabeth."

After that encounter, I completely agree. However, my curiosity is piqued. As strangely bizarre as I think Fallon is, he intrigues me.

"But he's your friend."

"It's complicated."

Okay.

Changing subjects, I ask, "What was it you said you wanted to tell me? Oh! Julien has good news, but I won't spoil it and will let him tell you. Would you mind driving him home, so Jayson and I can leave?"

"Yeah, I can do that. Why are you leaving? I just got here."

"I'm not up to partying tonight."

Ryder nudges me back over to the porch swing, and we both sit down.

Ever perceptive, he says, "I feel like there's more to that than you're letting on."

"Too many bad memories," I reply, knowing he'll understand. "So, what's up?"

By his stiff posture and morose expression, I can sense something is weighing on his mind.

"I broke up with Maria."

Well, that came out of left field. Maria hasn't said a word to me about it. Actually, Maria hasn't responded to any of my texts, and now I know why.

Knowing it's none of my business, I ask anyway. "What happened?"

He exhales with a shrug. "She needs to be free to find someone who will be able to give her what she needs. I'm not that person.

And it's not fair of me to keep leading her on when I know things are going nowhere between us."

I feel like it's my fault.

Ryder and I have this push-pull between us, like we're stuck on opposite ends of a bungee cord, and the farther we try to run away from each other, the stronger the snap-back is. Jayson has planned this grand future for us. How can I truly commit to that future when part of me is still in love with Ryder? It's not fair to either of them. Why can't I just let him go?

Suddenly exhausted, I slump back on the bench swing and look at him. "What are we doing, Ryder?"

Those warm, copper eyes meet mine. "I wish I knew, Elizabeth."

The front door bangs open, and the music blaring from inside the house blasts outside when Jayson and Julien emerge.

"There you are." Jayson notices Ryder next to me. "We've been waiting on you. When'd you get here?"

"Just now. Saw Elizabeth. Heard you had some good news, Jules."

"Such good news. CU"—he hiccups—"offered me a full ride."

Jayson stops him from toppling over. "Dude, you're so drunk."

"I know. Isn't it awesome?"

"Whatever you say, brother. No more, okay. Mom and Dad will flip their shit if Ryder brings you home like this."

"Same could be said about you," I tell him.

Jayson's mouth curves in a wobbly, tipsy smile. "Yeah, but I don't plan to go home because I'll be sleeping in your bed."

Ryder rakes a hand down his face before getting up and taking Julien's arm.

"I've got him. He won't drink anymore tonight. Congratulations, Jules. You deserve it."

"Damn straight, I do." He burps and makes a disgusted face. "That tastes awful."

"Let's see if we can't get you some coffee. I'm sure Curtis has some somewhere."

"You ready to go, baby girl?" Jayson asks me.

Hell, yes.

"I'm driving. Give me your keys."

I hug Julien bye, but when I go to hug Ryder, he presses his cheek against mine.

"Good night, Elizabeth."

"Good night, Ryder."

He helps Julien back inside, and we watch until they disappear into the house.

Jayson only trips a few times on the way to the truck.

"I'm starving."

I check to make sure he's buckled before I start the engine. "I'll stop by the Dog House on the way. Chili dogs. My treat."

"No onions."

"Why?"

"Because I'm having you for dessert."

I'm suddenly woken from a deep sleep. Cracking my eyes open, I look over at my alarm clock. Three in the morning.

I listen intently for a few minutes and swear I hear someone crying. Pushing off the covers, I sit up, but Jayson hooks his arms around my waist and pulls me back down.

"Go back to sleep, Liz," he murmurs into his pillow.

"I think Hailey is crying. I'm going to take a quick peek into her room."

Jayson lifts his head. "I don't hear anything."

His hand moves down my bare stomach.

"I swear I heard crying."

I cock my head to the side, trying to locate the sound but all I hear are the sheets rustling as Jayson moves lower, inching my tank top up and taking a nipple into his mouth.

"I thought you said I had to go back to sleep."

He bites down gently and everything inside me clenches, desire pooling between my legs.

"Not sleepy anymore."

He rolls over on top of me. Pulling my hands above my head, he thrusts into me with ease. The only sounds now are the hushed tones of our quiet moans as Jayson fucks me.

Chapter Thirty-Six

ELIZABETH

INSTEAD OF GOING to our morning breakfast meet-up before school, I tell the guys I'm driving in with Hailey so we can track down Maria. She's ghosted me for days, and I'm starting to wonder if she's mad at me or just upset about her break-up with Ryder.

"Mom! Did you sign that permission slip for school yet?" Hailey yells from upstairs.

I take a bite of my muffin.

"Oh crap," Mom mumbles. "Signing it right now, sweetheart. Lizzie, where's a pen?"

I take one out of my bag from the floor at my feet and hand it to her.

"Do you remember where I put the permission slip?"

"Table in the entryway."

"Thanks, honey." She runs out of the kitchen.

"Hales, we need to leave. Come on, slowpoke!" I shout.

"Coming. Geesh!" I hear her feet stomping down the stairs.

She takes a black hair band held between her teeth and ties her hair into a ponytail.

I mentally critique what she's wearing. Long capri pants and a long-sleeved button-down shirt.

"It's going to be in the mideighties today. Aren't you going to be hot in that?"

"I'm good." She slides on her shoes and grabs a muffin. "Okay, I'm ready."

Mom meets us at the door and hands Hailey her permission slip.

"Thanks."

"Be good, girls." Mom kisses both of us. "Who's picking you up from work today?" she asks me.

Hailey and I share a car. It makes things a little difficult to schedule when we have different things to do after school.

"Jayson." I kiss her cheek. "See ya!"

As soon as we get into the car, Hailey says, "So, how are we doing this? Ambush style or straight up gangsta?"

I chuckle at her enthusiasm. "Maria usually gets to school around seven and helps out in the main office."

To graduate, every senior has to accrue a hundred hours of volunteer credits. My job at the library counts toward mine.

"You still don't know why she won't talk to you?"

"I have a pretty good suspicion."

Hailey shovels the rest of her muffin in her mouth as she drives. "And?" she says after she swallows.

My sister is like a damn Hoover when it comes to food.

"And I think it has to do with Ryder breaking up with her."

"You think she blames you?"

"Yes."

"That's bullshit."

"Is it?"

Hailey slows down for a stop sign, then turns right.

"I'm not dumb. I'm also not blind. I know the deal when it

comes to you and the guys. But I also know that you and Ryder have not once crossed the line with each other since you and Jay hooked up." I grimace, and her eyes grow big. "Or have you?"

I remember what I said to Ryder in my bedroom after Fallon's party. How he held me until I fell asleep.

"Technically? No. Lines have not been crossed, but they've definitely blurred."

"Blurred is not crossed."

"Isn't that just semantics?" I press my forehead to the window glass and sigh. "I don't know, Hales."

"Exactly. You don't know. So, let's go find out."

We pull into the senior lot at school, and I see Maria's car already parked.

"She's here."

"Want to be Riggs to my Murtaugh?" Hailey asks.

"Honestly, I think we're more Lloyd Christmas and Harry Dunne from *Dumb and Dumber*."

She laughs as she gets out of the car.

Just as I'd hoped, Maria is in the main office standing in front of the copier machine.

"I'll wait out here," Hailey says, taking a seat on the metal bench.

Here we go.

I pull open the glass door. Mrs. Teasdale, the school receptionist, greets me with a smile.

"Good morning, Elizabeth. How can I help you today?"

Maria looks over her shoulder and scowls. Not a good sign.

"Good morning, Mrs. Teasdale. May I talk to Maria for a second?"

"Of course, dear. Maria, I can take over until you get back."

Not happy, she literally skulks right by me without a word. When she notices Hailey, she scoffs.

"Great. You're tag teaming."

"What's going on, Mar? Why have you been avoiding me?"

She crosses her arms. "Like you don't already know."

"No, I really don't."

Another scoff, this one angrier. "Ryder broke up with me."

"He told me. I'm so sorry."

"Of course he fucking did," she snaps.

Hailey jumps in. "Cut it out. Why are you mad at Lizzie? She didn't do anything."

That sets her off, and Maria explodes. "Are you kidding me right now? It's always been about her! It's been almost two goddamn years since she started dating Jay, and Ryder's still in love with *her*. He still wants *her*. I never stood a chance."

"Maria—"

Eyes blazing, she smacks me across the face. "It's all your fault, you stupid bitch!"

Hailey is off the bench in an instant and shoves her away from me. "Don't you dare touch her again."

Several students walking by slow down to watch the drama unfold.

"You chose Jayson. The day Ryder asked me out, I was like, finally, he saw me. He saw me, and not you. I have bent over backward for years trying to get him to notice me. I was an idiot. He never wanted me. I was just a distraction for him while he continued to pine away for you!"

Stunned that she hit me, I'm rendered mute, not able to say anything to defend myself against her accusations, so Hailey does it for me.

"She's not responsible for your relationship problems."

"*She* has Ryder and Jayson wrapped around her finger. Their princess. Isn't that right?" she says, glaring hatred at me. "You're a selfish bitch. You want everything and have to give up nothing."

Her verbal daggers hit their target. My whole world has revolved around those boys. Ever since I was six years old, it's been me and them. I don't know how to exist without them.

And maybe that's the problem.

Hailey gets in her face. "You're the one being a petty, selfish bitch. I can guaran-*damn*-tee you that nothing has ever happened between her and Ryder. So, if Ryder wanted to dump your ass, that's on him. Lizzie has done nothing but support you. You don't deserve her friendship."

"That's fine with me. We're no longer friends...bitch," she hisses.

Mrs. Teasdale pokes her head out into the corridor. "What's going on? Do I need to get Principal Waters?"

Did she not see Maria hit me?

"We're good," Maria says cheerily, acting like nothing happened.

"Elizabeth?" Mrs. Teasdale asks.

I cup my stinging cheek and say the dumbest thing. "I need to go to the bathroom."

"Me, too," Hailey says and quickly ushers me toward the girl's restroom. "Enjoy the show, assholes?" She growls at a few of the onlookers, who have their cell phones out.

Wonderful. I'm sure this will be posted before the first bell rings.

Once inside the restroom, Hailey does a quick check of the stalls.

"All clear."

I burst into tears. "What the hell just happened?"

She tears off a paper towel, wets it, and hands it to me. I rub underneath my eyes to wipe away the mascara smears. I don't wear a lot of makeup, but I don't want raccoon eyes.

"Screw her, Lizzie. Just screw her. That was the biggest pile of denial bullshit I have ever heard."

"She's one of my best friends, Hales. I didn't know she was so angry with me. Why didn't she come talk to me? I don't understand. I never interfered with her relationship with Ryder. I may not have liked it, but I supported it and stayed out of it."

Fabulous. More tears. I rip off another paper towel.

"Can you imagine what you would do if Brea did that to me?"

"I'd kick her ass. Wouldn't matter that she's Ryder's sister."

"Exactly. Be lucky I didn't do just that."

"Hopefully she'll come around," I say.

I wash my hands and splash water on my face. I've got some makeup in my bag that should cover the bright red handprint Maria left.

"I know how you love to shoulder the blame. This is not one of those times. You did nothing wrong," my sister insists.

"But I kind of did. Maria was right about me being selfish. The guys have been my everything for so long. Our relationships are not normal."

I know this. We're too affectionate. Too close. I'm in love with two of them. Not normal.

Hailey smothers me in a hug. "Who's to say what's normal? There is no right label to slap on love. Your heart wants what it wants. Whatever you and the guys have, it works. *That's* your normal."

But it doesn't work, and that's the problem.

My phone rings, and Jayson's name pops up.

"I think shit's about to hit the fan," Hailey says.

My voice is a bit throaty from crying when I answer. "Hey."

"Liz, what the fuck? Are you at school right now?"

"Yeah."

"I'm with the guys at Ruby's. You're on speaker. Please tell me what we just saw did not happen."

Well, that was fast. Sometimes I hate social media.

Hailey yanks the phone out of my hand. "Where's Ryder?"

"I'm here," he says over the speaker.

She paces to the other end of the bathroom when I try to take back my phone. "You broke up with that crazy bitch, so she's your problem. She comes near Lizzie again, all bets are off."

"I'll deal with it," he coldly states.

Jayson comes back on. "We're on our way. Hales, take her back out to the car and wait for us. I love you, baby. Everything's going to be okay. Be there soon."

"Okay."

He hangs up.

"Come on, sis. Let's go wait for your boys."

Chapter Thirty-Seven

JAYSON

I MISSED SEEING Liz this morning, but I understand she wanted to get to school early. Maria is being a bitch to my girl by ignoring her, and Liz wants to find out why.

"Can I get you guys anything else?" our waitress, Pauline, asks us.

"A black coffee and a cinnamon scone to go, please?"

If Liz has already eaten, she can save the scone for lunch. I know she'll drink the coffee immediately.

"Sure can, hon. Be right back."

Settling back in the booth, I ask Ryder, "I know you broke up with Maria, but what gives?"

He's been cagey about the whole thing, and getting any information from him is like pulling teeth. I never liked her, but I don't like that he broke up with her. I felt safer when they were together. Kept him busy and away from Liz.

"Wasn't going anywhere. Broke up with her. End of story."

"I always thought she was a bit odd. Too loud and obnoxious for me," Julien says. "No offense."

"None taken," Ryder replies.

Julien pours syrup over his french toast. "But why is she ghosting Liz?"

Ryder rubs his hand over his face and scratches his head. "Beats the hell out of me."

I sip my coffee. "Did you cheat on her? She cheat on you? People don't break up for no reason."

He seers me with a hot look. "No, I didn't fucking cheat on her, Jay. You know me better than that."

The waitress drops off my to-go order, and Julien pays the check. Ryder crumples up his napkin and flings it on the table.

"She was getting clingy and wanting more than I was willing to give her." He flicks his gaze at me, then away. "She started talking shit about Elizabeth, and it pissed me off. I got fed up with all of it, so I dumped her."

"What the fuck did she say about Liz?"

"Nothing I'm going to repeat to you."

The urge to punch him is strong.

"You're a dumbass."

Our phones chime simultaneously.

"I didn't want things to be weird between Elizabeth and Maria, so I tried to end things as amicably as I could."

"Clearly, it didn't work."

He gives me the finger.

"Check your phones. We need to go," Julien says.

Ryder and I take out our phones. A video was posted five minutes ago and in the comments are the hashtags #nolongerfriends #theotherwoman #sayitisntso #bitchslap. Ryder and I must hit play at the same time because we hear Maria's voice in stereo. As we watch her tear into Liz, I literally see red. And then Maria slaps her. The video ends.

I glare murder at Ryder and call Liz.

"Hey."

"Liz, what the fuck? Are you at school right now?"

"Yeah."

"I'm with the guys at Ruby's. You're on speaker. Please tell me what we just saw did not happen."

Hailey's voice comes on. "Where's Ryder?"

He leans over the table. "I'm here."

"You broke up with that crazy bitch, so she's your problem. She comes near Lizzie again, all bets are off."

"I'll deal with it," Ryder tells her. He looks pissed.

"We're on our way. Hales, take her back out to the car and wait for us. I love you, baby. Everything is going to be okay. Be there soon."

"Okay."

I hang up.

"Jules, you're with me. Ryder, fix this mess. If you don't rein in your ex, I will. Maria is not going to mess with Liz because you broke up with her. That's bullshit."

Ryder throws down a twenty and heads out without a word.

Julien picks up the coffee and the paper bag with Liz's scone. "Liz must be devastated."

I double-tap the unlock button on the key fob. "Hurry up and get in."

I peel out of the parking lot, not caring that I'm speeding.

"Who are you texting?" I ask Jules when his fingers fly over the screen of his phone.

"Elijah. I'm rallying the troops. Liz is going to need us."

"Good idea. See if he can come over tonight. I'll pick up Liz from work and bring her to the house. We can order pizza or something and watch a movie. All of us."

"E says yes. No work tonight."

We arrive at school and park next to Liz and Hailey's car. The passenger door is open, and Liz is sitting in the seat, head back against the headrest, eyes closed. Ryder's car is already here, but he's nowhere in sight.

"Hey, baby doll."

I caress her cheek.

"I'm glad you're here." She turns her face into my hand.

Her eyes are puffy and red from crying, but she's still the most beautiful girl in the world.

"Come here, Princess."

Lifting her out of the car, I sit down with her on the parking lot gravel. I cuff her neck and wrap my other arm around her back and just hold her.

"Love you," I whisper into her ear and kiss her temple.

Once I feel her relax and her breathing even out, I pull back to assess her.

"Better?"

"Much better. Thank you."

"My pleasure." This time I bring her in for a real kiss, a slow kiss, gentle and reassuring. "Ryder is going to talk to her."

"I just feel like it's my fault. Perhaps I wasn't as a good a friend as I should've been to her."

Maria hits her, and *she's* the one who feels guilty. My girl's heart is so fucking big.

"No baby. You were a great friend. She should be ashamed of herself. I hope for your sake she apologizes. I know how much you care about her. But my concern right now is taking care of you. If she wasn't a girl, I would've already found her and punched the crap out of her."

Liz shakes her head. "What is it with boys thinking everything can be solved with their fists?"

"They can't? News to me." I grin and tighten my grip on her. "Hold on, baby. This ride's about to get bumpy."

I stand up with Liz still wrapped around me and start walking toward the school.

"What are you doing? Jayson, put me down before someone sees us."

Hailey grabs Liz's bag from the ground, and she and Julien silently follow behind us.

"Would you prefer caveman style?"

"Absolutely not. I think one video with me in it is enough for one day."

"Oh, these motherfuckers ain't seen nothing yet."

I kiss the shit out of her, and a chorus of catcalls and whistles erupt all around us. Liz giggles and smiles against my mouth.

"Fine, you can carry me."

I'm glad I could put a smile on her face.

Julien hands her the coffee we brought from Ruby's.

"You can put me down now. Caffeine comes before kisses."

"Keep telling yourself that, Princess."

Hailey hands off Liz's bookbag, and we head to our first period class. Still no Ryder in sight. Right before the tardy bell rings, he rushes to his desk. Class starts, and I hide my phone in my lap, making sure the teacher doesn't notice. Opening my group chat with Julien and Ryder, I type out a quick message.

Me: We're rallying the troops for Liz. Our house tonight at 7.

Ryder: Will be there.

Julien: E's coming too. Let's get Hailey and Brea in on it.

Ryder: Will text Brea later.

Me: Don't want Liz upset anymore so no talking about Maria in front of her. R, did you talk to her?

Ryder: Yeah. Didn't go well. Will tell u about it later when Elizabeth isn't around.

Chapter Thirty-Eight

RYDER

I SHOULD HAVE KNOWN Maria would lash out at Elizabeth. Asking her out was a stupid mistake. I thought she was funny. She made me laugh, provided me short reprieves from my thoughts of Elizabeth.

I knew Maria wanted more, but I figured, what the hell, so I asked her out. Almost immediately after our first date, Maria started dropping subtle, snide comments about Elizabeth. I never said anything about it, not even to Julien. Maria kept pushing me for sex, and after the Jacinda incident at the bonfire party, I was not going down that road again. Was I tempted? Yeah. Did I love Maria? No. And I made a promise to myself after Elizabeth saw me with Jacinda that I would never be that guy again, the one who uses a girl just for sex.

So, I kept my hands to myself, which only made things worse. I'm an idiot for not ending our relationship sooner. Julien was right. I should have broken up with her months ago. Now, I have to fix the mess I created. To say that I'm pissed at Maria after watching the video is an understatement.

I know exactly where she is when I get to school, but we're not having an audience for what I need to say to her.

I gesture for her to come out when she sees me outside the front office window.

She throws up her hands and mouths, *What?*

Come here, I mouth back.

She shakes her head no.

Come. Here.

Her eyes roll, but she's walking toward the door. As soon as she steps outside the office, I grip her elbow and lead her down the hallway to the A/V storage room. Once inside, she jerks out from my grasp.

"What do you want, Ryder?"

I flick on the overhead light. It casts an eerie glow in the enclosed space. Carts filled with equipment line the wall, and bundled cables lie on the floor.

"What the hell is wrong with you?"

"Did Lizzie come running to you, wanting a shoulder to cry on? Figures."

"No. Your little tirade was posted online."

She has the audacity to smile.

"Good."

I gape at her with incredulity. "That's it? That's all you're going to say?"

Maria stares at me, unblinking. No remorse. No apology.

"That was a shitty thing to do to your best friend."

Her chin dips, her eyes hard. "She is *not* my best friend."

"Yes, she is. She's been your friend since the third grade."

"I *hate* her."

My head recoils like she just slapped me. "How can you say you hate her? You two have been best friends for years."

"You are so fucking dumb. You know nothing."

"Explain it to me."

She's starting to really piss me off, and I don't know how much longer I'll be able to keep my temper in check.

"We might have known each other since the third grade, but I only started hanging out with her in junior high to get close to you."

She must see the confused look on my face.

"Lizzie had the monopoly on what I wanted, so I used her as my in with you." She kicks a mop bucket and sends it crashing against the metal shelving. "All the good it did me."

"That's the biggest pile of shit you have said to me. You're going to stand there and tell me that all the years you and Elizabeth were friends, it was because you wanted me to—what? Notice you?"

Maria comes closer, invading my space. "I want you, Ryder. I've wanted you for a long time. You want me, too. I know you do. You wouldn't have asked me out if you didn't feel something for me. For *me*, not her. Don't throw away what we have over that bitch." She slides her hands up my chest, and I'm too dumbstruck to stop her. "I'm better than she is. I can make you feel so good if you'll let me. Please let me."

With my mind whirring, Maria slips her hands to my belt buckle. Clarity returns, and I snatch her wrists.

"Stop."

"No."

She falls to her knees in front of me and tries to wrench her hands out of my grasp to unbuckle my pants.

For fuck's sake, not this again. I look down at her and see images of Jacinda doing the exact same thing. Appalled with what she's trying to do, I let go of her wrists and back out of her reach. My shoulder knocks into a shelf, and the resulting crash of metal hitting the floor shrills its echo between the walls.

She hobbles closer and goes for my zipper.

"I said *stop*."

On her knees, she gazes imploringly at me, but all I see is duplicity and hate. I really was an absolute idiot to fall for her lies.

"Why can't you love me like I love you? It's all her fault! She doesn't give a damn about you! She takes and takes and takes. She has Jayson. It's not fair! She shouldn't get you, too."

How could I not have seen this about her? How could I not see her hatred for Elizabeth?

"You know what? I'm fucking done. We're done. Over. No longer together. I'm not your boyfriend anymore. And you're right. I don't love you. I never did love you. I'm sorry if asking you out led you to think I wanted more. That's on me, and I apologize. But what you did to Elizabeth, what you just said to me now, that's all sorts of fucked up."

Maria rises from the floor, anger making her tremble with pent-up fury. "Fuck you, Ryder. And fuck Elizabeth."

"Stay away from Elizabeth. I'm warning you."

"Like you said. We're no longer together. You don't get to tell me what to do."

With that, she flings open the door, and storms out.

I rub a hand over the back of my neck, but it does nothing to ease the tension. If what Maria said is true—that this entire time she just used Elizabeth to get to me—Elizabeth isn't going to understand. It's going to devastate her.

Chapter Thirty-Nine

JULIEN

"TODAY COULD HAVE BEEN BETTER," I tell Elijah when he arrives at my house.

Knowing Jayson has to pick up Liz from work, I texted Elijah and asked if he could come over at six instead of seven. I wanted some alone time with him before everyone showed up.

We're sitting on my bed in my bedroom with the door closed and locked.

Elijah hugs me. "Unfortunately, everyone at Highland saw the video, too. I'm so sorry, Julien. Liz didn't deserve that, and she definitely didn't deserve to have it aired publicly like that."

He leans in, takes my face, and kisses me.

I melt into him and pull him closer. Mouths fused, we fall sideways onto the bed, our heads sharing my pillow.

Giving him one final swipe of my tongue, I brush my nose against his.

"That's not the worst of it. Ryder tried to talk to Maria. She said she hates Liz and was only her friend so she could get access to him. Apparently, Maria has had a crush on Ryder for a really long time."

Elijah plays his fingers through my hair. "You're kidding, right?"

"Wish I was."

"It's amazing what jealousy does to people. Take us for example."

I give him a quizzical look. "What about us?"

Elijah chuckles and kisses me softly on the lips. "Sorry, that didn't come out right. Maria is jealous, and she's taking it out on Liz. But that's completely on her and it's wrong for her to do it. I could allow myself to be jealous of Liz."

I can't stop my knee-jerk reaction or the hard tone of my voice. "Why the hell would you be jealous of Liz?"

"Because you love her," Elijah states quietly.

Still defensive, I reply, "Well, of course I fucking love her. I always have. She's my best friend. What does that have to do with us?"

We covered all this when we started dating. He knows I love Liz, but it's a deep friendship kind of love, and nothing like the love I feel for him. They're two completely different things.

"You're bi, and I'm not," he explains. "I could worry that one day you'll leave me to be with a woman or another man. If there was anyone else who I could see you with, it would be Liz. Does that make sense?"

"No."

Is he saying that he's afraid I'm going to dump him for Liz?

Yes, I'm bisexual, and yes, if I wanted to have a relationship with a girl, I would definitely have wanted it to be with Liz. But I don't. I want him. I'm damn lucky to have found Elijah, and I'm even luckier that he loves me in return. I'm happy. My life is good. I have so much to look forward to, even if I'm afraid of the future that awaits me.

"I could let my insecurities and jealousy control me, but I

don't. I trust what we have together, Julien. I trust you. Maria couldn't do that with Ryder. She's been swimming in her own pit of jealousy for so long, it taints everything in her life."

Needing to dispel his insecurities, I reach for his hand and hold it to my lips.

"I love you. Only you. Got it."

Elijah's eyes soften, the colors shifting to a deeper green than brown.

"Got it."

"That was the most godawful best-*est* movie I have ever seen." Liz is laughing so hard tears stream down her cheeks.

Brea wipes tears from her face. "Whose idea was it again to watch *VelociPastor*?"

Jayson raises his hand.

"You're the best, Jayson!" she exclaims.

Mom calls from the kitchen. "Who wants more pizza?"

You would think after we devoured the four large ones she already made, along with two dozen cookies, we'd be full.

Mom sets a meat lover's pizza on the coffee table, and four sets of hands dig in.

"Thanks, Mom," I tell her, fighting Elijah for the slice with the most cheese.

"You know, we should do this more often," Brea comments, munching on a cookie. "I mean, I know you guys have your breakfast thing every morning now *that we aren't invited to*"—she sticks her tongue out at Ryder—"and you guys will be off to college soon, leaving me and Hailey here to fend for ourselves. It would be nice to do stuff like this together before you all leave to become adults and all."

"I second that," Hailey agrees.

"I don't see why not," Ryder says, picking up a slice, the gooey mozzarella creating strings that stretch from the pan to his hand.

I lick grease off my fingers. Elijah watches me with smoldering eyes. My dick hardens at his heated gaze, and I roll over onto my stomach to hide my growing erection.

"I've got one for you guys. It's called this or that. You have to pick your favorite from a choice of two things. Like beach or mountains."

"Mountains," Ryder, Elijah, and Brea say.

"Beach," from Liz and Hailey.

"*Black sand* beach." Jayson smirks at Liz, waggling his eyebrows, and she giggles.

"Oh yeah. Definitely black sand beach," she agrees.

"Are we missing something?" Brea asks them.

"I am a vault," is Jayson's remark.

"My turn," Hailey jumps in. "This one's for the boys. Boxers or briefs?"

I don't answer because I usually go commando, and that's information I'm not going to share with my friends.

"Boxers," Elijah and Ryder reply.

Liz pokes Jay in the side. "He's definitely a briefs man."

"Okay, smartass," Jay counters. "Thong or underwear?"

Brea and Hailey reply, "Underwear."

"Neither," Liz says.

I point at her. "You have to choose. Which is it?"

Liz shocks the hell out of us when she says, "Neither because I'm not wearing any."

The girls burst out laughing, Ryder sucks in an audible breath, and Jay suddenly lurches up off the couch and tosses Liz over his shoulder.

"Not this again! Jayson, put me down!"

He takes off with her and heads for the stairs. "Be right back. I have to see if she's telling the truth."

Liz pushes up from his back. "Can someone please help?"

I smile. Hailey and Brea send her a finger wave.

"Traitors!" she shouts.

Tapping my watch, I call out, "You have nine minutes!" Then laugh my ass off when Liz gives me the finger.

Chapter Forty

ELIZABETH

Prom

"FOR FUCK'S SAKE!" Hailey yelps.

I think she's burned her fingers four times already, trying to straighten my hair. I have a lot of it, and she's been at it for an hour. My butt is numb from sitting still for so long. My squirming has gotten worse over the last twenty minutes, and Hailey is about to smack me with the straightening iron to stop wriggling.

Using a hand mirror, I apply the finishing touches to my makeup, painting my lips a bloodred as she glides the hot iron over the last section of hair. Why do girls do this to themselves? We primp and spray, fit our bodies into skinny jeans, and teeter around on four-inch sticks for shoes that blister our feet. Guys just pick up some pants and a T-shirt off the floor, do a sniff test to make sure the smell isn't too bad, and they're done.

"When I get through with you, Jayson won't know what hit him." She spritzes more glossing serum on my hair, then sprays it with hairspray and stands back to observe her work. "There. Perfect. What do you think?"

Relief is the first thing I feel because I get to stand up and stretch. When I do look in the full-size bathroom mirror, my mouth drops open. My long hair is naturally wavy, which is why I never take the time to straighten it or do much with it other than a quick dry with the hair dryer. Hailey has turned my wavy hair into a glossy, sleek waterfall of spun gold. I run my hands through the ends, and it feels like I'm touching silk.

"Oh my gosh, it feels so good. It's gorgeous, Hales." I swish my hair from side to side and watch as it falls back into place.

"Just one more finishing touch," she says and goes into her bedroom. When she comes back, she's holding a square box. "This is from me and Mom. I hope you like it."

Curious, I remove the lid and pull back pearlescent tissue paper. Sitting on the bottom is a black tiara headband with tiny red flowers. Beside it are five small red flower clips.

"These are beautiful, Hailey." I hug her tight and kiss her cheek.

"Here, let me." She takes the items out, one by one. She weaves my hair through the tiara headband to create some volume at the top of my crown, then clips the tiny flowers in various strands throughout. "Now you really do look like a princess. A smoking hot, sexy princess."

We giggle as we look at my reflection in the mirror.

"Let's get you in that dress and down to your guy."

Going shopping for my prom dress was a tad depressing. Maria and I always went clothes shopping together. I miss her. She still won't talk to me, and to make matters worse, she's gotten chummy with both Jacinda and Samantha. Instead of being my best friend, she's become my bully. She has pushed me into lockers, dumped soda on me, and tripped me in the girl's locker room after PE.

I haven't told the guys what has been going on at school. If they found out she did that stuff to me, they would lose it. So, I've kept quiet. She doesn't mess with me when the boys are around, and I've gotten very good at making sure one of them walks me to each of my classes in order to avoid her.

But I don't want to think about Maria tonight. Tonight, I want to dance and laugh and have fun.

Hailey helps me put on my red spaghetti strap high-low gown. It has a plunging neckline with flower appliqué beading on the bodice. The high part of the gown is in the front, and I love how it shows a lot of leg. Mom let me borrow her ruby drop earrings and matching bracelet. After slipping on my black satin heels, I turn a pirouette. Hailey wolf whistles and takes some photos of me with her phone.

"This will be you next year, little sis. And then I can be the one to dress you up."

While Hailey zips up the dress in the back, a bright light appears outside my bedroom window.

"Jayson must have turned on your tree lights. It's just like that Valentine's Day."

My man is so freaking romantic.

Male voices filter in through the window from outside, signaling the guys have arrived.

"It's showtime!"

I grab my black clutch purse and the small gifts I made from the bed and make my way down the stairs.

I've been looking forward to seeing all three of them in their tuxedos, but I never expected to be greeted by a wall of utter male hotness. Holy hell. I don't think I've ever seen a trio of more drop-dead gorgeous men in my life.

Jayson's tux is black, and underneath he's wearing a dark charcoal dress shirt, a black bowtie, and a deep red cummerbund to match my dress. Ryder is wearing all black—of course. He's in a classic satin peak lapel tux. Julien has on a light silver-gray tux that matches his eyes and a dark gray bow tie and red cummerbund. He has spiked the front of his hair into a short faux hawk.

Several gasps interrupt my lingering perusal. I hadn't noticed our entryway was filled with our parents, cameras at the ready. Heat climbs up my neck when three sets of male eyes land on me in various stages of admiration, appreciation, and dirty eye-fucking. My belly flips violently, and my breath hitches. I may end up in a puddle of goo before I make it to the bottom of the stairs.

Jayson reaches out to take my hand.

He whispers in my ear, "You are a goddamn goddess."

I suck in a sharp inhale when his teeth nip my earlobe.

"Liz, you look phenomenal," Julien declares and kisses my cheek.

My eyes find Ryder's.

"There are no words," he tells me, a half-tip smile curving his mouth.

I understand what he means, because right now, I'm having trouble finding the right words to say.

"You guys look so handsome. You all make me breathless."

Seven different cameras have been snapping pictures the entire time, the flashes bouncing off the walls like heat lightning during a summer thunderstorm. Jayson's dad hands him a small box. He opens it and takes out a delicate wrist corsage made of red and black satin ribbon and red flowers. Holding my hand in his, he slides it onto my wrist, then raises my hand and kisses it.

"Love you, baby."

I sniff the corsage.

Ryder's mom gives me three matching boutonnieres.

I approach Julien first to pin his and surreptitiously lean in close, so that no one can hear me.

"I'm so sorry that Elijah isn't the one doing this for you. But he did give me these to give to you. Put them on after we get into the limo."

I discreetly place the silver cufflinks into Julien's hands. Elijah had them specially made with Julien's initials inlaid in black onyx. He curls his fingers around them.

Next, I step up to Jayson with his boutonniere. I look into his mesmerizing metallic eyes and say, "*You aren't just a star to me, you are my whole damn sky.*"

He breathes deeply at my words before taking my lips in a deep, soul-shattering kiss, not caring one bit that we have an audience of parents. I send up a silent thank you to whoever invented smudge-proof lipstick.

After pinning his flower with shaky hands, because, *Jesus*, he just blew my mind with that kiss, I hand him a paper origami star like the ones he often gives me. Inside I have written him a love poem. Hailey helped me with it.

Last, I come to Ryder. "Hey you."

"You look beautiful, Elizabeth."

I pin his flower to his jacket and smooth the lapels down. He gives me a hug, and when we part, I hand him a roll of paper tied with ribbon.

"This is for you. It's not much."

I wrote him a song. I've been working on it and perfecting it for over a month. Even Dad hasn't heard it because I wanted the song to be Ryder's, and no one else's.

Freda sniffles. "My boys are all grown up."

Julien and Jayson groan. "Mom, cut it out," they say at the same time.

Dad guts me when I see tears in his eyes.

"Come here, puddin'."

He takes me in his arms, and I am engulfed with his scent. My dad smells like clean linen and mint.

"I love you, sweetheart. Have fun tonight."

I nod, emotion clogging my throat. "I will."

"You boys take care of my little girl."

"We will, sir," Ryder replies.

The families walk us out to the awaiting party bus they rented for tonight. We loiter for more hugs and pictures until we're finally able to leave.

"Fuck yeah!" Jayson whoops when he climbs into the limo bus.

Seriously? There's a stripper pole inside the party bus?

"Not in this lifetime, and most certainly not in this dress," I warn him.

"I bet I can persuade you."

He takes my hips and pulls me down into his lap.

The bus is equipped with long curved leather bench seats that stretch from the front to the back on one side. The other side has a minibar and controls for the overhead video screen and stereo. Bright colorful neon lights glow throughout. It's tacky as hell, but that makes it so much fun.

"Let's get this party started."

Julien turns on the stereo and cranks up the music.

Prom, here we come.

Chapter Forty-One

RYDER

I THINK my heart stops when I see Elizabeth standing on the staircase, looking absolutely stunning in her red dress, her long legs openly showcased. The tiny red flowers in her hair make her look like a forest fairy, and the deep red color of her dress contrasts with her green eyes. My gaze moves to her mouth painted a scarlet red.

I have to hand it to Jayson. He really stepped up for Elizabeth. When he first came to me about all of us taking her to prom, I didn't know what to say. Julien and I planned to go anyway because we knew Elizabeth would want us there. Jay said all he wanted was for her to be happy, and he knew that Jules and I being a part of her prom experience would make her happy. The thought of getting to hold her close tonight, take her in my arms, even if it's just for one dance, makes all the years of waiting worth it. For one night, I can pretend that she's mine. Hold her like she's mine.

The bus pulls up to the hotel where our school prom is being held. We idle in a line of limos and luxury sedans and watch hotel bellmen greet each arriving vehicle to help the passengers out.

As soon as we step off the bus, two girls I recognize from school rush over and hug Elizabeth.

"You look so fab!" one tells her. I think her name is Beth.

Keith and Davis, offensive linemen on the Fallen Brook football team, walk over to stand with the girls. It's then I remember the other girl's name is Celeste.

We walk inside the hotel and check in with a parent volunteer sitting at a table in the front lobby. After marking off each of our names from a list, our hands are stamped with a dye that will glow under a black light.

"What the fuck is he doing here?" Jayson growls next to me.

I follow the direction he's glaring and automatically shift my body in front of Elizabeth's, my fists clenching for a fight.

Julien comes to my side. "Not tonight. Tonight's about Liz."

Elizabeth is talking to Celeste and is oblivious to Maria and Marshall looming our way.

"Isn't this sweet? Lizzie finally got her wish for a threesome."

Elizabeth stops mid-sentence and turns around.

"We aren't doing this tonight," I tell Maria.

Marshall is smart enough to keep his mouth shut. It's not only me, Jayson, and Julien, but also Keith and Davis creating an impenetrable wall of "don't fuck with us" attitude. Marshall mumbles something to Maria and hauls her away, but her eyes remain locked on Elizabeth.

"Well, this night just took a turn," Elizabeth says.

"Nope. Not going to let that happen, Princess. This night is about you, and we will make damn sure that it's a night to remember," Jayson promises.

He takes her in his arms and kisses her. "I want to dance with my sexy-as-fuck girlfriend."

Careful of her dress, he lifts her in his arms and carries her into the hotel ballroom.

"Elizabeth is never alone tonight," I tell Julien.

I have a bad feeling that Maria will try something, and I will not let that happen.

"Not for a second," he says.

The hotel ballroom is decorated with different replicas of tourist attractions from around the world. A lit up twenty-foot Eiffel Tower stands in the middle of the room, a water wall that says Niagara Falls next to it. There's also London's Tower Bridge, and mini skyscrapers that represent the New York City skyline. Photographers are stationed at each one, ready to take photographs.

"Babe, you guys did such a great job," Davis tells Celeste.

She shimmies to the beat of the music thumping out from the tall, stand-up speakers placed in front of the DJ's table.

"Thanks, babe."

"You did this?" Julien asks her.

"Not just me, but yeah. I'm on the prom committee along with Beth."

"Nice!"

Beth laughs. "You would never believe what Samantha wanted to do—a cowboy theme with a mechanical bull."

Celeste rolls her eyes. "She wants anything she can ride, if you know what I mean."

"Celeste!"

"You know I'm right."

Elizabeth and Jayson leave the dance floor when the song ends, and she rushes over to me.

"Dance with me?"

I glance at Jayson, and he nods his okay.

"I'll go grab us something to drink. Come on, Jules. I can use the extra hands."

Dancing isn't my thing, but I'll suck it up and look like a fool for Elizabeth for one night. She links her pinkie with mine and walks us to the middle of the dance floor. As soon as she turns around and I take her into my arms, the lights dim and the DJ plays "Helium" by Sia.

And just like that, everything around us falls away.

The lyrics of the song begin, and something shifts between us. Some intangible emotion, chaotic and unrelenting. Like opposite magnetic poles, our bodies pull together, inch by slow inch. With our linked hands between us, pressed to my heart, she places her other hand flat against my chest. Her touch lights a spark that grows into a wildfire, and my fingers convulse with need as they curve around her hip.

Her sweet breath puffs against the side of my face when she rests her cheek against mine and sighs. My eyelids close of their own accord, every cell in my body electrified and pulsing, reveling in the feel of her in my arms. This moment. This girl. This is everything.

"Do you feel it?" she says, her words a warm flutter against my already heated skin.

My fingertips dig into her dress. "I do."

She shakes her head in confusion. "Will it always be like this between us?"

I don't know how to answer her. Because for me, the answer is yes. Yes, to the invisible power that always seems to inevitably bring us colliding back to one another. Yes, to the love between us that we never act on. Yes, to the overwhelming emotions that punch me in the gut every time I see her or hear her voice. Yes to it all.

The music fades, and Julien taps me on the shoulder. "My turn."

I reluctantly release Elizabeth and leave her with him. Jayson hands me a bottle of water when I reach him.

"She having a good time?"

"Yeah."

I search the crowd for Maria and Marshall and spot them at the Eiffel Tower with Jacinda, Samantha, and their dates.

"I'm going to steal Liz later for a bit. Didn't want you to think we skipped out and leave without us."

Do I want to know? I mean, we are in a hotel, so of course my mind goes to the obvious conclusion that he's reserved a room just for the two of them.

Jay sees the look on my face.

"Not what you're thinking. Also, none of your damn business even if it was."

Don't ask. Don't think about it.

For the next two hours, we dance and hang out with Davis, Keith, Beth, and Celeste. No matter what, we never leave Elizabeth's side. If she goes to the restroom, Beth and Celeste go with her. The guys and I keep a constant watch on where Maria and Marshall are. The girls have fun pulling us to the different world displays. We take goofy pictures at Tower Bridge and group pictures at Niagara Falls and the New York City skyline.

At the Eiffel Tower, Julien takes Elizabeth in his arms and dips her. The photographer gets the perfect shot of them. She's arched over his arm, their noses almost touching. Julien says something to her, and she tips her head back, a full-bodied laugh escaping.

Once Julien is finished, Elizabeth waves me over.

"Where do you want me?"

She worries her bottom lip, then reaches for my hand. "I want a photo of us just like we were when we danced. I want to capture that moment."

She tucks her hand against my chest next to where my heart is pounding staccato beats, because holy hell, she's touching me again. She wraps my fingers around her waist. My dick jumps in my pants, a surge of lust racing through me. As if in slow motion, she glides her fingertips along my neck and stops when her thumb curls under where my jaw meets my ear.

"Thank you, Ryder, for tonight. You guys have given me the perfect prom."

She pushes up on her tiptoes and softly kisses the side of my mouth. I can hear the clicks of the photographer's camera. I don't know whether it's the fact I stop breathing when her lips barely touch mine or the way she's looking at me, but I'm lightheaded and a bit punch-drunk.

I step away from her when I notice Jayson and Julien are watching us. Julien with a quizzical expression, Jay with a harsh scowl.

I walk her off the platform, and the twins ask the photographer to snap a few pictures of them together. Elizabeth stands next to him, wanting to see the shots he takes.

"They really are identical twins," the photographer says to her, looking at his camera display. "If they didn't have different hairstyles, you wouldn't be able to tell them apart."

"Count the freckles," she says, and he gives her a questioning look.

Jay lifts his fingers to his lips and lets out a sharp whistle. The shrill sound bounces off the ballroom's high ceiling, and a few people stop what they're doing to see what's going to happen.

"Come here, Princess."

He pulls her in front of him, his hands enveloping hers, and he grins.

Elizabeth's brow furrows. "Um, aren't we going to do photos?"

Jay's grin spreads. "Wait for it."

Suddenly, the upbeat rhythm of the dance music cuts off, replaced by the slow, soulful croon of a woman's voice.

Elizabeth's face lights up in recognition. "That's our song! Oh my god!"

It's Roberta Flack's "The First Time Ever I Saw Your Face." The song Elizabeth sang at our end-of-summer camp out.

And then to my horror, Jay drops down on one knee.

"What the fuck is he doing?"

Julien's shock mirrors mine. "I don't know."

"Did you know about this?"

"No."

Elizabeth's face drains of color, the joy in her eyes evaporating. She tugs at Jay's hands, trying to pull him to his feet.

"What are you doing?" she hisses.

The entire ballroom comes to a standstill. No one is dancing anymore. All eyes are fixed on the scene unfolding in front of the fake Eiffel Tower.

Holy shit. Holy shit. This can't be happening.

Chapter Forty-Two

ELIZABETH

JAYSON GOES DOWN on one knee, and all I feel is panic. Overwhelming panic.

I frantically pull at his hands. "Jayson, what are you doing?"

"Elizabeth Penelope Fairchild. I have loved you since the first grade. The happiest day of my life was when you said yes. Yes to us. Yes to me. Yes to everything. My heart is not whole without you. My life is not complete without you in it. In the tradition of all our next times, I want to forever promise you my heart and my love. Will you wear my promise ring, knowing it represents my promise to you for our happily ever after?"

A promise ring. He's not proposing. I'm going to kill him.

Several sighs erupt around us from various girls.

Keith asks, "Does he do this stuff all the time?"

Beth exclaims, "That is so freaking romantic!"

And then I hear Celeste. "Why don't you do stuff like that for me?"

Jayson winks at me and stands up. The necklace he dangles between his fingers is a simple gold chain. Hanging on it is a thin gold band with four small, red inset rubies. He unclasps the fastener and loops it around my neck, tucking the necklace next to the rose quartz heart pendant I've worn every day since he gave it to me.

"It's engraved," he says, showing me the script on the inside of the band.

In tiny cursive letters are the words: *All Our Next Times.*

"It's lovely. Thank you."

And it is.

I'm still going to kill him.

He grabs my face between both hands and swoops in with a kiss to end all kisses. Several cheers erupt around us, and I blush in embarrassment. I hate being the center of attention.

"I've got another surprise." He twirls me under his arm like a ballerina. "Be back in a little while," he tells the guys.

My gaze cuts to Ryder and Julien. They look as shell-shocked as I feel.

"Jayson, wait—"

He hurries me out of the room and into the elevator.

"Where are we going?" I ask as soon as the doors slide closed.

"Patience."

"Jayson—"

He kisses me to shut me up.

The doors whoosh open on the third floor.

"Up you go."

I'm lifted bridal style in his arms.

"Jayson, what—"

He cuts me off again with another hard kiss.

I'm both exasperated and turned on.

"Will you stop doing that?"

"Doing what? Kiss you?"

He kisses me a third time before lowering me to my feet.

"A hotel room?" I ask when we stop in front of a door.

"Sort of."

Sort of?

He fishes out a card key from his dress slacks. Swiping it, there's a click and a green light. When he hip bumps the door open, I'm greeted with a path of red rose petals scattered all over the floor, and he's draped my favorite fairy lights from wall to wall.

"Dance with me?"

Taking out his phone from the inside pocket of his tuxedo jacket, he swipes a few times and presses play.

I'm so confused.

"You couldn't dance with me downstairs?"

"Not the way I want to."

"How do you want to dance with me?"

Jayson doesn't answer me. He shows me.

He slips off his jacket, followed by his cufflinks and bow tie. Never taking his moonlight eyes off me, he undoes the buttons on his shirt, each one popping through the buttonholes like cannon fire exploding inside me.

I can't help my body's response to seeing him undress.

He opens his shirt, and my hungry gaze goes to his muscled, tanned chest and travels down to his Adonis belt. I stand hypnotized as he walks around me, stopping when he's at my back.

I feel the heat of his lips against my shoulder when he pulls the zipper of my dress down. The flowy material cascades down to the floor and pools at my feet. His calloused hands paint my skin with his fingertips, tracing the line of my spine from neck to lumbar.

Coming back around, he kneels and lifts each of my feet, one at time, to help me step out of my dress.

"We'll keep the shoes on," he says and kisses the triangle of lace that covers my pubis.

My stomach muscles contract when he hooks his fingers in my panties and slides them down my legs.

He tips his face back. "You are so fucking gorgeous."

I'm on fire, throbbing with need by the time he kisses his way up my body.

"Now for that dance."

He takes me in his arms, and it feels so good to be pressed skin to skin.

I'm a tactile person, and I love the dichotomy of our bodies. Hard and soft. Masculine and feminine.

"I love you, Liz," he says, turning me in his arms.

He skims a hand down my stomach and between my thighs, whispering seductive words in my ear, then slips one finger inside me, then another, fucking me slowly, his thumb rubbing circles on my clit.

When his other hand moves to my breast, teasing my nipple with sharp tugs, a myriad of sensations catapult me into a ridiculously quick orgasm. My back arches, head thrown back against the dip of his shoulder, and I cry out his name. When my legs buckle, Jayson throws me onto the bed. Rose petals scatter and float back down around me.

He settles between my legs, laving my breasts with his tongue and mouth.

"Again," he says, pushing my thighs apart and deep tonguing my pussy.

I'm floating on a cloud, racing higher and higher with each thrust of his tongue. It takes less than five minutes before I climax again. And he's still not through with me.

"Again."

I moan, so drunk with desire, over-sensitized, and thoroughly sated from my last two orgasms, that I don't know if I have another one in me to give.

My voice slurs. "Jayson, I can't."

He nips love bites between the juncture of my thigh and hip.

"Yes, you can," he says.

He holds me down and sucks my clit with hard, punishing pulls.

Oh god. Oh god. Oh god.

"*Jayson!*"

I climax once again with a long, delirious moan.

"Again."

Holy shit.

The fourth orgasm breaks me, and I think I black out.

By the time he's through with me, I'm barely conscious. Not having enough energy to lift my head, I reach down and thread my fingers through his hair.

"I think you broke me."

The deep rumble of his laughter vibrates through me. "Best dance ever."

Yes, it was.

Chapter Forty-Three

ELIZABETH

Fall From Grace

AFTER PROM, Maria started a rumor at school that I was pregnant. For a week, she, Jacinda, and Samantha hazed my locker and car with baby pacifiers and diapers. Julien caught them in the act, and once the school administration saw the pictures, Maria got a week's worth of detention. Jacinda and Samantha didn't get any punishment after the cheerleading coach spoke to the principal. Figures.

I know I should be over it, but it still hurts when Maria does mean stuff like that to me. I'm used to Jacinda and Samantha being world class bitches. But Maria? That stings the worst. I keep wondering what happened to the girl I thought I knew—the girl I thought was my friend.

Glancing at the clock on my nightstand, I groan when I see the time. I'm too psyched from yesterday's news to sleep. Jayson was offered the swimming scholarship he'd been hoping to get from Carolina University. If his news wasn't awesome enough, Ryder and I both received our acceptance letters from CU in the mail, making it a triple surprise. Our plans for going to college together are finally a reality, and my brain won't shut off. Is this the future I want? Or am I just doing it because it's what the guys want?

Pushing the covers off me, I climb out of bed. Might as well work on my AP Lit paper that's due next week.

I'm pulled back by a strong, warm arm.

"Where are you going?" a sleepy Jayson asks.

"I can't sleep."

"Don't go," he mumbles against my neck. He breathes in deep and moans. "You smell good."

I roll over so I can look at his face. I graze my fingers across his morning stubble and push his hair back behind his ears. Jayson really is wonderful to look at, especially when he's asleep, his face relaxed and calm. I see glimpses of the boy he used to be in the man he has become. I'm still so wildly attracted to him, even after twelve years of knowing him. Jayson absolutely takes my breath away.

"You are such a beautiful man," I say out loud, continuing my exploration with light caresses.

"Baby, you keep sweet-talking me like that..." He trails off and shifts me on top of him.

I'm instantly wet, and if his erection is anything to go by, he's more than ready for me. Bracing my hands on his chest, I lift up and slide down effortlessly on his hard length, our lovemaking slow and languorous.

When the clock displays four in the morning, Jayson climbs out my window before my parents wake. They have to know by now that he sneaks in almost every night. Maybe not Dad. He'd lose his shit if he knew Jayson and I were sleeping together.

I take a quick shower and then work on my school assignment. Luckily, it's Friday so I'll be able to catch up on my sleep over the weekend. There's another bonfire party tomorrow night. Maybe

I'll skip it. I'm tired after a long week and want a weekend of lying in and catching up on my TBR.

The shower turns on in our jack-and-jill bathroom, alerting me that Hailey is up. Crap. I lost track of time and am going to be late meeting up with the guys for breakfast. I pack all my school stuff in my bag and go to brush my teeth. As I wipe off the condensation from the mirror, I happen to look up when Hailey turns off the shower and pulls the curtain to get out.

My gaze catches her in the mirror, and she freezes. Her eyes flare in surprise and something else, something like shame. She snaps the curtain back to hide herself, but she isn't fast enough.

I saw them.

"Jesus, Hailey!" I shout, yanking the shower curtain hard enough that it pops three of the rings holding it on the bar.

Hailey desperately tries to wrap the towel around herself, but I'm not having it. I pull it away, exposing her naked body to me, modesty be damned.

"What the hell, Hales?"

"It's nothing. Honest."

"Nothing? I wouldn't call those bruises nothing. What happened?"

I manhandle her to get a better look at the huge purple and green bruises decorating her upper thigh and hip. On her shoulder is what looks like a circular burn mark that has blistered and scabbed over.

"I fell during PE. Like I said, it's nothing."

She steps out of the shower and snatches the towel from me, wrapping it tightly around her chest.

The ghost of Mom possesses me, and I give her Mom's patented incredulous eye stare that we get when she calls our bullshit.

"It's not nothing. Does it hurt?"

"No."

She walks out the other side of the bathroom to her room with me hot on her trail.

"You're making a big deal out of nothing. Please, drop it."

"Enough with the flippant remarks." I touch her shoulder. "What about this one? Get that at PE, too?"

"That's from my curling iron."

She throws open several drawers and grabs various articles of clothing, one of them a long-sleeved shirt. She's been wearing those for a while now, even when it's hot outside.

"Hailey."

She pivots around, giving me a brilliant, happy smile, but I'm not stupid.

"I fell down and had a hair mishap. Do I lecture you when I see all the hickeys that Jayson gives you, or the fingermarks I sometimes see on your hips when you're wearing your bathing suit? Which by the way, I really do not want to know what you and Jayson do to get those."

She has a point, but then again, she knows those marks are ones I get in the heat of passion from my boyfriend. Hailey looks like she challenged a semitruck and lost.

"Aren't you going to be late?" she reminds me. "I'm surprised Jayson isn't already beating down the door wondering where you are."

I consider her for a minute, concerned and feeling utterly helpless. "Hales, you know if you need to talk to me about anything, I'm here."

She sucks in her cheek, biting the inside, then gives me another one of those brilliant, fake smiles.

"I know. If there was anything to tell, I'd tell you. But there's not. So, stop worrying."

Hailey squeezes me in an overenthusiastic hug and pushes me

out of her room. “See you at school!” she says, closing her bedroom door in my face.

Maybe, I’m worrying for nothing. If there was something going on, she would tell me. Right? I’ll ask Ryder to talk to his sister, Brea, since she and Hailey are best friends.

Another thought pops into my head. Is Hailey being bullied at school? Is Maria messing with her, too? I wouldn’t put it past her to hurt my sister to hurt me. If Maria has put her hands on Hailey in any way, she’s going to regret it.

Chapter Forty-Four

RYDER

"DO NOT SAY A FUCKING word to Liz about what happened at the bonfire," Jay warns us once again.

He has given us the same threat every fucking day since the bonfire party.

I glance across the parking lot where Elizabeth is talking to Beth and Celeste.

"If you don't tell her, she's eventually going to find out."

Julien hops up onto the tailgate of the truck. "I agree with Ry. Tell her. Get it out there, act like it's no big deal, and move on. Liz doesn't need another Jacinda or Maria incident."

"Don't you know that I know that already? She's stressed enough as it is with all her AP exams coming up, work, and getting ready for her music competition. She doesn't need another thing to worry about," Jay replies in frustration. "She hasn't been sleeping, and now she's worrying about Hailey, but she won't give me specifics."

"I hate to say he's right, but..." Julien says, flip-flopping his opinion.

"You just told him that he should tell her."

He shrugs. "He made a good point. I'm allowed to change my mind."

I shove my hands inside my pockets. "Do what you want to do, man, but I disagree. Then again, it wasn't me Jacinda was climbing all over, so it's not me Elizabeth will be upset with."

I stop talking when Elizabeth approaches. Jayson reaches out to grab her, but she spins out of his reach and jumps onto my back, piggyback style.

"I can't wait to see you race tonight."

Elizabeth took the week off work, Julien doesn't have a match, and Jayson doesn't have a swim meet, so everyone's coming to watch me race.

Her legs squeeze around me when Jayson tries to pull her off.

"Hands off my girl, Ry."

Because he's being a dick, I want to mess with him.

"Hold tight," is the only warning I give her, and I take off across the parking lot toward my car.

Elizabeth hangs on for dear life, laughing hysterically. Jayson doesn't find it funny at all. He may be a fast swimmer, but I'm a faster runner. I have Elizabeth in my car, doors locked, and engine turned on by the time Jayson pounds on my window.

"Open up, fucker, and give me my girl!"

I raise my middle finger and rev the engine. Elizabeth waves goodbye, and we peel out of the lot.

"He is so going to beat your ass when he gets to the track."

I grin at her. "Worth it."

"Am I a bad person to like it so much when you mess with him?"

"He deserved it."

"Why do you say that?"

I change the subject. "I can't believe we only have a month left before we graduate."

"I know! It all feels so surreal."

"Eavesdropped any info about where the parentals are taking us for summer vacation?"

Elizabeth's grin is wicked. "I found a London travel book half hidden under my dad's newspaper this morning."

"You're shitting me? We're going to England?"

"I hope so. I was right about Hawaii."

She swipes through my music files. She loves cranking up rock and roll when we're driving in my car together.

"Ryder, has Brea said anything to you about Hailey acting weird?"

I shake my head, eyes on the road. "Nothing. Sorry. I did talk to her like you asked me to, but she said that other than Hailey having a secret boyfriend, she's been the same old Hailey with her, maybe a little more standoffish than usual."

"I think her secret boyfriend is hurting her. Forget I said that. I'll figure it out."

I slip my hand off the gearstick and take her hand.

"Hey, if anyone is hurting her, we'll stop it."

There's a flurry of loud honking, and I look in my rearview mirror. Jayson's truck is coming up fast.

Elizabeth turns in her seat to peer out the back windshield.

"Wonder what took him so long."

I push down the gas and speed away. No way will he catch up to us now.

We arrive at the Fields minutes later. Cars and trucks are already parked along the side of the dirt road. Things won't really get busy until about seven, so we have over an hour to kill.

Gravel flies up when Jayson slams on the brakes and parks his truck behind us.

"Come here, Liz," he says when he gets out.

She uses me like a human shield, hiding behind my back. Julien casually walks over and lifts Elizabeth into his arms.

"Stop being a possessive ass," he tells his brother.

"Fucking Christ. Will everyone stop touching my girl?"

If her giggles are anything to go by, Elizabeth is enjoying the game of *pass the girlfriend*.

Elijah shows up, and Julien hands Elizabeth over to Jayson.

"Hi." She grins at him.

Jayson attacks her mouth with a kiss. I turn to pop the hood of my car, feigning checking the engine. It gets harder and harder for me to watch Jayson kiss Elizabeth because, *shit*, I want to be the man kissing her.

"I hate to be the bearer of bad news," Elijah says. "But word is, Marshall is racing tonight. Haven't seen him yet, so here's to hoping he doesn't show up."

Julien lets loose a few choice curse words.

"College can't come soon enough. I won't have to see that asshole anymore for the rest of my life."

I spot Fallon's Porsche 918 Spyder coming up the road. I swear that guy goes through cars like he does women. Jayson drags Elizabeth off, and Julien and Elijah walk away, deep in conversation.

Since my hood is up, I look over my engine.

"Hey, Ry!" Fallon shouts.

"See you brought the Porsche."

Elizabeth's blonde hair slides into my periphery. While Jayson is talking with a group of guys from our school, Elizabeth is closely watching Fallon and me.

"That car is fucking awesome. Want to give it a spin?"

That snatches my attention. "The Porsche? You serious?"

"You're the only one I would trust driving her."

"Fuck yeah. When and where?"

Even if he offered, I'm not idiotic enough to take an almost one-million-dollar car out on a dirt track in the middle of a field.

Fallon twirls his keys around his index finger and slips them in his front jeans pocket. "I'll set something up for this weekend at the track in Raleigh."

"Sounds good. When did you get back?"

After he graduated from Highland High last year, Fallon took a gap year. For the last few months, he's been gone who knows where, and I haven't seen him in a while.

"Got back a couple of weeks ago. I spent some time with Tati."

Tati is his older half sister, who lives in Spain.

He leans against my Hellcat. "You're racing Marshall tonight."

My head bumps up, and I almost smack it against the underside of the hood.

"Why the hell would you set that up," I say, not as a question but as an accusation.

Fallon takes out a joint and then puts it back in his pocket when he sees Elijah's dad.

"Why? You worried?"

"Hell, no. I can drive circles around that asshole with my eyes closed."

Fallon tilts his head when he notices Elizabeth looking and stares at her. She cocks her head to the side, imitating Fallon, and stares right back at him.

I frown. "You keep looking at Elizabeth like that, and you and I are going to have a problem."

I've always known he's had a thing for her. It's why he and Jay hate each other.

"She's a fascination. Hot as fuck, too."

"Fallon," I warn.

"I know she's hands off."

My gaze follows him as he walks over to her. He leans in to whisper something in her ear, then saunters off, a smile on his face.

When she joins me, I slam the hood down.

"Want to tell me what that was all about?"

Her gaze slides his way. "Just Fallon being Fallon."

Chapter Forty-Five

ELIZABETH

I Will Never Let You Go

MY NERVES ARE ON EDGE, every muscle in my body tense. Why in the hell is Ryder racing against Marshall?

Ryder's car growls to life as he pulls up to the starting line, Marshall idling next to him in his shiny new Mustang—a departure from his usual Camaro. The sleek lines of the cars catch the glow of the pole lights, but the sight of chrome and glossy paint only churns my stomach more.

When I start gnawing on my nails, Julien's hand shoots out and forces my arm to my side.

"Marshall doesn't stand a chance."

I know that. But it's not only the race that's making my skin prickle—it's everything else. I hate Marshall with a passion that's hard to put into words, and this nagging, uneasy feeling won't let go, especially after Fallon started with his cryptic "secret for a secret" bullshit. Fallon's always looming, always watching, and I refuse to let him see how much he gets under my skin. He stares at me, and I stare right back.

Fallon strides onto the track, but he doesn't do his usual theatrics to hype up the crowd. No showboating or grand gestures. Instead, he stands in front of the cars, arms raised high, signaling for the drivers to get ready. The engines roar, shaking the air like rolling thunder before a storm. Through the tinted glass of Ryder's Hellcat, I spot his left hand gripping the steering wheel so tightly his knuckles turn white. That single detail makes my stomach twist even tighter.

Fallon drops his arms and shouts, "Go!"

The cars propel forward in a roar of engines that split the night like gunshots. Dirt flies up as their tires spin to gain traction, and then they shoot off in a blur. My pulse hammers as the cars tear down the track, headlights cutting through the swirling dust.

"Go, Ryder!"

The words rip from my throat, but the cacophony swallows my voice. It doesn't matter that he can't hear me; I scream anyway.

As they hit the first corner, Marshall veers too close and clips the back of Ryder's Hellcat. The car fishtails, spinning wildly toward the grass. My breath catches, panic flaring white hot in my chest—but Ryder pulls it back, regaining control just in time.

Ryder pushes hard, gunning it to catch up on the short straightaway. He edges wide, ready to pass, but Marshall swerves, trying to sideswipe him.

My hands fly to my mouth, helpless anger flooding my veins.

Marshall's playing dirty, risking more than just a race. One wrong move, and Ryder could wreck—or worse.

As Ryder flies past the finish line well ahead of Marshall, all I see is red. I don't remember running out to the track. I don't hear Jayson or Julien calling my name. I don't hear Ryder yelling for me. I don't remember much of anything until I am at Marshall's car.

"You son of a bitch!" I shout when he gets out.

I pull back my clenched fist and punch him in the face.

A crunching sound is audible above all the noise of the crowd, but I don't know if it belongs to him or me because, *holy shit*, that hurt.

"Ow! Fuck!" I yelp, shaking my hand out.

Marshall cups his nose, blood dripping between his fingers. "You crazy, stupid bitch!"

Did I break his nose? Part of me is very impressed with myself.

Oh crap. Marshall lunges for me.

To my downright shock, Fallon is the person who jumps between us and pushes Marshall away from me.

"Don't you fucking touch her."

Fallon protected me. *Fallon*. I'm at a loss.

I'm yanked backward by several pairs of hands.

"Jesus, Liz," Jayson pants, breathing hard. He folds me into his body and holds me tight, palm gripping the back of my head.

Julien takes my injured hand to inspect it. My knuckles are already swollen and bruised but I don't give a shit.

Jayson crushes me to him to the point I can't breathe. "What the hell were you thinking?"

My anger is too vibrant right now, and I know I need to calm down before I do something else crazy, like attack Marshall again. I want to give him two black eyes to go with his bloody nose.

Ryder storms over and slams Marshall against his car.

"You come anywhere near her again and I will kill you."

Elijah's dad and the other deputy who are here tonight push into the chaos to figure out what's going on.

"Everything okay here?" Mr. Barnes asks us.

No one says a word. We know to keep our mouths shut. If the parents think fights are happening at the Fields, they may shut it down, and that's something we will not allow to happen. This place means too much to all of us.

Mr. Barnes looks at me. "Do you need medical attention?"

I shake my head no.

He asks Marshall, "What about you, son? Looks like you broke your nose."

"I'm good. I'm leaving anyway."

Fallon shoves Marshall into his car.

Mr. Barnes's sheriff's gaze slices to Ryder.

"Nothing happened."

"Uh-huh." He adjusts his badge on his belt. "Okay, then. I think that's enough excitement for tonight. Pack up and head home, kids. Races are over for the evening."

The crowd groans their displeasure, but everyone turns around and heads to their vehicles to leave.

"I've got an ice pack in the first aid kit of my car. Elijah will bring it," Mr. Barnes tells me.

"Got a mean right hook, kitten," Fallon remarks as he walks by.

Ryder grabs hold of his arm and stops him. "Did you know he was going to pull that shit tonight?"

Fallon's face morphs from cocky to threatening.

"No. I'll deal with him. Send me the bill for the damages to your Hellcat."

My muscles tremble as my adrenaline crashes.

"Baby, let's get you home and get that hand looked at. Julien, can you grab the blanket from the back of the truck and bring it for Liz?"

"Yep. Be right back." Julien kisses my temple and leaves to get the blanket.

Elijah jogs over, holding the ice pack from his dad's car. "That was the most awesome thing I have ever seen. You are such a badass, Liz."

"If I wasn't so mad at you right now for scaring the shit out of me, I'd agree," Jayson says.

My knuckles sting when I hold the cold pack to them. "He tried to hurt Ryder."

"Elizabeth, I'd rather he hurt me than you. If Fallon hadn't been there, Marshall would have hit you."

I wiggle out of Jayson's arms and approach Ryder. He looks down at me. My amber-eyed daredevil.

I crash myself into him, holding on. "No one will ever hurt you or take you from me. Ever," I tell him vehemently.

Chapter Forty-Six

JAYSON

Present Day

HAVE you ever thought to yourself after you've experienced one of the shittiest days of your life, *I wish I could go back in time and have a redo?* How can your morning start out so normal, but the day end as your worst fucking nightmare?

If I knew today would be that day, the one that forever altered my reality and scarred me in a way that would damn my soul to hell—the one that shredded every part of me into jagged, fragmented pieces and then burned them to ashes—I never would have left Liz's bed that morning. I would have held her tight, kissed her forever, fucked her completely, shouted I love you, and then I would have repeated it all again, over and over.

So, that's how my morning starts—a slice of normal. I reluctantly leave Liz's bed so she can get ready for choir practice before school. I know she's excited about her upcoming music competition, but fuck, if I won't be ecstatic when it's over with. I hate her early morning practice days because it means that I'm forced to give up an hour of being snuggled next to her in bed. I will never get tired of waking up to her gorgeous, smiling face, her soft kissable lips, her light green eyes that I willingly fall deeply into. My hands never know which part of her to touch first. They are absolutely obsessed with every inch of her tall, slender figure.

I've been looking online at cheap apartments near campus at CU. I plan to move her in with me as soon as we get there. I love Liz so damn much. I meant what I said. I plan to ask her to marry me. I want a family, a lifetime, a forever with her. I've been looking for a ring. Liz is it for me. My soulmate. Always has been.

My girl is also a fucking boss. The way she sucker-punched Marshall last night was a sight to behold. Pride swells my chest for my fierce princess. Then it turns to fear and rage and shame. Marshall went after her in retaliation, and I wasn't close enough to stop him. Thank God for Fallon—words I never thought would leave my mouth.

On the way to school, the guys and I stop at Ruby's for breakfast, and I make sure to get Liz her favorites—coffee and a scone. I have a smile on my face, knowing I'm going to see my girl soon. Even a minute away from her is too long.

When we get to first period, my smile falls when Liz sees a text from Jacinda meant for me on Julien's phone. Jacinda is a manipulative bitch. She knows I can't stand her, especially after what she did.

And then, Liz finds out about what happened at the bonfire. Ryder warned me to tell her, but I'm the asshole who thought I could protect her by keeping it from her. The morning gets worse when Hailey skips school, and Liz can't get in touch with her.

That leads to now.

I check my watch.

Instead of going home, I decided to stick around the library and use one of the study rooms to finish my homework while I wait for Liz to get off at six. I text Julien to let him know I'm taking Liz to dinner when she clocks out. Ryder's at the garage working on getting out the dents and scratches on his Hellcat.

"I hope I'm not the reason for that scowl."

Liz props her shoulder against the doorjamb, purse hanging from her hand, looking like the most beautiful creature ever to exist on this planet. She slays my heart. Every. Single. Time. My scowl turns to one of perplexity.

"It's only five. Are you on break?"

She pushes away from the door and slips inside the room.

"Nope. They're letting me off early today. Nothing to shelve."

When she gets close enough, I pull her between my knees.

"You know we need to talk about the text, right?" she says.

"There are better things we can talk about. Or not talk at all."

I tug her closer, and she places her hands on my shoulders, looking down at me in the chair.

"Jayson," her voice is soft, but commanding.

I sigh. "I know."

I stand up and spin us, so she's sitting on top of the table. Grasping the back of her head, I angle it so I can kiss her.

"No necking in the library," Mrs. Peters calls from outside the room.

Liz giggles. "Yes, ma'am."

"How about we head on home, and I cook you dinner while we talk."

Liz's eyes brighten. "You had me at cook dinner. Let's go."

Fifteen minutes later, we're back at my house and parked in the driveway. My parents had texted me and Jules earlier saying they would be late.

"Be right back. I'm going to grab a clean shirt," I say as soon as we walk inside.

I've already stripped my shirt off by the time I get to the closed bedroom door. But I wasn't expecting to see my brother kissing Elijah when I opened it.

"*What. The. Fuck!*"

Chapter Forty-Seven

ELIZABETH

I GRAB two sodas from the fridge.

"*What. The. Fuck!*"

Jayson's booming, angry voice makes me jump, and I drop one of the sodas. The can explodes on impact, spraying my legs and feet.

I grab some paper towels to clean up the mess.

"Jay, it's not what you think. Let me explain."

Oh, shit!

Tossing everything into the sink, I run as fast as I can up the stairs. Jayson's rigid body blocks their bedroom doorway.

"Elijah, get the fuck out of my house!"

"Don't talk to him that way!" Julien shouts.

I grab Jayson's arm. "Jayson, please. Calm down. Just sit and listen to Julien. Please."

If I thought I saw Jayson angry before when he was beating on Marshall at Fallon's party, this is much worse. And it's directed at me.

"You knew about this?" His voice is cold and sets me on edge.

I swallow convulsively, wanting to tread lightly with how I answer that.

"Yes," I meekly reply, nodding slowly.

"You *knew* about this!"

I startle and stumble backward.

"How long, Liz? How fucking long have you known?"

Julien comes out into the hall. "Jay, let's go downstairs and sit down and talk. We owe you an explanation."

Jayson doesn't say a word. He jerks his shirt over his head and stomps downstairs.

Tears streak down my face at Julien's devastated expression.

"Julien, I'm so sorry."

He pulls me into his side and kisses my hair. "You have nothing to apologize for, Liz. Nothing. You hear me? He's just in shock. Once he calms down and we talk things through, I'm sure he'll understand. If it's anyone's fault, it's mine. I should have told him a long time ago."

The short descent down the stairs and into the living room is rife with anguish.

The room is as morose as the mood. Dark shadows dance along the walls, and an orange hue from the setting sun faintly illuminates the beige walls with somber hues of dark orange and red.

We find Jayson hunkered down in one of the armchairs, knees splayed, forearms resting on his thighs. His hands fist his hair, and he's breathing hard. As soon as I get close, he bolts out of the chair.

"Jayson."

"Don't."

His angry rejection increases the tears that fall down my face. I don't know what to do, so I just stand there.

"Jay, sit down so we can talk. Please," Julien begs his brother.

Jayson goes to the opposite side of the room from where I am and sits down on the sofa. My heart breaks. I want to hold him so badly right now. Give him comfort.

"Talk," he snaps.

Elijah and Julien take their seats on the other side of the sofa, hands clasped with one another's, a show of solidarity. I'm so proud of Julien right now. I know how scared he must be and how hard having this conversation with his twin brother is.

"I'm gay. If you want to be technical about it, I'm bisexual. And I love Elijah. I have for a long time."

"How long?" Jayson murmurs, his voice barely above a whisper.

"How long have I known I was bi, or how long have E and I been dating?"

Jayson waits for Julien to continue.

"We've been dating for a while. My feelings for Elijah were what made me finally come out to Liz."

"When?"

"When?" Julien looks up at the ceiling and then at me before moving his gaze back to Jayson. "Um, I told her the summer we went to Topsail for July Fourth."

"We go to Topsail almost every summer," Jayson says.

"A few years ago. I knew before then. Just never told anyone. I was scared, I guess."

Elijah brings their clasped hands to his lips and softly kisses the back of Julien's hand.

"Why didn't you? Why didn't you tell me, Julien?" Jayson's face is etched with agony. "I'm your twin brother! I should have been the first person you talked to. Why Liz? Why her and not me?"

Julien looks helplessly in my direction. I smile, trying to give him the courage he needs.

"I don't know. Liz is just the person I go to when I need to talk. I don't know why I've been afraid to tell you all these years. I guess I didn't want you to be disappointed in me."

Jayson looks horrified when he stares at his brother in disbelief. "You thought I would be...why would you...*fuck*."

Jayson closes the two feet between them and jerks Julien into his arms.

"I would never be disappointed in you. *Never*, Julien. I love you. You're my brother. I love you. No matter what."

Years of pent-up uncertainty release like a dam bursting. Julien breaks down in racking sobs in Jayson's arms, his hands convulsively tightening around his brother's back. The scene before me is so earth-shattering, so real and emotional, I openly sob with them. Jayson reaches out to Elijah, who has been sitting silently witnessing them together, and pulls him into the embrace. For several minutes, I watch them cry.

"Thank you for loving my brother, E," Jayson says.

"That's the easy part," Elijah replies.

The three boys release one another, swiping the tears from their eyes with the backs of their hands.

"Have you told Mom and Dad?"

"No." Julien dries his face on his shirt. "Would you mind being here with me when they get home tonight?"

"It would be my absolute honor, Jules."

Jayson embraces Julien again for one long hug.

"I can stay, if you want me to," I speak from my corner of the room.

Jayson turns indignant eyes toward me. "You need to leave."

"She can stay. She has every right to stay. She's been there for me and E—has supported us the entire time. We wouldn't know what to do without her."

Jayson's handsome face contorts into something...ugly.

"Basically, what you're confirming is that my girlfriend has been lying to me for years."

"No, it's not like that," I protest. "I couldn't tell you without breaking my promise to Julien."

"But I'm your fucking boyfriend, Liz! The one person you're supposed to love and trust more than anyone else! How could you keep a secret like this from me? From *me*, dammit! It should have been *me* he came to first. *Me* he talked to first. Not you!" he yells.

"She's right. It wasn't her secret to tell. It was mine. And the fact that I told her first shouldn't be a factor. She was there for me when I needed her."

Jayson shakes his head back and forth, his dark chocolate locks falling into his eyes when he looks at me.

"All I see in front of me is someone who has lied to my face for years. I can understand why Jules was afraid to tell me, but what I don't understand is why you locked me out and kept it from me. How many opportunities did you have to tell me to talk to my brother? That there was something going on with him and he needed me. He needed me, too, Liz, and you took that away from me. You stole that from me. You stole years of me being there for him."

Jayson makes a strangled sound and sits back down, looking defeated.

"Get out. I can't look at you right now. I can't speak to you right now. Just get out. I want to be alone with Julien before our parents get home, and I don't want you here."

"Jayson, please. I'm sorry."

I try to reach for him.

"Get out! Now!" he shouts.

My face crumbles. I run out of the room, grabbing my purse off the foyer table. Going out the front door, I dash across the yard to my house, tears making everything look blurry. Julien calls after me, but I don't stop.

I spot our car in the driveway. Hailey must be home.

Of fucking course she's home now after ghosting me all day when I tried to find her and talk to her. Dealing with my sister will have to wait.

Unlocking the car door with my key fob, I get in and turn the ignition. Damn tears. I wipe them away because I can't see well enough to drive.

I don't understand Jayson's anger. Doesn't he get that I couldn't say anything to him without betraying Julien and breaking my word? I never lied to him. Did I? Fantastic. He has me second-guessing myself now. Well, fuck him. I did the right thing. I won't apologize for it. Jayson has kept things from me. Look at what I found out today about Jacinda. He's a hypocrite. He's lied by omission several times. And instead of talking to me tonight, he kicked me out of his house. He yelled at me. Well, fuck him.

My mental tirade has me shaking and incensed. I need to get out of here.

Putting the car into reverse, I slam on the brakes when Julien runs to the driver's side of the car and pulls on the handle, only to find it locked. His voice is muffled through the rolled-up window.

"Liz, come back inside. He didn't mean what he said. Please come back in with me."

"He doesn't want me there. And it's not about me. I love you. I'm so proud of you for telling him tonight. It's good that he knows. Go back inside and be with him."

"Liz, wait."

But I'm already backing down the driveway.

Chapter Forty-Eight

ELIZABETH

My Choice

AFTER DRIVING AROUND AIMLESSLY for an hour, I find myself parked in front of Randy's garage. The bay doors are down but the lights are on, and I can hear noises and music coming from inside. I open my car door. It's late enough that the business should be closed, but I see Mr. Cutton sitting inside at the counter, typing away at the computer. I knock on the glass door, and he looks up, a smile splitting his face when he sees that it's me.

He walks over and unlocks the door. The familiar smell of oil and rubber hit my nose as soon as I walk inside.

"Well, hey there, Elizabeth. What brings you by tonight?"

His smile falters when he notices my teary eyes.

"Is Ryder around?"

"Yeah, sweetheart. He's in the garage. Hold on a sec. Let me get him for you."

A minute later, the music turns off and Ryder walks in, a rag in his hands as he wipes the grease off them. Mr. Cutton says something to him that I can't hear, then goes into his office and quietly closes the door.

"Good to see you're alive. Julien and Elijah have been blowing up my phone for the past hour. I tried texting you as well."

I nod but don't reply.

Ryder throws the rag on the counter, his golden eyes giving me a thorough examination.

"Come on. Let's go in the back so we can talk in private."

I follow him into the garage bay. He pulls up a stool and offers it to me. I shake my head no, needing to stretch my legs after being in the car for an hour. Ryder retrieves a bottled water from the mini fridge, twists the top off, and brings it to me. I take it, grateful, because my throat is sore and parched from crying.

"Want to tell me what's going on?"

Holding the bottle with my left hand, since my right hand is still too sore from punching Marshall, I tip the water back and look at him. I mean, *really* look at him. He looks good. Strong and vital and so damn handsome. I never allowed myself to really see him before. Not just the superficial things that I'm attracted to, like his copper-colored eyes that I know have flecks of green in them. Or the way his arm muscles bulge when he crosses them over his chest like he's doing now. Or the cupid's bow on his full, top lip. His tanned skin or his devastating smile that I'm lucky to be the recipient of often. Those are only superficial qualities.

What I see now, perhaps truly for the very first time, is how he always stands by me and supports me no matter what. How he has gifted me with his love and with his heart and not once expected anything in return. How he must love me so much, he was willing to give me up to be with Jayson and still remain my best friend, even though I know it must kill him every day to see me and Jayson together. I see all the years we've shared, all the times we keep finding our way back together. How even though I love

Jayson so very much, my love and my heart have always belonged to Ryder.

I sit down on the stool he offered as my mental fatigue morphs into physical exhaustion.

Ryder drags another stool over in front of me. He takes the water from me, setting it down on the floor, and cups my bandaged hand.

"I never really thanked you for defending me last night."

"He deserved more. How is your car?" I tilt my head in the direction of his car that's currently perched on a lift.

"Minor stuff I can handle easily. I've been working on it all afternoon."

"That's good. I'm glad."

Ryder peels back the gauze to inspect my swollen knuckles. His thumb lightly rubs over each one before he pulls the gauze back down.

"You should call Julien. He's worried about you but wouldn't tell me why. Where's Jay?"

Where to start?

"Jayson is with Julien and Elijah at the house."

"Why aren't you with them?"

"Jayson kicked me out."

Ryder's head tilts, not understanding. "Why the hell would Jay kick you out of their house?"

"He's angry at me. He thinks I've been lying to him for years."

Ryder bites on his lower lip, considering things. "This wouldn't have anything to do with Julien and Elijah, would it?"

I peer into his face, and it hits me. "You know?"

"Pretty much."

"Did Julien tell you?"

"No. I kind of clued in a while ago. I figured when Jules was ready, he would tell me himself. But, yeah, I figured it out. Wasn't that hard. You can tell how much he and Elijah love each other. How happy Julien is whenever Elijah is around. It's obvious."

Doesn't that beat all, I think to myself, chuckling out loud. All this time, Ryder had it figured out while Jayson said he had no idea. I'll have to add perceptive to Ryder's list of qualities.

"Julien is going to tell his parents tonight. Jayson's there with him."

"You should be there, too."

"I want to be, but Jayson is so angry with me. He said some hurtful things that he won't be able to take back. Things that I won't be able to easily forgive him for this time."

Ryder pulls my stool closer to his, the sound dulled by the epoxied flooring. He lifts my chin until we are eye to eye.

"Loving someone isn't easy, Elizabeth. I should know. There are so many good days that even the few bad ones can't lessen them. Today is just one of the bad ones. You and Jayson have loved each other a long time. That kind of love doesn't disappear at the first sign of anger or because you're fighting."

Leaving the stool, I pace the garage.

"He keeps things from me all the time. Stuff about Jacinda. Stuff about Marshall. Stuff with Fallon. I gave Julien my word. What kind of friend would I be if I broke my promises?"

I stop in front of Ryder. He's watching me from his place on the stool.

"Why didn't you fight for me?" I shout at him, my emotions all over the place. Anger at Jayson. Loving Jayson. Anger at Ryder. Loving Ryder.

"What?"

"Why didn't you fight for me? When Jayson snuck into my bedroom that night, he told me how he felt about me. Why didn't you? You told me at the Fields you wanted to talk to me about something important. Why didn't you say anything? Why did you give up so easily?"

Ryder's mouth opens and closes several times.

We face each other in a standoff. He's not willing to answer my question, and I'm not willing to let it go. You know what? Screw it. Screw it all. I feel like choices have been stolen from me. Who I'm allowed to love. Where to go to college. Who I'm supposed to marry. How I'm to live my life. The mess with Maria. The fucked-up mess with Jacinda and Marshall.

I've always been meek and pliable, doing what I'm told, letting others decide for me and never speaking up for myself. The stereotypical good girl. Last night when I punched Marshall—that felt good. I felt strong, and capable, and free. I made the choice to hit him. My choice. Now, I'm choosing this.

Before I have a chance to change my mind, I'm straddling Ryder on the stool and touching my lips to his.

My choice.

There's a second of hesitation from him before his arms band around me and his mouth opens to mine. I immediately tangle my tongue with his, his lips so soft yet firm, and oh, so wonderful. He makes a guttural moan, fusing our mouths tightly together. I started out the aggressor but now he's the one taking control. A decade's worth of unrequited love and passion erupt into this kiss.

And it was my fucking choice.

Chapter Forty-Nine

RYDER

AS SOON AS Elizabeth's tongue touches mine, I'm done for. My desire for her overrides my conscience. I'm tired of fighting this. Tired of always being the one to walk away. Tired of watching Jay take what should have been mine. Because she's always been mine, even when she wasn't. If this is my one opportunity to kiss her the way I have fantasized about, the way I crave, I'm taking it. Consequences be damned. Jayson be damned.

I seize control of our kiss. Elizabeth needs to know what I've been holding back all these years. What could be hers if she takes the chance, takes that leap with me. So, I lay my heart bare, giving her everything I have in me with this kiss.

I cuff her neck to angle her head, delving deeper into her warm, luscious mouth. She tastes like sunshine, and I'm instantly addicted. I want more, and apparently so does she.

Her little mewling moans are driving me fucking crazy. I stand up with her clinging to me, her mouth ravenous as it licks and kisses along my neck and face. She's as hungry for me as I am for her. And neither one of us is willing to stop.

Our bodies slam against the wall, pressed so intimately

together, you wouldn't be able to tell where she begins and I end. She grabs at my shirt, ripping at it.

With my weight molding to her soft curves, I shift her higher with one arm, while reaching over my shoulder with my other hand to pull my shirt off. Her light green eyes spark with desire. She releases her grip from around my neck to explore my bare chest. Her hands mold to every inch of my skin, mapping every muscle and dip she finds.

"I've always loved looking at you. You're beautiful, Ryder," she says in a husky voice.

Her hands feel incredible. She splays her fingers wide over my upper torso and rubs her thumbs across my hardened nipples. My cock jumps and expands painfully behind my zipper, begging to be buried deep inside her.

Elizabeth reaches down and lifts the hem of her shirt, eyes like wicked verdant fire lighting me up, daring me to touch her in return.

A flash of red catches the light, and like flames doused with cold water, my goddamn common sense rears its ugly head and tells me to apply the brakes.

"Elizabeth, we can't."

God, that's so painful to say. I feel like my heart is being ripped out of my chest.

"What?" she asks, utterly confused.

Because I'm a bastard, I press a kiss to her neck before I release her. God, she smells good. I guide her long legs from my waist and slowly lower them down until she's able to stand.

"We need to stop."

"Why?" she asks, that one word filled with the pain of rejection.

I gently tug her shirt back into place and carefully pull out the chain dangling around her neck. I lift it up with a finger and hold

Jayson's promise ring between us, making sure she sees it. The four red rubies mock me, reminding me that Elizabeth is not mine to take.

"This is why."

She looks down at it and tucks the necklace back under her shirt.

"Ryder, my heart has been as much yours as Jayson's since the day we met. And I'm done letting everyone make decisions for me. I won't do it anymore. Jayson keeps making plans for our future. Plans I don't want." She rubs her fingertips across her forehead. "How do I know what I want if I'm never given a chance to decide for myself?"

Elizabeth encircles her arms around my waist and rests her cheek against my chest.

"I want you, Ryder. I want to be able to explore what this is between us. I don't want to live with any more 'what ifs.' Watching Marshall try to run you off the track...something snapped inside me. The thought of losing you, of not having you in my life..." She chokes up, not able to continue.

My pulse is hammering so hard it shakes my body. The words my dad said to me come back. He told me that Elizabeth needed to be given time to figure out what she wanted. She needed to be allowed a chance to choose her future.

"What about Jayson?"

"I love Jayson."

The dreams that were beginning to swirl, scatter at her words.

She brings her lips up to mine and says, "But I love you, too. So much. I need you, Ryder. I need to know our 'what if.' Things can't continue the way they are now."

"Jayson isn't going to sit back and allow you to be with me and not him. You know that. And I'm not sneaking behind his or Julien's backs."

"I would never do that, and I would never ask you to. Jayson already accused me once tonight of lying to him. I won't keep this from him. The only thing I need to know right now is, do you want to be with me?"

"God, yes," I answer without hesitation. Because I can't resist any longer, I pull her face to mine and kiss her. "I love you, Elizabeth."

Her breath hitches and tears spring to her eyes. "That's the first time you have ever said that to me."

We hold each other for a while, suspended in our own reality, one that not even time can penetrate. Dad comes in an hour later to tell us he's closing shop. I help Elizabeth into her car, and because my dad is watching, I don't kiss her good night like I want to. Instead, I press a kiss to her forehead.

"Are you ready for this?" she asks.

I link our pinkies. "I've been waiting for you my whole life."

Chapter Fifty

ELIZABETH

The Things That Break Us

I'M SO MENTALLY exhausted by the time I get home. I had shut off my phone when I ran out of the Jameson's house earlier tonight. I turn it on. It's flooded with text messages and voice mails. I need some sleep before I try to tackle the mess that awaits me. Perhaps I'll skip school today and stay home. Perhaps Ryder will skip with me. It would give us a chance to talk about how I'm going to tell Jayson.

Walking to the side of the house, I look up at the twins' second-story window—Jayson and Julien's room. The glass pane is shut, and the drapes are cinched closed. Everyone must be asleep.

I hope everything went well with Freda and Mitch. I know their parents will accept Julien for who he is, just like Jayson did.

Jayson.

The boy I have loved since I was six. The boy I shared all my firsts with. Every awkward, beautiful first. Images of us flicker like an old film in my mind: the sweetness of falling in love, the laughter we shared, the friendship that came before everything else. As difficult as our relationship was, the good outweighed the bad, and I don't regret a single moment with him. Not many people get to experience first love with their best friend.

Standing here in the dark, my chest tightens with guilt. I'm about to break his heart, tear apart the world we've built together and the future he's planned for us. How do you hurt someone you've loved for so long, just to follow your own heart?

I squeeze my eyes shut, fighting back the ache rising in my throat. Jayson doesn't deserve this. He doesn't deserve to have his heart shattered by the person he trusts most. But I can't lie to him. I can't lie to myself. We've both been doing that for far too long.

I'm so sorry. I love you. Please forgive me.

The neighborhood is eerily quiet, as if the world itself is holding its breath. Stumbling up the porch steps, I get my key out of my purse and unlock the door, then close and re-lock it once inside. The house is pitch black.

I stop.

Something ugly slithers its way up my spine, and my heart painfully crashes against my rib cage as if adrenaline is being mainlined directly into my bloodstream. Before I'm even able to register movement, I'm tackled hard to the ground. I open my mouth to scream, but I'm silenced in a chokehold when a punishing hand squeezes around my throat.

"Welcome home, sweet Elizabeth."

Pain shoots across my head, and everything goes black.

Oh god, my head. It hurts. I struggle to open my eyes. Why do I hurt so much? I try to move my hands but can't. I try to move my legs and arms and get nothing. Fear. Panic. Why can't I move? I scream and scream, but no sound comes out. There's something covering my mouth.

Oh god. Oh god. Help! Someone, please help!

My senses click on, one at a time. I'm in a chair, my arms and ankles bound. Duct tape covers my mouth. I'm in the house.

No. *NoNoNo!*

Hailey! Mom! Dad!

Get free. Save your family. Do something!

With every ounce of strength I can muster, I buck against my bindings. The chair teeters precariously but I don't stop.

Get free. Save your family.

The chair topples sideways with me strapped to it. My shoulder and head hit the floor and intense pain like none I've ever felt before detonates inside my skull.

"Oh, good. You're awake."

Black tennis shoes appear in my blurred vision. Hands roughly lift me upright.

"I'm running out of time," the voice says.

Terror fills me as the sharp edge of a knife is dragged up the middle of my chest like a caress, sliding between my breasts and under my chin. The tip of the blade nicks my jugular, and I jump in response.

"Look what you made me do, Elizabeth."

How does he know my name?

I can already feel blood trickling down my neck, the small slice of skin stinging.

"I said look!" he screams.

I don't know what he wants me to look at. What is happening? Why is he doing this? Where are my parents? Where's Hailey?

I try to capture images of his face, what he's wearing, anything that I can give to the police if I'm able to make it out of here alive.

He's tall. Not as tall as Jayson, more Ryder's height. He's wearing all black and has a black face mask covering his hair and face. However, even with the dim light, I'm able to see the color of his irises. His pupils are blown but the rims around each are visible. One light blue, one brown.

I whimper and try to tell him that I don't know what he's talking about. He fists my hair with a severe grasp and jerks my head at an odd angle. I try to look away from the utter horror he forces to see, but he won't let me.

Lying motionless on the living room floor are my parents. There's enough light coming in through the separation of the curtains from the streetlamps outside for me to see the carpet is painted a dark crimson. My mother's vacant, cloudy eyes stare at me, unblinking, my father next to her, his face I can't see. I scream behind the duct tape, thrashing around wildly, desperate to get to them, to save them, even though I already know they're both dead.

"Now you see, my sweet Elizabeth. But that's not all I have to show you."

He releases my face and walks over to the pantry and opens it. I hear a loud thump and then a noise like something is being dragged across the floor. The man appears in front of me again, his hand curled around Hailey's hair as he slides her limp, naked body in front of me and tosses her down on the floor at my feet. Her body is covered in cuts, bruises, and burn marks, and if she didn't make a tiny moaning sound when she hit the floor, I would have thought she was dead, too.

I vomit inside my mouth but there's nowhere for it to go. I swallow it back down—the burning, acrimonious taste making me gag and want to vomit all over again.

The man starts talking frantically, his words a jumble my mind has trouble processing. I ignore him and focus on Hailey. *Get up! Get up, Hailey!* My muffled words plead to her. *Get up!*

The man bends down and flips Hailey over onto her stomach. Her muscles twitch but she barely moves, her skin sticky with congealed blood. I'm watching my sister die right before my eyes and am helpless to do anything about it.

Hot, overpowering rage rises, aimed at the man in front of me as he hovers over her. If I can just get free, I will rip every bone from his body.

A yellowish-orange spotlight passes over Hailey's pallid, blood-streaked skin as the early morning sun filters through the windows. Ryder said he would come by this morning. Ryder will save me. I just have to hold on until he gets here.

"Do you see, Elizabeth? Your pathetic sister could never take your place. You're my butterfly. My beautiful broken butterfly."

He's not making any sense.

If I thought seeing my parents dead on the floor and my sister's life draining out of her right in front me was enough to break me, what he does next obliterates me, leaving nothing but a husk of myself remaining.

The man lowers his zipper and climbs on top of Hailey as she lies prone on her stomach, not moving. *This is not happening. This is not happening. This can't be happening.* I shut my eyes, not able to watch him defile my sister in the most horrific way.

"Elizabeth," he coos.

I shake my head. I won't watch. I won't.

"*ELIZABETH!*"

My eyes pop open.

He plunges a knife into Hailey's side, over and over.

My mind fractures. I scream so loud and so long and so hard that my vocal cords shatter. Tears pour down my face, clouding my vision and mixing with the blood covering my neck.

"Shh," he says, stroking my hair. "I'm almost done."

"Don't touch me! Don't you fucking touch me!" But nothing comes out. I have no voice. He stole my voice.

I whimper when he slides the knife across my leg bindings. He's going to do to me what he did to my sister. A second of clarity hits me. This may be my only chance to escape.

"Don't you see how much I love you, Elizabeth? She wanted to be you. She could never be you. I've been waiting for you."

Once my legs are unbound, I rear back and smash my head into his face as hard as I can. Stars explode behind my eyes. *Jesus, fuck!*

I hear him yowl in pain as dizziness swamps me. Using my legs, I push down with all my might, trying to stand and run, but my wrists are still taped to the chair. The man grabs my ankle, and I careen into the dining room table, striking the side of my face against the wooden edge, the chair shattering beneath me.

"Why, Elizabeth? Why did you do that?" the man screams at me.

He sits on my chest and pins me down, and I lose it. I fight with everything in me, kicking, biting, thrashing. Voices come from outside, and I try to scream but only a whisper comes out, then a gurgling noise like coffee percolating. My head lulls to the side. The man pulls the knife out of me.

He croons to me in a soft voice. "Hush now, sweet Elizabeth. It will all be better soon." He slides the knife into me again, twisting it. Ripping the duct tape off my mouth, he kisses me softly. "My beautiful broken butterfly."

When the voices get louder, he climbs off me. I hear his footsteps running toward the back of the house.

My body is floating, but I feel no pain. I try to take in a labored breath, but it's too hard to pull in air. My eyes track to the dining room window, searching for Jayson's window, but the old oak tree is in the way.

Jayson. I see my swing and remember the Valentine's Day he gave it to me. The night he made love to me for the very first time. My gorgeous silver-eyed boy. The boy who owns all my firsts. Memories of Jayson and all our next times float in rapid succession across my vision. I think of my jar of stars as I try to touch the chain around my neck, wanting to feel my promise ring.

Daddy. I feel my dad's arms wrap around me. I'm sitting in his lap. His hands cover mine as he helps me pluck the guitar strings. I hear his deep voice singing to me. I hear him call me puddin'.

Mom. I can feel my mom's love. She wraps it around my body just like she wrapped me in hugs every day. Her soft whispers telling me it's going to be all right.

Hailey. My sweet baby sister. I try to slide my hand across the blood-slicked floor to reach her.

My vision fades out, then back in. A gurgling cough erupts up my throat, and I taste something thick and metallic. I blink.

Julien. So handsome and brave, his smiling face hanging upside down from the tree branch in front of our old tree fort. Julien in his gray tux as he dips me in front of the Eiffel Tower. My best friend.

"Elizabeth! Are you in here?"

That's my sweet Ryder's voice. I picture us in his car, the wind in my hair, his golden, amber eyes always filled with love when he looked at me. How free I feel when I'm with him. He kissed me tonight. He said he loved me.

My beautiful, wonderful boys. My three princes. I've lived a lifetime of happiness with them by my side. They are my family. Wait, no. Not all my family. My parents. My sister. Gone. He killed them. Why did he kill them?

There's a tug on my torso, and I hear Ryder's voice, faint and far away, calling my name. My eyes are too heavy to open, and my limbs won't work. Jayson is here with him. I need to tell them before the darkness takes me away. I need more time. I can't leave them. I'm not ready.

Ryder's frantic eyes swim in front of my vision.

With my last, gasping breath, I rasp out, "I love you."

Chapter Fifty-One

JAYSON

AFTER A SHITTY NIGHT tossing and turning, I'm fucking tired and running on fumes. As I've said before, my parents are just plain awesome. Elijah and I sat with Julien as he told our parents about their relationship. Of course, they welcomed Elijah into our family with open arms, and Mom insisted Elijah stay for dinner. Elijah's dad showed up, and while the parents talked in the kitchen, me, Jules, and Elijah watched movies in the living room.

It was good, *really good*, to see my brother happy and relaxed. He and Elijah held hands, smiled, and kissed with the biggest smiles on their faces.

Elijah and Mr. Barnes left around midnight, and Julien and I stayed up for a couple more hours talking. We eventually conked out on the sofa. Not the most comfortable place to sleep, hence the restless night.

Julien talked me down from my anger at Liz. Just another tick mark on how many times I'm going to fuck up when it comes to her. I feel horrible about the way I yelled at her, and the guilt has been eating me up ever since.

I noticed headlights and heard the sound of a car around one in the morning. I wanted to run out of the house and grab her in my arms, beg her forgiveness, and tell her how much I love her. But I didn't because I needed more time before I faced her.

At six, I hear Ryder's Hellcat pull up outside the house. Since I'm already dressed for school, I step out onto the front porch and watch as he parks his car behind Liz's in her driveway.

"What are you doing here so early?"

Ryder stops mid-step up the pathway and turns toward me. I jog down to meet him halfway.

"How's Julien?" he asks me.

"He's good. Did Liz tell you?" I wait for his answer before I blow a gasket because if she told him when she wouldn't tell me, I will absolutely lose it.

"Nah, man. I already knew. She didn't have to tell me anything."

"You knew? Did Julien tell you?"

"No, Jay. I figured it out a long time ago. It wasn't that hard to see what was going on."

His pointed jab scores a direct hit. I'm Julien's twin brother. I should have known. I should have been there for him, and I wasn't. Another thing to feel guilty about.

"You saw her last night?" I ask.

"Yeah. She came by the garage, and we talked."

"What are you doing here now?"

"Jay, what's with the third degree? I can see Elizabeth whenever the hell I want. I don't need your damn permission."

I eye him suspiciously because I feel like something's up.

"Is Liz okay?"

"No, she's not." Ryder glares at me for asking such a stupid question.

Of course, she's not okay. I treated her like a grade-A asshole last night.

"I would love to stand out here and shoot the shit with you, but I promised Elizabeth that I would pick her up for school this morning." He starts walking.

"Shit. Ry, wait. I need to talk to her. I want to apologize."

He keeps walking. "Maybe you should give her some space."

"I'm not going to give her some space. She's my fucking girlfriend. We had a fight. I want to apologize."

Ryder spins around and pushes against my shoulder to stop me from following him.

"If she wants you to leave, you leave. Understand. Otherwise, I'm not letting you take one step inside."

I grit my teeth in annoyance but acquiesce. "Yeah. Fine. Got it. I just need to see her."

We walk up the steps onto her porch, but Ryder suddenly stops and presses his face to the sidelight window next to the front door. He rips his keychain out of his side pocket and unlocks the door.

"Ry, it's early. Why don't you knock first?"

He ignores me and throws the front door open as soon as he turns the key. The first thing that hits me is the smell.

"What the fuck is that smell?"

"Elizabeth! Are you in here?" Ryder shouts in a panic.

I grab Ryder. "Holy shit! Holy fuck!"

There's blood everywhere. I gag. Ryder pulls his arm out of my grasp and runs upstairs. He calls for Liz and yells for her to answer him.

"Liz! Liz, you in here, baby?" Terror claws at me from the inside out. I follow the trail of blood from the foyer into the living room. "Jesus Christ! Ryder!"

His footfalls pound the wood as he races down the stairs. He collides into me, and we both stand there, frozen at the sight, not knowing what to do. A small sound has us both racing from the dining room into the kitchen. I take out my phone and dial nine-one-one. I don't know what I say to the dispatcher, but I'm pretty sure I give them the address.

Ryder's anguished cry makes me drop my phone. I rush to where he's kneeling on the floor.

I must be asleep or something. This isn't real. I'm having a nightmare and when I wake up, I'll be cuddled next to Liz in her bed. I'll kiss her bare shoulder before tangling my fingers through her long blonde hair. I'll hear her sweet giggle before I roll on top of her to get lost in her beautiful green eyes.

Ryder's heart-wrenching cries pierce through my mental fog. He lifts Liz's limp body into his arms. *Jesus, there's so much blood.* And then I see Hailey. I can't look. I think I'm going to be sick.

"*No, no, no*. Elizabeth. Please, baby. Please. Please don't leave me. Please, Elizabeth. I can't live without you. I love you so much. Please, baby," Ryder sobs. He raises his head and screams at me, "Jayson, call an ambulance!" He looks back down at her. "Hold on, baby. We're here. I'm here, sweetheart. Just hold on."

I can't move. No. That's not my Liz. He's mistaken. That's *not* my Liz. The girl I love more than life itself.

He shouts her name again in agony, and my legs give out. I fall to the floor next to them. Her body dangles limply in Ry's arms. She can't be dead. Not my Liz. Not my girl.

I slide next to Ryder and take Liz's head in my hands and press my face to her blood-crusted hair.

"Liz, baby girl. We're here. You're safe. We've got you, Princess. Just hold on. Help's coming."

The sound of sirens in the distance gets louder as they come closer. I try to give her hope.

"See, baby. Just hold on. Help is coming. Hold on. Don't leave us. We need more next times. I'll hang a thousand stars on our tree. I'll fill a million jars with stars just for you."

Ryder and I are mirror images of one another—sobbing, pleading, praying, making promises, begging, telling Liz we love her.

Before the paramedics forcibly pull us away from Liz, I swear I hear her whisper, "I love you."

Ryder and I try to push our way back to her, not wanting to leave her for a second.

One of the paramedics yells out, "We're losing her!"

Epilogue One

RYDER

A Little Over a Year Later...

JULIEN WALKS INTO THE KITCHEN, takes a cold bottle of water from the fridge, twists it open, and guzzles the entire thing down. His shirt and shorts stick to his skin, drenched with sweat.

I stand at the stove and scramble eggs to go with the bacon I just took off the burner. Julien grabs a strip and leans against the counter island.

"Jay up yet?"

"Yeah. He's on the phone."

Julien perks up at that. "Any news?"

I shake my head no and divide the eggs onto three plates, then add bacon to each one. Sliding Julien's over, he grabs it and shovels a forkful of food into his mouth. He's usually starving in the morning since he gets up at five to run ten miles, rain or shine. Julien needs it. Running for him is an outlet, ten miles that allow him to shut his brain down and just be in the moment. Normal moments have been few and far between for the three of us this past year.

My release is racing. I need the adrenaline rush to steady my thoughts and keep me grounded. There's a professional race track a half hour from here where I spend most of my evenings.

Jayson is a different story. His escape used to be at the bottom of a liquor bottle. Now his emotions are channeled through his fists in an underground fight club.

We hear Jayson walking toward the kitchen. "Yeah, yeah, okay, man. Thanks. You know the drill. Call anytime if you find something. Yeah. Good. All right, man. Talk to you soon."

He tosses the phone on the counter, grabs his plate, and falls onto the stool next to Julien. "Fucking hell."

"Why do we keep paying that guy again? It's been months, and he hasn't been any more successful than we were."

Which means the PI has found absolutely nothing.

Jayson spreads his arms across the counter, dropping his head with an exhausted sigh. "I know. I fucking know."

I notice his cut and swollen knuckles. I open the freezer to grab a bag of frozen peas and hand it to him. He fought last night, and I'm surprised he isn't more banged up. He usually comes home with a black eye or two or a busted lip, or bruised ribs. I'd rather he used his fists to fight his demons than get cirrhosis of the liver. He was a fucked-up mess for a while.

Soon after Elizabeth disappeared, Jayson started drinking heavily to the point he would black out most days. I envied him. I would have given anything to escape the pain I woke up to every damn day she wasn't in it. But I needed to be strong for her and do what I know she would have wanted. That meant helping Jay, giving him a reason to live.

There was a time when Julien and I thought we would lose him. It took a lot of tough love from all of us, our parents included, to lift him out of his deep depression and bring him back to the light. He's surviving, barely. It's good enough for now.

Julien has fared a bit better than his brother. He has Elijah. Elijah helps take some of that weight off my shoulders. He keeps Julien grounded, keeps him going. I will never be able to thank him enough for that, for giving up his dream of going to Stanford to come here to CU to be with Julien. Elijah's a good man.

I think about the past year. The year without Elizabeth. You always hear people say that time moves on. Days turn into weeks that turn into years. Seasons change, people change. Time stopped for us when Elizabeth disappeared, when she was taken from us to who knows where. Our families struggled with the pain of losing her, of losing Hailey and their parents. Their killer was never found. No resolution, no justice. Nothing.

I don't think any of us will ever recover. I don't think Jayson and I ever will. We were the ones who first found all of them. Found Elizabeth gasping for breath on the blood-smeared floor, red pooling all around her, staining her blonde hair an ugly scarlet. I can still feel the weight of her limp body in my arms as I watched her life drain away. Her parents dead in the living room. And Hailey. God, Hailey. A fucking nightmare. It never ends. Just plays like a goddamn horror movie set on repeat in my head, day after day after day.

After Elizabeth's attack, we visited her every day in the hospital until an incident between Jayson and a staff member got us all kicked out and banned. A short forty-eight hours later, Elizabeth was gone. Since we weren't family, no one would tell us anything, other than some relative had showed up. Who? We don't fucking know.

We now live in an empty void, wondering what happened to her; if she's still alive, if she exists only in the shell of her body, if she ever came out of the coma. Does she dream about us? Is she scared? Does she think we abandoned her? Every night we fall asleep with thoughts of her. Every day we wake up to the same. We hunt for any clue online that she is out there, praying that one day there will be something to go on—a picture, a post, a news article, hell, even an obituary—anything that tells us what happened to her or where she is.

Several months ago, we hired a private investigator, the guy Jayson was talking to on the phone. We will never give up until we have answers.

Jay, Jules, and I live together in a condo off campus. Our parents leased it jointly so the three of us could live together. We kept our promise to come to Carolina University, but honestly, I don't remember most of last year or if I went to half of my classes. We were just trying to survive day to day. I'm surprised we made it to our sophomore year, but here we are, three weeks away from the start of the first semester.

Jayson bailed on his swimming scholarship, but his parents were more than happy to fit the bill for his education. Anything to help Jay from tumbling back down into the soul-sucking darkness again. Julien kept his and is a center forward for the CU soccer team. I still plan to get my MBA. Elizabeth was so excited for me to do that, and I won't let her down.

I tip back the rest of my coffee, rinse the cup out, and grab my keys and wallet off the counter.

"I'm out of here. I need to stop by the student store and pick up a textbook."

"Elijah's going to pick me up in an hour."

"What's on the agenda for you today?" I ask Jay.

"Sleep. Web search. Work out. The usual." Yep. That's our new normal now.

"I'll help you when I get back. Give me about an hour."

"No rush."

Loping down the stairs, I jog over to where I parked my Hellcat. I remember the first day I took Elizabeth out in it. She named it Stella. I laugh at the memory. God, that was a good day.

I park Stella in one of the student pay-by-the-hour lots on campus, rest my head back, and shut my eyes. I can picture Elizabeth sitting next to me in the passenger seat, her long flaxen hair flying around her face. Her squeals of joy and excitement when I raced around the track at the Fields. The way she smelled. Her fucking delicious scent of jasmine and sunshine. I miss her so goddamn much.

Taking a deep breath, I shake my head to stave off the sadness that will overtake me if I allow it to. As I walk to the CU student center, I encounter other students and faculty members milling about the grounds, the campus full of people doing summer courses.

The sun is out, puffy white cumulus clouds dot the sky. It's a gorgeous day. The weather is typical for early August, the heat of summer bearing down, hot and sticky. The mingled smell of dirt, grass, and honeysuckle vines is pungent. Girls are lying on towels spread out in the grass. Some in bathing suit tops and denim shorts trying to get a tan, others reading or working on their laptops. Some guys toss a frisbee back and forth, trying to be nonchalant as they check out the girls walking by.

Life goes on, but unfortunately, I'm not in the mood to enjoy it. I never am anymore.

"Ry! I've been yelling your name for the past two fucking minutes. Where's your head at?" Fallon jogs up to me.

Out of all the people I would have expected *not* to go to college, Fallon coming to CU shocked the hell out of me. Yet, here he is, also a sophomore like us since he took a gap year after graduating high school. Come to find out, his parents went to school here, and they donate a shitload of money to the university. One library and an academic hall are named after them, and Fallon is a legacy member of his dad's old fraternity.

"Surprised to see you here"—I look at my watch—"before noon."

He throws his arm around my shoulders as we walk.

"Have to get the frat ready for incoming rush. Fucking freshman."

"Thanks for reminding me why I never want to join a frat, ever."

Fallon barks out a laugh. "I have a proposition for you."

"And that would be?"

"I bought a new car. Want to drive it around the track to see what she can do?"

Typical Fallon. I think this makes number four so far this year.

"What car did you buy?"

Fallon pops a stick of gum in his mouth. "A Radical RXC."

"Hell yeah! I'm in. When?"

"This weekend good?"

"Send me a text. I'll be there."

We get to the student center and walk in. Fallon spots a group of girls and veers away to chat them up. Just like in high school, he's as much of a manwhore in college. I head to the back of the store where the textbooks are located and search for the one that I need for Marketing Analysis and Development. After seeing how much it costs, I debate whether I should find the book used online.

Feminine laughter catches my ear, and the hairs on my arm stand up. I look around. I hear it again. My feet follow the sound like I'm a fish caught on a fisherman's line being reeled in, and there's nothing I can do to escape its pull.

I see Preston, a guy I know from one of my classes last year. He spots me heading his way and says something to me, but I don't hear him.

Sweat breaks out all along my forehead. My palms go clammy. My heart begins to pound out of my chest. A sick feeling swirls in my gut. I feel like I'm about to pass out or explode into a million jagged pieces, my body can't decide which. My vision blurs, and I use the backs of my hands to wipe them. Am I crying? Am I even breathing? My legs have stopped moving but I feel like I'm flying. It's a strange sensation. I blink a few times to clear my vision. Each blink is like the click of a camera shutter.

I swallow thickly, my mouth bone dry. My gaze is frozen. Unmoving. Locked onto the person standing next to Preston.

My brain can only process a few words.

Holy fuck.

Holy shit.

Holy fucking shit.

I must have said the words out loud. The person in front of me turns around. Moss-green eyes, pale-blonde hair tipped with pink, full lips, and the most beautiful face I have ever seen. A face that has haunted me for over a year. A face I have loved for most of my life.

She's *here*.

"Elizabeth?"

Epilogue Two

ELIZABETH

THEY SAY WHEN YOU DIE, your life flashes before your eyes. You see a bright light, and a warmth wraps around you. You feel at peace.

I wouldn't know any of that.

Because I can't remember a fucking thing.

A Look at Book Two

PAPER STARS REWRITTEN

A shattered past. A forgotten love. And a future rewritten.

It's been over a year since my world changed forever. After waking up thousands of miles from home, I was forced to start over, guided by scars I didn't recognize. It hasn't been easy, especially when life keeps pulling me toward a past I can't fully grasp.

Now, a twist of fate has brought me back, thrusting me into a world I don't remember. At college, I run into Ryder—someone who swears he knew me before, someone whose eyes spark a connection I can't explain. Then there's Jayson, whose pain and anger cut through me like shards of a forgotten past. And Fallon, the enigmatic playboy who shouldn't make sense in my new life but somehow does.

They all want pieces of the girl I used to be. But I'm not her anymore.

If life offers you a second chance at love, how hard will you fight for it? My story is far from over—and this time, I'm writing it my way.

AVAILABLE MAY 2025

A Letter to Readers

Dear Reader,

Thank you for reading *All Our Next Times*. I would say that I'm sorry for that cliffhanger, but I'm kind of known for them. I hope you're ready, because Elizabeth, Jayson, Ryder, and Fallon's story is just beginning. Fallon? Oh, yes. Fallon. Just wait.

All Our Next Times is the first book baby I ever published, but some characters and some stories, like theirs, stay with you and won't ever let you go, even for the author who wrote them. These characters hold a very special place in my heart. As with all my books, I leave a part of myself on the pages. Character quirks. Settings. Life experiences.

And in case you were wondering, Fallen Brook and Highland are fictional towns I created in my beloved home state of North Carolina, and Carolina University is based off UNC-Chapel Hill, my alma mater.

Just wondering, did you cry at the end? I sure did. I bawled my eyes out when I wrote the last chapters. If you're new to me and my stories, just know that I love to throw shocking twists at you and tug at your heartstrings. Don't worry. I make sure to tie everything up in a nice bow at the very end and give you a swoon-worthy HEA.

Also, hi! Nice to meet you.

If you don't know me yet, here's a little bit about myself. I'm a North Carolina native. My favorite Southern foods are fried okra, biscuits and molasses, and collard greens (with or without apple cider vinegar). I'm addicted to coffee. I love butterflies and men with tattoos. I hoard book boyfriends. I can do a fairly reasonable Scottish accent, but my British one is better. Get me excited about something and my Southern accent comes out big time, y'all. Yes, I can be both a UNC Tarheels fan AND a Duke Blue Devils fan, no matter what anybody says. I love dipping my potato chips in spicy brown mustard (I gave Elizabeth that trait).

I also love my FMCs strong & sassy and my MMCs morally gray and beautifully broken. I've been crowned by readers as the Queen of WTF Twists (not sorry one bit), Queen of cliffies (again, not sorry), Queen of book hangovers (love those!), and an author who loves to drink the tears of her readers (I even have a travel mug from a reader that says so). I wear my crowns proudly. From my swoony, steamy small-town romances to my walk on the dark side with my dark rh/why choose romances, there are plenty of must-have book boyfriends to choose from, stories to get lost in, and love stories to cheer for. If you want to know more, there's some additional stuff listed in my author bio.

And now for my thank yous.

Thank you to my husband and son for always supporting me and being my biggest fans. I love you both so very much.

Thank you to Ellie, my longtime editor at My Brother's Editor, for her love and support of my books.

Thank you to Nala for being the plotter to my pantser. Our weekly goal meetings have helped me so much over the years.

Thank you to my wonderful team of ARC readers and to my awesome street team who hype my books.

Thank you to the wonderful Instagram book community and to the book bloggers who tirelessly pimp my books out to the world. I couldn't do this crazy job without you!

And thank you, dear Reader, for coming along this journey with me. I hope you're ready for *Paper Stars Rewritten* because it's going to be one hell of a ride.

Happy reading,
Jennilynn

About the Author

Crowned the queen of plot twists by her readers, Jennilynn Wyer is a multi-award-winning romance author whose accolades include Rudy Award winner for romantic suspense, two-time HOLT Medallion Award winner, contemporary romance Writers Reader's Choice Award winner, seven-time contemporary romance Writers Stiletto Finalist, four-time HOLT Medallion Award finalist, Carolyn Reader's Choice Award finalist, and an international Amazon best-selling author of romantic fiction.

Jennilynn writes steamy, small-town romances as well as dark why choose romances. She also pens young adult romance under the pen name J.L. Wyer. Her favorite characters are women who are strong and sassy, and men who are morally gray and beautifully broken.

Jennilynn is a sassy Southern belle who lives a real-life friends-to-lovers trope with her blue-eyed British husband. When not writing, she's nestled in her favorite reading spot, e-reader in one hand and a cup of coffee in the other, enjoying the latest romance novel.

Discover Jennilynn Wyer's books at www.jennilynnwyer.com.

www.ingramcontent.com/pod-product-compliance
Ingram Content Group UK Ltd.
Pitfield, Milton Keynes, MK11 3LW, UK
UKHW022248170125
453711UK00007BA/37

9 798895 679463